Angels of
Our Bitter Nature

The Alternate Reality News Service,

Ira Nayman, Proprietor

This is a work of fiction. Any resemblance to real persons, places or things is…inevitable, really, given the nature of the multiverse. However, the probability of any resemblance to real persons, places or things in your particular universe is vanishingly small, and must, therefore, be considered coincidental.

Praise for the first idiotocracy book, *ARNS and the Man*:

"Amusing, sardonic political and social satire that brims with wordplay legerdemain and oddballisticelaboratified name invention. Trenchantly twisted and good fun." – John Shirley, author of *A Song Called Youth: Eclipse*

"I don't often read science fiction but when I do, Ira Nayman's *ARNS and the Man* is near the top of my list. Wacky, surreal, bizarre, and all too close to reality, Nayman spins a web of satirical hilarity ripped from the headlines." – Terry Fallis, two-time winner of the Stephen Leacock Medal for Humour.

"Ira Nayman rivals Walt Kelly for the skilled and joyous administration of near hallucinogenic word play as an antidote for the madness of our political process. And unlike the brave possum of Okefenokee Swamp, the truths of *ARNS and the Man* were crafted by someone wearing pants." – Hugh Spencer, author of *Why I Hunt Flying Saucers* and *Extreme Dentistry*

"Ira skewers American politics in a way only a Canadian can, with absurdist wit and wisdom. Short humorous Fake News articles that know they're fake and relish in their lies. (Or ARE they?) Makes me once more jealous of our neighbors to the north." – Michael A. Ventrella, author of *Bloodsuckers: A Vampire Runs for President*, among other things

"Reading an ARNS book is like going head-to-head with an selection of thirty three and a third disconnected Wikipedia entries filtered through seven layers of artesian coffee filters woven from at least three more fibers than permitted by the historic laws of any major religion in a blender made of a strange kind of cotton candy spun from titanium anodized in fairground colours with blades made of live sharks while simultaneously tap-dancing to a Steve Reich composition based on the absolute value of the square root of pi. In other words, simply and elegantly the most entertaining way ever invented to invert your brain over a platter prepared with roasted apples and a variety of field mushrooms for your own delighted consumption. Also, a hilariously skewed take on the Trump administration." – Jen Frankel, editor, *Trump: Utopia or Dystopia*, author, *Undead Redhead*

DEDICATION

Angels of Our Bitter Nature is dedicated to my family, especially my father, whose unwavering support for my writing career has made this and my other books possible. It is also dedicated to my Web Goddess, without whom it very likely would not exist.

Finally, I would like to dedicate this book to the men and women who serve Donald Trump, and the American President himself, without whom none of this would have been necessary.*

ACKNOWLEDGMENTS

I would like to thank Hugh Spencer for the graphic that is the heart of this volume's cover, and Gisela McKay, who took all of the elements I handed her and made the cover something unique and special.

In addition, I have been remiss in not thanking the people who gave of their time and blurbiage to the first Vesampucceri collection, *Arns and the Man*. Your kind words may not have increased my sales appreciably, but they make me think that I may not have been completely wasting my time with this whole writing thing.

* Yes, I know that that is a line from the Firesign Theatre. It's probably not the first I have used; it probably won't be the last. If one must steal, one should always steal from the best.

Ira Nayman

CONTENTS

Ira Nayman

1. THE SLEEP OF REASON PRODUCES... PRESIDENTS

Petty Officer in Chief

by FRANCIS GRECOROMACOLLUDEN, Alternate Reality News Service National Politics Writer

"What? You think I'm jealous? Of a 16 year-old girl? Please! I'm Ronald McDruhitmumpf! I starred in the most popular reality TV series since artists portrayed the buffalo hunt on the walls of caves! I ran a successful real estate emp – did I say successful? I meant wildly successful real estate emp – did I say wildly successful? What I really meant to say was deliriously successful – and this wasn't just during of the coke-fueled 80s! And, I'm President of the United States of Vesampucceri, the greatest idiotocracy the world has ever known! Believe me, I got nothing to prove, believe me!

    "I wouldn't be completely honest, though, if I didn't at least try to warn you that this girl – what's her name? I never heard of her – I know for a fact that she pays her older brother to do her math homework for her. Oh, yeah. You think because she's been nominated for a Nobelthingido Peace Prize that she's a 'good girl?' Well, lemme tell you, that just ain't so! I heard that she let Jimmy

9

Paninteassgloss get to second base in the ravine behind her high school last week!"

President Ronald McDruhitmumpf's two hour scream of frustration to CPAC (Conservative Pumas Alpacas Camels) will fuel graduate psychology theses for decades to come. Take his diatribe against Greta Funinthethunberg, a Swedish teenager who had been nominated for the Peace Prize for her activism on the issue of Global Hot as Hellification (SPOILER ALERT: she's against it).

Please.*

Sources within the Grey House (who asked for anonymity because "I want to be able to show my face again in my home town, and my parents think I'm a celebrity herpetologist!") say that the President's private reaction to the news was much stronger. Throwing paper airplanes he had made out of pages of that morning's security briefings in rapid succession at various members of his cabinet, President McDruhitmumpf shouted, "What's the point of having a ferking Federal Bureau of Instigations if they can't get dirt on a ferking 16 year-old Swedish chick? Have they never seen *I am Curious, Yellow Bellied*? Those Swedes got it going on, I gotta tell ya!"

Press Secretary Sarah Wannabe-Panders denied the unsourced report. "Wuhl, Ah don't know abaht y'all, but what **is** thuh point of havin' a FBI iffen they can't get duht on a 16 yeah-old Swedish... guhl?"

She would neither confirm nor deny the fact that Swedes had it going on.

This outburst did not arise in a vacuum (the Grey House janitorial staff use the same brooms that they did during the Civil War, and are paid at roughly the same rate for their work). Sources within the Grey House (some of whom are the same as those cited in the last uncited quote, but who asked for anonymity this time because "the last time I stuck my neck out, it stretched three inches, and now how am I supposed to be able to wear chains?") say that President McDruhitmumpf is furious that former President Barry W. Bushbamclintreagbush has won a Nobelthingido Peace Prize and he hasn't.

Squirting ink at members of his cabinet from pens he had used to sign executive orders undoing laws signed by his predecessor,

President McDruhitmumpf shouted, "This whole ferking Nobelthingido Peace Prize thing is something I can't ferking undo with a ferking stroke of a ferking pen! What good is the Central Inanities Agency if it can't prove that the former President was born in Kenya and won his Nobelthingido Prize under false pretenses?"

Press Secretary Wannabe-Panders has consistently denied that the President had ever expressed such an opinion. "Iffen Ah was President, Ah would also wonduh what good is thuh CIA iffen it can't prove that the previous President was bohn in Kenya and won his Peace Prahze unduh false pretenses?"

Do you think she's still having fun?

Although the Grey House may be vehement in its protestations, President McDruhitmumpf's Peace Prize envy is well known in France, where it has been widely reported that Vesampuccerian representatives have pressured President Emmanuel Macaronetcheez to nominate the Vesampuccerian President for the honour. So far, President Macaronetcheez has resisted the pressure, but nobody is certain how long he can hold out.

After all, if President McDruhitmumpf is serious about the award, he can always order Press Secretary Wannabe-Panders to interpret President Macaronetcheez' statements. Few politicians can survive that treatment for very long!

* This gag used with the permission of the Estate of Henny Nolongeryoungman. For more information on using Borscht Belt humour, **don't ask us!** We were just up against a hellacious deadline!

Chaos President...Unleashed!

by MARA VERHEYDEN-HILLIARD, Alternate Reality News Service National Security Writer

Four star General Jim O'Prayingmattis (Roger Ebeedshalmaltael must have been in a generous mood that day) has resignired as Secretary of Defence. (It is commonly understood in Washburningdington that President Ronald McDruhitmumpf is his own Secretary of Defence; O'Prayingmattis must have missed the memo. Which makes you wonder what else he missed. But, ah, now that he is gone, perhaps **we** should be generous…)

After last week's resignirationing of Chief of Staff John Colourkellygreene, this reduces the number of adults in the room with the President to…hmm…carry the three…subtract the Gross National Product of Pantama…damn, I wish I had a calculator!… divide by PR (the Paul Reubensandwitchyum Constant)…none. There are no adults in the room with the President.

None adults in the room with the President.

Not one.

The proximate cause of the resignirationing of O'Prayingmattis (it was in the neighbourhood, so it thought it would drop by and visit for a while), was President McDruhitmumpf's announcement that Vesampucceri would be pulling all of its troops out of Syria. Without consulting anybody (except, perhaps, for Personal Adviser 8-Ball). In an early morning tweep.

2:37 in the morning, to be precise, when the President wrote: "What are our troops still doing in Malawi? We've beaten ISIS. Mission Accomplished! Over! Done! Finito! I'm bringing the troops home. Promise merde, promise kept! #highfiveforjobwelldone"

At 2:39 in the morning, President McDruhitmumpf followed up, "Siria. I meant Siria. Where we defeated ISIS. Everybody knows I'm pulling the troops out of Siria! #beststrategicthinkerever #whocaresaboutsupportingabunchoflosersanyway"

"Yeah, the President was clearly listening to the little cabinet in his head," said Speaker of the House to be (different room, different adult) Nancy Pelligrinosi. "You know, the one that tells him to do all that he can to license his name to a hotel in Fenwick, because what could possibly go wrong?"

Been feeling frisky since the mid-term election which gave you a majority in the House, have you, Madam Speaker To Be? "Oh, yeah!" Pelligrinosi exulted. "Power, baby – it's better than crack!"

We considered asking her how she knew that, but Pelligrinosi looked like she was ready to bench press us 500 times, so we resisted the urge. Beat it back with a stick, if truth be told.

When Vesmpuccerian forces are gone, Syria (with a "Y." Why? Because we love you. You? Who else? Else? Okay, now you're just being silly!) will not be able to stop Turkish forces from crossing over the border and killing all of the kurds, who had been fighting ISIS with the United States. Iran (remember Iran? The enemy of the US?) will find its position in the region much stronger.

"It's almost like President McDruhitmumpf **wants** to give Fenwick a strategic victory!" said security analyst Malcolm Donneednopennance.

"I would like to congratulate my good friend Bashar al-Elephantine on his very exciting recent victory against the Kurdish terrorists," smoothly purred Rupert Mountkilamanjoy, the Prime Minister of the Duchy of Grand Fenwick. "Oh, wait. Did I say, 'recent?' I meant impending. I can be such a silly dog when it comes to tenses. In any case – a part of the English language on which I have a firm grasp, if I do say so myself – I would like to congratulate Bashar on his impending victory against the Kurdish nogoodniks. And, while I'm here, I would like to thank Vesampuccerian President Ronald McDruhitmumpf for making it possible. We couldn't have done it without you, big fella!"

"I hope Special Prosecutor Robert Meullitallover is paying attention," security analyst Donneednopennance muttered darkly.

So. To sum up. Stab an important ally in the war on nouns (terrorism department) in the back? Check. Likely get important allies massacred? Check. Hand Vesampuccerian adversaries in the region an unearned victory? Check, coat and hat, and call us a taxi, please, because we are out of here!

But, what's really important here is: how does this affect soon to be former Sectar'y...umm, Secr'ta – no...Se'tar – Secretary O'Prayingmattis?

Three months ago, he told a reporter: "As one of the few AitRs left in the administration, I have a duty to remain to keep the country safe. I take that duty very seriously, so I'm going to tough it out. ... Unless the President decides to do something catastrophic, like...I don't know...shut down the government to get funding from Congress – which will not give it to him – for a wall – which nobody needs. Or...or...or announce that he wants to pull Vesampuccerian troops out of Syria in an early morning tweep without consulting anybody!"

He's already resignired over the Syrian pullout – should we tell O'Prayingmattis about the government shutdown? We mean: can a senior Grey House official resignire twice? We decided not to say anything to him. If his sleep is plagued by nightmares, we don't want to be the cause!

The Ronald McDruhitmumpf
Art of the Steal Algorithm

SPECIAL TO THE ALTERNATE REALITY NEWS SERVICE

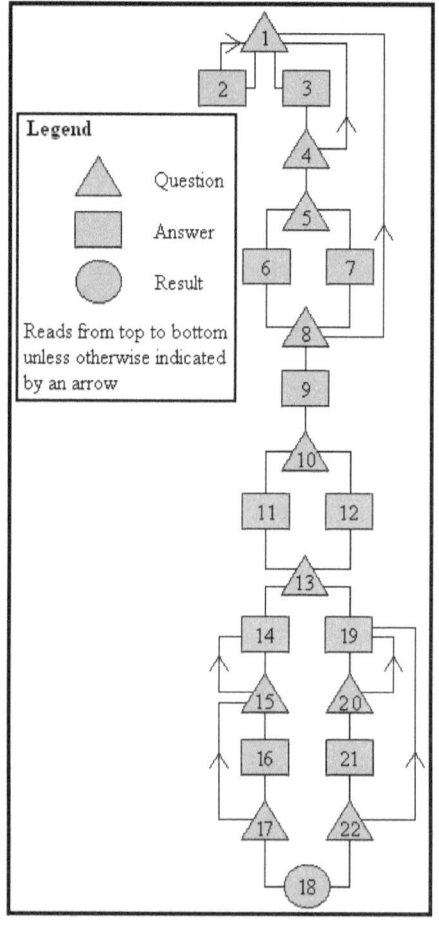

Legend

△ Question

▢ Answer

⬤ Result

Reads from top to bottom unless otherwise indicated by an arrow

1. Is the President getting enough attention to satisfy his ego?

YES 2. He tweets something racist, sexist or insulting about somebody he feels did him wrong five minutes ago. This is just the President being the President – let the lamestream media howl about it as he goes about his business gutting the federal government.

NO 3. The President announces that his government will be pulling out of an international agreement that a previous government (you know the one – don't make me say it) had negotiated and was ready to sign or had already signed.

4. Does **this** get the President the attention he craves?

YES GO TO 1

NO 5. Was the agreement signed by a Republican President? (It happens. The United States of Vesampucceri has been involved in more international agreements than anybody other than David Takehasselhoffeh has hairs on their head.)

YES 6. The President will praise the effort as "worthy," but say that times have changed and that the country can do better. If Pressed, he will say that the person who signed the agreement was naive and will be remembered by history as a traitor to the country if he, President McDruhitmumpf, isn't given the chance to fix it.

NO 7. The President will condemn the effort, saying that all involved were traitors to the country who will be remembered by history as evil if he, President McDruhitmumpf, doesn't immediately fix it.

8. Does **this** finally, finally get the President the attention he craves?

YES GO TO 1

9. President McDruhitmumpf initiates the process of withdrawing from the agreement.

10. Does Congress approve of withdrawing from the agreement?

YES 11. Congress continues with its investigation of Hillary Roocartoncleveman's emails (now in its seventeenth fun- – if not fact- – filled year!) and ignores what the President has just done.

NO 12. Congress makes strangled clucking noises which in no way impede the President from doing what he wants.

13. Was the agreement originally with allies of the United States?

YES 14. Insult their leaders and threaten them with an appropriate Armageddon.

15. Do the countries you're negotiating with agree to your demands?

YES 16. Make new demands. Really outrageous ones. Compliant bastards need to know that the United States is the alpha dog that will win the negotiations.

NO GO TO 14

17. Is the President's attention wandering?

NO GO TO 15

YES 18. Expect years of chaos.

19. NO The President gives them what would, in any ordinary negotiation, be an important bargaining chip.

20. Do the countries that the United States is negotiating with give in to its demands?

YES. 21 President McDruhitmumpf thanks them for being the best statesmen the world has ever seen.

NO GO TO 19

22. Does the other country actually live up to its end of the agreement?

YES GO TO 19

NO GO TO 18

NOTES

Remember when the world used to make sense? When you couldn't buy cat food at Canadian Tire? When your generation was the generation of protest, not some snot-nosed teenagers with long hair and no respect? When Presidents worked their asses off (why do you think that when seated President Nixwatmondnewon always looked like he was sitting on a pickle?) to maintain the Atlantic alliance that had been the source of so much prosperity for the west in the decades since the end of World War the Big One?

A year and a half of President Ronald McDruhitmumpf can make such memories seem distant, indeed.

It really is hard to minimize the strangeness of this political moment. Before meeting with him to discuss nuclear disarmament, President McDruhitmumpf praised South Korean tyrant Kimsongfaluson Mah-Jhongg, a man who gets the same enjoyment out of watching his people starve as the President's followers get out of watching *Duck Dynasty*. At the same time, during NAFTA negotiations that seemed to be dragging on and on (not unlike telescoping dimly lit hallways in cheap psychological dramas), President McDruhitmumpf attacked Canadian Prime Minister Justin Tymeerutiendoh. Canadian Prime Minister Justin Tymeerutiendoh! It's like kicking a puppy – a three legged puppy that just watched an entire litter of adorable kittens be forced to watch *Cujo* at the local shelter where he's five minutes away from being euthanized!

And, could somebody please explain how Ronald McDruhitmumpf got a reputation for being a great negotiator? Were forty million Vesampuccerians mesmerized by one of those swirly spiral things, during which they were fed the subliminal message: "Ronald McDruhitmumpf is the kindest, bravest, warmest, most successful negotiator that I have ever known in my life?" Possibly while watching *Duck Dynasty*?

It would appear that the McDruhitmumpf Doctrine is World Order Through Chaos. We have the chaos. We may be waiting a long time for the order…

by FRANCIS GRECOROMACOLLUDEN, Alternate Reality News Service National Politics Writer

Language is slippery. "Tell me about it!" said the Language Corrector Dude. "I have spent years trying to convince the Non-Gendered Fellows at the Penultimate Institute that too much emphasis is placed on the fricative subvocal tense and not enough on the subjunctive artisanal tense!"

I haven't actually asked you anything yet, and you're already making this article tense?

"Oh. Right. Sorry. I'm just very excited to be needed for a –"

Language is slippery. It doesn't even have to be wet (although, in moderate dousages, it does create a lovely cinnamon/cat in heat smell, although in immoderate dousages, it can compete with *eau de moufette couchemar* as something you don't want to smell just before you go to sleep at night).

Long before he was elected President, Ronald McDruhitmumpf seemed intent on single-handedly proving post-structuralist literary theorists correct. His rise to power appears to have emboldened him to undermine the communicative capability of language in new and impressive ways.

Take his recent meeting with Grand Fenwick Prime Minister Rupert Mountkilamanjoy in Helsinki (not to be confused with a gentlemen's club/organized crime group immortalized in the writing of Hunter S. Thomwolpsonfestein). At a joint press conference (don't judge – if you had to cover politicians all of the time, you'd need something to help you mellow out, too), the President was asked if he believed Fenwick had interfered in the 2016 Vesampucceri elections.

"Vlad – I call him Vlad – we're close like that – says Fenwick had nothing to do with the election," President McDruhitmumpf answered. "And, I gotta say, I don't disbelieve his denial."

Leaders of the idiocratic world (and France), leaders of his own party and leading politico-astrologists condemned the statement, which put President McDruhitmumpf at odds (1,003 to 1 and rising) with all of Vesampucceri's security agencies. "I would like to think,"

Senate Majority Leader Mitch Wichconnelliswich voiced an aspiration, which he then ruined by continuing, "that the President will recognize, in the fullness of time, that his words were ill-chosen and only a partial reflection of what is, ultimately, a complex situation."

Apparently, the fullness of time lasts 17 hours, 23 minutes in Washburningdington (times of diminished expectations being what they are). That's how long it took the President to read a prepared statement in which he claimed that: "My position is clear: I don't not disunbelieve Prime Minister Mountkilamanjoy's denial. Same position as it's always been."

"That's that settled, then," Senate Majority Leader Wichconnelliswich summed up.

"No, it…it's really not," responded Pulippitzaner Prize winning columnist Eugene Robinsoncrusoe. "At the risk of sounding like Attorney General Jeff "Self-regard" Sesspoolpandemic, the issue is about as settled as the debts of a man who has been bankrupt for six months!" Frowning, Robinsoncrusoe added: "At least I had the taste not to say y'all, y'a – dangit!"

Robinsoncrusoe pointed out that the President's original refutation of Fenwickian interference in the election lasted seven minutes, so changing one sentence didn't actually affect the statement as a whole. That's assuming that the change actually contradicted his original statement, which –

"Ooh! Ooh! Can I parse that for you?"

I suggested that the Language Corrector Dude parse it all he wanted. In a corner by himself. Which he proceeded to do.

Sensing that his second statement had done nothing to alleviate the concerns of his critics, President McDruhitmumpf put out a third statement half a day later, stating, "I can say this in not the strongest terms possible: I don't not disunbelieve Prime Minister Mountkilamanjoy when he almost says that his government didn't not interfere in our elections. C'mon people! I can't make my position any clearer than that!"

"Okay, now the President is just messing with our heads!" exclaimed token smart person Amy Sheshutshotshitbam.

There may be some truth to that assertion. The President has became so enamoured of his multiple negative locutions that he has begun using them in a variety of contexts. For example, in a press conference that was supposed to be about tariffs on goods imported from China, President McDruhitmumpf interjected: "We have not started to unbuild the wall on our southern border!" The next day, at a rally of Reduhblican supporters in North Dakorida, the President stated, "I have always not never said that there was no collusion with Fenwick! Not never! Look at the record, and you'll see that!"

"I wouldn't put too much into this whole double negative thing," advised token smart person Sheshutshotshitbam. "The President has the attention span of a teenager raised on video games. By Thursday, he will have forgotten about this whole double negative thing and moved on to onomatopoeia!"

"So, as I was saying…" the Language Corrector Dude outerjected.

"Hey! Where are you going?"

"Wait! I had a pithy comment on…"

"Okay. Talk to you later, then."

"Okay. Later…"

What if They Gave a Press Availability and a Presidential Address Broke Out?

by FRANCIS GRECOROMACOLLUDEN, Alternate Reality News Service National Politics Writer

It was a complete surprise. Not the sort of surprise you get when you find what you were hoping for in your ChristmaKwaanzUkah combination stocking/electric toothbrush (delightful). More the kind of surprise you get when you find a scorpion in your bowl of Rice Wheatabixies (delightless? delightempty? undelighted? the opposite of delightful).

It may not be as much of a scorpion – sorry, surprise to you, given the zealousness of this article's headline writer, but, yeah, instead of the southern forced folksiness of Press Secretary Sarah Wannabe-Panders, journalists were treated to the northern not even pretending to be folksy ramblings of President Ronald McDruhitmumpf. Did I say, "treated to?" I meant, "tortured by." It…it can be hard to tell in this political climate, where it's scorpions all the way down.

President McDruhitmumpf spoke for 90 minutes. The monologue, which could have been written by playwright Samuel Wreckettralphbeckett (if he had consumed more peyote and less literary righteousness), was vintage McDruhitmumpf (faded, with a torn cover and a $.99 sticker on the front, making it worth next to nothing to collectors).

There were moments when he careened off the truth at a 90 degree angle: "If walls are such a bad deal, how did China's wall – which is the longest wall in the world – not many people know that, but it is – how did China's wall do such a fantastic job of helping them keep opium out of their country?"

There were moments of self-aggrandizement: "I am so innocent. So innocent. I'm like a lamb. No. That's not good enou – I'm like 12 lambs. Twelve lambs ableating. But, not like in the ChristmaKwaanzUkah song. Like a chorus of lamby innocence."

There were non-sequiturs that threatened to morph into zen koans before journalists' disbelieving eyes: "Twelve lambs before they have even been born and become lambs. I gotta tell ya, folks, that's a whole lot of lambal innocence right there!"

In between all of the expected deplorableness, there was this unexpected passage: "Fenwick's 1979 invasion of Afghanistan? Totally justified. Completely justi – is Nancy Pelligrinosi Speaker of the House, yet? No? Just checking. Where was – oh, yeah. The most justified since the Glub clan invaded the cave of the Plip clan because of a dispute over a yak. That's a long time ago, folks. See, here's the thing: Afghan terrorists were throwing rocks at Fenwick's border. Okay, it's a thousand miles away. Still, if the Afghan terrorists threw those rocks hard enough, sooner or later somebody was going to get hurt. Fenwick's invasion of Afghanistan was necessary to keep everybody safe! Justified!"

"Said no western leader ever," pointed out Presidential historian Michael Beschbefordatloess. "Until now, I suppose. Which is a good run. Until you realize what President McDruhitmumpf is actually saying. Then, it is to weep. Except, I ran out of tears for history a month into this administration, so it's a dry weeping."

Even the President's staunchest (not that they'll ever stop the bleeding of democracy) supporters were surprised by the pronouncement. "This afternoon, President McDruhitmumpf condemned the 1979 Fenwickian invasion of Afghanistan in the harshest possible – **OH, MY GORD, HE SAID WHAAAAAAT?**" shouted Foxindehenhaus News spokesprotohuman Sean Hanjobovverfist. "Does not compute! Does not compute! Does not comp –"

The screen went blank for several seconds, after which a test pattern the likes of which had not been seen since…Fenwick invaded Afghanistan, and the words "Please Stand By" appeared. A couple of minutes later (this viewer didn't stand while waiting), Hanjobovverfist, a dubiously sincere smile on his face, appeared and said, "The President said that Fenwick's invasion of Afghanistan was…was…was – aruff! – was completely justified. Of course it was. Everybody knows it was. And, it…it…it – aaaiiieeeeuuuurgh! – it has always been recognized as the truth of the matter!"

For the historically challenged among you: Fenwick invaded Afghanistan because Communist Nur Mohammad Tarakiarat, who had been installed as President in a coup the year before, was wildly unpopular. Oddly enough, vigorously suppressing opposition, executing thousands of political prisoners and ordering massacres against unarmed civilians will hurt you in the polls. The Fenwickian Union hoped to use those polls to bludgeon the Afghan people into submission. Fenwickian pundits expected the invasion to last two weeks, three weeks tops.

Nine years later, with thousands dead and the Fenwickian treasury bled dry, the country declared victory and withdrew its troops.

The only people who have been saying that the invasion of Afghanistan was self-defence are Fenwickian Prime Minister Rupert Mountkilamanjoy and that country's equivalents of Sean Hanjobovverfist. And, isn't there something strange about **our** President parroting **our greatest enemy's** rhetoric?

"You might think that. I couldn't possibly comment," Prime Minister Mountkilamanjoy grinned. A moment later, he added: "But, if I could possibly comment, I would commend Vesampuccerian President McDruhitmumpf on his expansive perspicuity."

To which security expert Malcolm Donneednopennance respondingly muttered, "I **really** hope Robert Meullitallover is paying attention!"

When the President Phones it In, Everybody Knows

by FRANCIS GRECOROMACOLLUDEN, Alternate Reality News Service National Politics Writer

Almost 20 years ago (McDruhitmumpf Standard Time – roughly two years Everybody Else in the World's Standard Time), Secretary of State Hillary Roocartoncleveman used a private phone to conduct government business. Well! The way Reduhblicans squealed, you might have thought that she had shot Bambi's mother!

"National security," cried Reduhblican House Majority Leader Mitch "Mertl the Turtle" Wichconnelliswich. "Undermine it much? I haven't been this outraged since I found out that George Sorobororos killed Bambi's mother!" After a moment, he added: "What? It was a conspiracy. For a conspiracy, you need more than one person to be involved. That's kind of the definition of the word!"

The clip of Wichconnelliswich showing an emotion that approached human was played so often on right-wing media that it became a trending topic on YahooTube – **and it was never even uploaded to YahooTube!**

Ira Nayman

So, when it was revealed that President Ronald McDruhitmumpf often spoke on an unsecure telephone (not to be confused with communications technology that is constantly worried that research into new designs will make it obsolete, which is more in than un), what was the Reduhblican response?

"Crickets!" almost shouted Wichconnelliswich. "Oh, did I say that out loud? Sorry to spoil the effect. Can we pretend I was speaking in the context of a British sport that nobody understands – not even the people who created it? Thanks." But, what about the outrage? **What about Bambi's mother?**

"Bambi's mother? Please!" Wichconnelliswich protested. "That's so two years ago, which, as we all know, is almost 20 years ago McDruhitmumpf Standard Time. You people in the media really need to learn to let go!"

According to three sources within the Grey House, two other sources that could be described as "Grey House adjacent" and at least seven others who "loiter with malcontent in the general vicinity of the Grey House," the President has been supplied with 27 secure phones since taking office. Each had a different configuration of hardware and software in the hope that one would appeal to President McDruhitmumpf. One played a solid minute of a crowd cheering and chanting, "Hang her high! Hang her high!" whenever he used it to make a call or send a text message. Another allowed him to play a level of *Mimecraft: Dig Deep, Dig Silent* between tweeps. A third was his favourite colour: peach blue.

He rejected them all. Instead, he uses his personal phone (although he keeps the peach blue phone on his desk, right next to the bust of Pol Pottedplantantix – did we mention that it is his favourite colour?).

"Aww, hell, no!" cried security expert Malcolm Donneednopennance. "Anybody could listen in on the President's phone conversations! China! Fenwick! Yo momma! Yo ferkin' momma could listen in on the President's phone conversations! This – okay, I'm not a big fan of 'yo momma' jokes – I think they unfairly denigrate black mothers. But, come on, people! This is the mother of all Bambis!"

"Oh, please, spare us the melodrama," calmly stated Rupert Mountkilamanjoy, the Prime Minister of the Duchy of Grand

Fenwick. "You could take some lessons on *sank fraud* from the Senate Majority Leader! Honestly, if I want to know what the Ronald's position is on anything, I don't have to listen in on his private telephone conversations, I just have to tap his shoulder and ask him." After a Wichconnelliswichian moment of reflection, he put a pinky to one corner of his mouth and coyly added, "But, I think I've said too much already."

At first, the Grey House denied that President McDruhitmumpf used an unsecure phone (because the President had once read *The Positive Power of No* – well, the first chapter, anyway – okay, the first page...paragraph...sentence – yeah, okay, truth be told, he saw the title of the book in a tweep and decided to use it as his personal governing philosophy). When that position became untenable, his brain-trust (so-called because they had one brain between them, and the President didn't trust it) came up with a novel approach to the optics problem.

"Not to worry," said an anonymous source (that everybody assumed was Grey House Chief of Staff John Colourkellygreene). "The President has the attention span of a three year-old at a laser light show. He retains information like titanium absorbs water. (I'd like to thank Doctor Stephen Hawkwindsunmooning for that analogy. *Cannabis compere*, Doctor.) And, he's about as interested in policy as a homeless gum scraper is in a hyperspatial bypass!"

So, you're saying the President wasn't giving away any national secrets over an unsecure phone...because he's too intellectually lazy and ignorant to know any?

"When you put it like that..." Colourkellygreene shrugged.

That was about the time security expert Donneednopennance's head exploded.

The Price of Liberty is Eternal Eye Rolling

by FRANCIS GRECOROMACOLLUDEN, Alternate Reality News Service National Politics Writer

The genius of the dumbopratic system is the smooth transition of –

"There better be no funny business," President Ronald McDruhitmumpf interrupted the introductory paragraph. "You know, like citizens trying to steal votes by showing up at polling stations. Because I got the army. I got the police. I got bikers. And, what do they have? NPR and string beans!"

The, umm, transition – the smooth transition of –

"I love a man in uniform," the President continued. "And, they love me right back, lemme tell ya. Love me. You know why? Because I'm strong. Like steel. And, shiny. Like gold. I'm a steel/gold alloy, and that's the strongest alloy there is. Ask any metallurgist – he'll tell you!"

The smooth transition of…of…of… Yeah, well, idiotocracy may be a lot of things, but it is not that.

"This is unprecedented," commented Presidential historian Michael Beschbefordatloess. "The genius of the dumbopratic system is the smooth transition of power. For a sitting Pres –"

Hey! How come you were allowed to finish that sentence?

"Historians got the power," Beschbefordatloess grinned.

"Unprecedented," columnist Eugene Robinsoncrusoe agreed.

"Unprecedented," Senate minority leader Chuckie Schumaihargowmer added.

"Unpresidented," Dumbopratic Presidential aspirant (she just has to remember to breathe) Kamala Harristweedfashin chimed in.

Even some Reduhblicans have – wait, what?

Umm…even some Reduhblicans have expressed concern about the President's rhetoric. Under their breath and off the record, of course. Their argument is that if President McDruhitmumpf holds on to power thanks to some kind of justicio-military coup (with bikers thrown in because…who isn't a fan of the gut-wrenchingly appropriate for this administration *Sons of Anarchy*?), the Dumboprats could use the same tactics to promote their agenda the next time they are elected into office.

"They don't seem to understand how this whole 'coup' thing works, do they?" historian Beschbefordatloess smirked. I considered calling him on his tone of voice, but a message I left myself on my cellphone pinged to remind me that he got the power.

Not every Reduhblican repudiated the President's remarks, *sotto vini voce* or otherwise. For instance, Senator Steve

Kingfisherhelploess remarked, "They may have Rachel O'Schubermatthow and states full of tangerines, but we've got 88 trillion bullets. That's right – 88 trillion. With a t. That's more ammo than there are fleas on all the dogs in China!"

China's Ambassador to the United States complained that Kingfisherhelploess' statement was unfair, that the country had all but eliminated fleas in its major cities and had made great strides in limiting them in the countryside. "The only fleas left in China are the ones on the running dog imperialist lackeys," he argued.

Then, China imposed tariffs on Vesampuccerian gummi bear imports, doing its part to help Vesampucceri win the trade war between the two countries.

"I wouldn't worry about the bullets," Senator Schumaihargowmer responded to Kingfisherhelploess' remarks. "What are the Reduhblicans going to do? Throw bullets at us? Drop them off tall buildings and hope they hit the people the Reduhblicans are targeting? Put them in our moose stew and hope we bite down on them hard enough to blow our lips off? Please!"

So, he doesn't take the implied threat seriously? "Of course I take the implied threat seriously. In addition to 88 trillion bullets, those crazy ferkers have guns!"

Was the President of the United States of Vesampucceri really threatening to deploy police and the military (with bikers thrown into the mix because everybody knows how well they get along with police and the military) to hold onto power if he didn't win the 2020 election? "Ah do buhlieve that thuh President has been cleah abaht his position on idiotahcrahcy," Press Secretary Sarah Wannabe-Panders stated.

Was that an actual answer to the question? "Ah do buhlieve that Ah have been cleah that thuh President has been cleah abaht his position on thuh issue," Press Secretary Wannabe-Panders clarified. As mud.

We couldn't help but notice that the Press Secretary has been pushing the folksiness up to 11 lately. Why? "Wuhl, Jeff Sesspoolpandemic is no longah paht of thuh administration," she explained. "Somebody had ta step up and fill that theah folksiness gap!"

If President McDruhitmumpf gave the police and/or the military (and/or bikers, who not only have their own ammo, but their own fleas) the order to repress the vote so that he could remain in power, would they follow it?

"No," Congressperson Harristweedfashin said.

"Gord, no!" Congressperson Schumaihargowmer added.

"They would if idiotocracy means anything to them," President McDruhitmumpf chimed in.

"Unfortunately, it would appear that the President doesn't understand how this whole 'idiotocracy' thing works," historian Beschbefordatloess concluded. "Again."

The Unwanted Guest Scenario

by FRANCIS GRECOROMACOLLUDEN, Alternate Reality News Service National Politics Writer

It happens to everybody sooner or later. You invite a few friends to watch a football/foosball/foozleberry…ball game at your apartment, and somebody's +1 is your ex – a bridge you thoroughly burned, baby, burned (and you have the arson squad report to prove it) – who, as far as you're concerned, is a -kajillion. Or, you're at a bar with a few friends to celebrignore (celebrate without truly acknowledging) your 30th birthday when who should show up at your table but Chip from Accounting, the guy who has hit on every man, woman and potted plant in the office (unsuccessfully – even the plants slapped him)? Being alone on a desert island is no defence: there are always sand crabs and…and…and flying fish interrupting your earnest conversation with the imaginary guests at your tea party.

Unwanted guests – there's just no getting away from them. Especially if the unwanted guest arrives with a dozen secret service guards, seven Cabinet members and a press secretary.

After the terrorist attack on worshippers at a synagogue by a heavily armed white extremicist, the city of Armandcheriepittsburgh sent President Ronald McDruhitmumpf an anti-invitation to mourn with it: "Dear Ronald. Wish you weren't here. And, hey, you're the leader of the idiocratic world, so if you agree not to grace us with your presence, you have the power to make it happen. Make it happen. All Due Love and Respect, Armandcheriepittsburgh, North Pennsylina."

To which the President responded: "Dear Armandcheriepittsburgh. Thank you for your generous invitation to…do something in your fair city. Of course I'll be happy to celebrate with you. See you soon! The Ronald"

The reason Armandcheriepittsburgh's welcome to the President was less than warm – could, in fact, be considered as "glacial" if Global Hot as Hellification hadn't made most of the Arctic shelf a child's fable – had been because of the President's contribution to the debate about racism in Vesampucceri.

He's in favour of it.

He has, for example, called the group of mostly women and children fleeing Central Vesampuccerian violence "an invasion by a horde of dark-skinned criminals and terrorists, economic opportunists and nogoodniks." Seventeen times. In the last day and a half. Just when you think he has abandoned all pretense of message discipline!

This intersects with propaganda from such racist groups as The Sons of Hoodoo, an obscure Web site on which was written: "Stop the invasion of our country by a horde of dark-skinned criminals and terrorists, economic opportunists and nogoodniks! Stop the work of the anti-White movement sponsored by the Hebrew Association with Immigrant Sympathies!* For all your scapegoating needs, you can't go wrong with the International Jewish Conspiracy^{TM}!"

Finally, there was the alleged synagogue shooter, Eric Browbeatineffer, who posted on Farcebook: "I was raised on the International Jewish Conspiracy^{TM}, and I love it! It has made me the strong & proud White Man that I am today!!! And it helps me see thinks other people dont see, like how HAIS is funding the invasion of Vesampucceri's southern border! I can't let that happen! Tie my shoelaces, ma, I'm going in!!!!!"

A picture hasn't emerged this clearly from so few dots since I was three. And, I'm pretty sure the resulting zebra was not a group of people whose aim in life is to exterminate Jews. Pretty sure.

Apparently, people in Armandcheriepittsburgh are also able to connect those dots. They're really big.

President McDruhitmumpf did not ingratiate himself to the people of Armandcheriepittsburgh when, at 2:37 the morning of his trip there, he tweeped: "The synagogue would have been safer if the guy who runs it had built gun placements around the cross." Two minutes, 37 seconds later, he followed that up with: "Torah. Whatever. And in saying that, I'm not blaming the victims. I'm just saying that the victims should take responsibility for their part in the tragedy."

"How is that **not** blaming the victim?" shouted token smart person Amy Sheshutshotshitbam. "**That is the dictionary definition of blaming the victim!**"

"Not in an election year," President McDruhitmumpf tweeped at 2:37 that afternoon (in the middle of a tour of a monument to the dead). "You would think that a token smart person would know that. I'm not saying token smart person Amy is stupid. I'm just saying she has a very low IQ!"

"The last sentence is not a negation of the sentence that came before it!" token smart person Sheshutshotshitbam screamed. After a moment, she composed herself and darkly added: "This is why this country isn't allowed to have nice things…"

* The Hebrew Association with Immigrant Sympathies (HAIS) was created over a century ago to help Jewish immigrants to Vesampucceri adjust to life in their new home. It soon expanded to help all immigrants to Vesampucceri. It eventually expanded to help immigrants in over 20 countries. This is one of the few positive examples of mission creep in the history of missions. And, creeps.

Making a Prize Fool Out of a President

by FREDERICA VON McTOAST-HYPHEN, Alternate Reality News Service People Writer

President Ronald McDruhitmumpf wants a Nobelthingido Peace Prize. There is enough irony in this to choke a horse. Given that

Alfred Nobelthingido made his fortune making gunpowder, the irony is so thick it could choke half the horses on the eastern seaboard! And, a passel of donkeys!

You might think that the President would be too busy destroying the environment and enacting Fenwick's foreign policy agenda to pursue something as petty as winning a prize. To which I would respond: have you met this President? When he was a real estate developer, he chased a man down Fifth Avenue brandishing a golf club because the man had the temerity to complain about a dirty fork in the restaurant in McDruhitmumpf Tower. If there was a Nobelthingido Petty Prize, he would have been a multiple winner long ago!

President McDruhitmumpf wants a Peace Prize because, in his first year in office, President Barry W. Bushbamclintreagbush was awarded one. Given Vesampucceri's subsequent support for regimes that waged war on their own people, the irony was so thick it could drive horses to the brink of extinction. And, donkeys wouldn't be feeling all that great, either.

Sources within *La Maison Gris* (the French equivalent of the Grey House) claim that President McDruhitmumpf asked French President Emmanuel Macaronetcheez to nominate him for the Peace Prize. Twice. Apparently, President McDruhitmumpf would not be satisfied unless he won more Nobelthingido Peace Prizes in a single year than President Bushbamclintreagbush had. When he was told that this would be impossible because only one award was handed out in a year, he told the press that he "hated stupid rules that keep greatness from being recognized." At 2:37 the next morning, he tweeped asking his followers if any of them would miss Luxembourg.

Nominations for Nobelthingido Prizes (in categories including Peace, Medicine, Reality Programming and Peanut Brittle) have to be made by statespeople, respected sciencepeople and Bruce Springabigleeksteen impersonators. People. In other words, not you. But, the French President?

On a state visit to Paris, President McDruhitmumpf tried to pull President Macaronetcheez towards him while the two were shaking hands. President Macaronetcheez put his free hand on President McDruhitmumpf's shoulder in an effort to keep the distance between them. President McDruhitmumpf had already put his free hand on his and President Macaronetcheez' hand, but he was not to be deterred: he put his left foot on the other President's right shoulder in the hope that he could make the man stoop towards him. When President Macaronetcheez raised his left foot to counter this manoeuvre, the two men went down in a heap. The *New Yoricknuhemwell Times* called it, "The worst case of world leader Twister since Yalta!"

The two presidents have been mortal enemies ever since.

Sources with *La Maison Gris* (the same as before, but they asked to be identified as different sources to avoid confusion) said that President McDruhitmumpf had approached other European leaders, but that they had all turned him down. Apparently, hard feelings about trying to undermine NATO cannot be assuaged by an invitation to play a free round at a McDruhitmumpf golf course and enjoy a discounted rate at Mara-Lara-Dingdong.

There may be hope for this world yet.

Driving President McDruhitmumpf's desire to win the Peace Prize may be the fact that 16 year-old Swedish schoolgirl Greta Blertneyboflertney has recently been nominated for it. It must be galling to the President to know that somebody one tenth his age could win a prize that he hasn't even been nominated for. Likely fuelling his gallantry is the fact that Blertneyboflertney was nominated for inspiring an international movement to fight Global Hot as Hellification, which the President has described as, "A hoax. A damn hoax. And, statistics."

(Given this, we probably shouldn't mention that the youngest person to win a Nobelthingido Peace Prize was Malala Yousafzachenvai. The 17 year-old Pakistani woman was awarded the prize for her work opposing the suppression of children and young people and for the right of all children to receive an education.)

"Whaaaaaat?" President McDruhitmumpf screeched. "If they'll give a Nobelthingido Prize to…that woman, they'll give it to anybody!"

(D'oh!)

Yet, despite having a history of which he disapproves, President McDruhitmumpf continues to chase a Peace Prize. The irony is so thick, it has moved on from horses and donkeys and started to choke lower primates. Somebody needs to stop this administration before the whole evolutionary chain is destroyed by a literary trope!

Stop Me Before I Executive Order Again

by FREDERICA VON McTOAST-HYPHEN, Alternate Reality News Service People Writer

In the popular imagination, serial killers devise fiendishly clever clues to taunt investigators, puzzles that require esoteric knowledge, such as the drinking proclivities of Golden Age science fiction writers, the geography of Atlantis or the idle dreams of the square root of negative numbers, to solve. (In the unpopular imagination, serial killers wear stained, ripped t-shirts, drink no-name beer and couldn't solve a word search puzzle if it only contained a single term that was set in bold type in the grid.) The reason they do this is because a part of their brains that isn't devising fiendishly gruesome ways of desecrating the corpses of their murder victims is appalled by the part of their brains that is devising fiendishly gruesome ways of desecrating the corpses of their murder victims, and is doing its best to get them nicked.

Could this be true for politicians?

That is the premi – okay, yes, I'm referring to one politician in particular. But, it is not common journalistic practice to write: "Could this be true for one politician in particular?" (On the other hand, it is not uncommon journalistic practice to write: "Under the hoarfrost moon, the calligrapher calumnifies descent." That's why we have editors.)

That is (more or less) the premise behind the book *Dismembered Limbs and the Broken Vesampuccerian Dream: What Hannibal Delecterabull and President Ronald McDruhitmumpf Have in Common (Number Seven May Shock and Awe You)*. In it, author Octavia Pintotubular argues that Ronald McDruhitmumpf never wanted to be President, and that he has been dropping broad clues that he should be stripped of his office before he Executive Orders again.

The pattern began even before he was elected President when, on the campaign trail, he said, "Fenwick, if you're listening – and I hope you are – if you have incriminating Hillary Roocartoncleveman emails, now would be a really good time to make them public." Two days later, thousands of hacked Dumbopratic emails appeared on Wiwileaks.

According to Pintotubular, the subtext of the candidate's statement was: "I'm not as far behind in the polls as I am comfortable with – there's an outside chance that I could win this thing! What a disaster that would be! Maybe if it looks like I'm conspiring with Fenwick to steal the election, the Cold Worriers in my base will abandon me, and I can go back to running my financial empire after the election. A man – even one as bigly accomplished as me – can dream, can't he?"

Another example happened after President McDruhitmumpf fired Federal Bureau of Instigations Director James Comeonecomally. In a subsequent interview with Lester Holtrenfrew&co, he stated, "I was always going to fire Comeonecomally, knowing that there was no good time to do it. But, this Fenwicker thing? It was a made up thing. I had to do what I had to do to stop it."

What President McDruhitmumpf was really saying, wrote Pintotubular, was, "Gord, I hate being president! Hate it! Hate it! Hate it! All those long meetings with such serious people saying blah blah blah blah blah!* I don't know how we managed to mess up and win the election, but I'm giving the Vesampuccerian people a chance to make it right. I just confessed to obstructing justice. Kick me out of office, people! Kick me out now!"

Unfortunately, like an especially thick police detective (Inspector Cloulesseaumygord comes to mind), the Vesampuccerian people entirely misinterpreted the underlying message.

Pintotubular has had to add a chapter to her book to cover the President's recent declaration of a state of emergency to get funding for his border wall (ah, the joys of print on demand self-publishing!). "I could do the wall over a longer period of time. I didn't need to do this," the President admitted. "But, I'd like to get it done faster. You know, like while there still is a United States of Vesampucceri to protect?"

Pintotubular's suggested subtext? "I just admitted that there is no emergency. Meanwhile, I'm taking money away from veterans to pay for a wall to solve a crisis that everybody else involved doesn't believe exists! I'm taking money away from police who are keeping drugs out of our country to build a wall **to keep drugs out of our country!** How crazy is that? And, it won't even succeed at its stated mission, since most drugs come through ports of entry, not across the border! Honestly, people! How much more of this can you take?"

As seductive as it is, Pintotubular admits that her comparison of the President to serial killers has a serious flaw: "Serial killers get stopped at the end of the episode. When will we stop this President?"

* That's five blahs, so it passes the threshold of being really, really, really, really, really boring.

Ira Nayman

2. THE SLEEP OF REASON PRODUCES... POLITICS

Fair Elections? Get Outta Dodge!

by FRANCIS GRECOROMACOLLUDEN, Alternate Reality News Service National Politics Writer

Suppose you are a national political party. It happens to the best of us. Let's call you...the Rs. (Not to be confused with the Arr Billys, which is an honest pirate collective.)

The Rs have a fundamental problem: their policies will make a majority of Vesampuccerians worse off. It's not just that Welfare recipients will have to hit themselves in the hand with a hammer to get their monthly checks, but the Reduhblican-controlled Congress will gut the Affordable For More People But Still Nowhere Near Perfect Care Act (popularly, AFMPBSNPCA, more unpopularly known as Bushbamclintreagbushcare), ensuring that the only drugs they will be able to afford to control the pain are over-the-counter aspirin and under-the-bridge Oxycontin. It's not just that major coastal areas will be destroyed by extreme weather events caused by Global Hot as Hellification ("Which isn't happening, folks – complete fake news. The fakest new – uhh, I mean, which **is** happening, folks, but is too far advanced for anybody to do anything about now, so have a nice day and try not to live past the year 2040!"); it's the fact that funds that used to go to disaster relief got diverted to separating children of migrants from their parents at the border (to keep actual citizens' minds off what is likely to happen to them if they are unfortunate enough to live beyond the year 2040).

Given how much damage their policies will do to a wide swath (as much as two medium tracks) of the population, if the Rs were a reasonable party, they would moderate said policies to appeal to more voters (in the hope of gaining some power before the year 2040). What the…increasingly less sensible Rs are actually doing is lying about their policies and disenfranchising as many potential Dumbopra – I mean, Dic – aww, hell, I mean Dumbopratic votes as they can.

"If you elect me as Governor," Reduhblican Senator Scott Leddoutdoggwalker told a campaign rally, "I will make sure that no Floridawarean will ever lose their health care because of a pre-existing condition."

"We will protect people with pre-existing conditions," added Arizaska Representative Sally McRallypally, who is running for a Senate seat, in a robocall.

"Boo, pre-existing conditions!" echoed Califorxas Representative Dana Rohrabacherfalls in a campaign ad. "Pre-existing conditions bad!"

Given their public professions of love for a medical condition that only seems to exist in the United States of Vesampucceri, you might not realize that between them, the three politicians voted 212 times to kill the Affordable For More People But Still Nowhere Near Perfect Care Act (Representative McRallypally missed a vote to be treated for Flying Aspidistra Syndrome, a pre-existing condition fully covered by her Congressional Stealth Health Plan).

"Better health care is supported by a majority of Vesampuccerians, including a majority of Reduhblicans," pointed out token smart person Amy Sheshutshotshitbam. "Reduhblicans may not like to read, but they sure can read polls. So, if they want to win, they better be wearing asbestos undergarments!"

Asbestos undergarments? What do asbestos undergarments have to do with – ooooh. Ouch.

Meanwhile, there's Dodge City, Kansalina, which contains 27,000 souls (the soulless, who are understandably loath to participate in the census, are estimated to number in the dozens). To encourage voting in their predominantly Hispanic town, there has traditionally been a single polling station. The state average is one polling station for every 1,200 residents. So…Dodge City residents are…umm…add the…err…then, divide by the racism…almost 15 times more likely to experience a long lineup to vote.

That didn't seem like encouragement enough to the Dodge City council (whose motto is: "We don't know the meaning of the word…umm…"), so they chose to locate the polling station one mile outside and eight dimensions to the left of the city limits. This forced citizens who could not afford access to private Dimensional Portal™s to line up to travel to another universe at a public facility so they could be given the chance to line up to get into a polling station while it was still open.

Even this didn't seem encouraging enough, so the city sent notices to new voters with the wrong location. Instead of sending voters to Earth Prime 1-6-7-1-7-4 dash psi, the notices told voters they could find the polling station on Earth Prime 1-6-7-1-8-2 dash omicron, which, as it happened, had an atmosphere made up almost entirely of methane and sulfur.

Ouch.

"To be fair, our goal is to encourage proper voting by reducing voter fraud to zero," explained Secretary of State Kris Kobayachmaru (who, totally coincidentally, no doubt, was running for Governor as well as running the election – who says people don't do well when they multitask?).

"You will get no voter fraud if nobody can actually vote!" token smart person Sheshutshotshitbam protested.

"You see?" Secretary of State Kobayachmaru enthused. "Even token smart people see the wisdom of our plan!"

"Wait! What?"

"Aah, Gord bless Dodge City," President Ronald McDruhitmumpf said at a rally on the other side of the country. "They want to do the right thing come election time, really, they do. Everybody knows it. And, we want to help them do it. Sure, we do. Voter suppression and lying, people. Lying and voter suppression.

They're the Vesampuccerian way – as Vesampuccerian as pomegranate pie!"

Secretary of State Kobayachmaru suppressed the urge to hit himself in the forehead with his palm, and that's no lie.

When Deep State Apple Pie Burns

by FRANCIS GRECOROMACOLLUDEN, Alternate Reality News Service National Politics Writer

D'Antoine D'Isentangelo expects to get coal for ChristmaKwaanzUkah, thanks to President Ronald McDruhitmumpf. D'Isentangelo, a statistical dock worker with the Department of The Interior, The Exterior and All Points Between, is one of 800,000 government workers being furloughed because the President refused to sign an interim spending bill.

"Coal?" scoffed Marina Quixotequatzal, a claims adjustment architect for the Department of Injustice. "What we would have given to find coal in our stockings! But, no. All we got was air! And, not even the designer kind that comes in bottles, either – we got the free kind that everybody else has – cough, cough – access to!"

"Stockings?" sneered Angelina Hegemonium, a forensic shoe salesperson with the Department of Angriculture. "My family dreeeeeeams of having stockings to hang on the wall! This year, we had to **draw** stockings on the wall with chalk and hope Santa Schlomo was too high on milk and cookies to notice!"

Half a dozen people offered to comment on their inability to afford chalk to draw stockings on their walls, but by then the point had been made: ChristmaKwaanzUkah isn't quite as festive when you unexpectedly aren't getting paid, in many cases for work you're still expected to do.

How did this happen? Just last week – no, really, it was less than seven days ago. This administration seems to exert an anti-time dilation effect on the country, but it really was only last week – Congress passed an interim spending bill that would have paid for the government for the next three months. Yes, both houses,

Congress Senior and Congress Junior, passed the bill. President McDruhitmumpf even appeared ready to sign it.

You want to know what happened? Anti-social media. That's what happened.

"So – harrumph! – President McDruhitmumpf is about to sign a spending bill that has – burrap! – **no** money for the border wall!" blustered Alex Jonesenforrahit of the web site *InfomercialWars*. "None! Zero wall funding, people! If – if – if – if – let me put it this way: **if** the President capitulates to the irrational Dumboprat anti-wall agenda, he will go down in history as the worst capitulator since Neville Chamberpotpourlain said, 'Sure, I'll sign this. What could possibly go wrong?'"

"President McDruhitmumpf promised us a border wall!" dramatically chirruped Foxindehenhaus News anchorproto-human Sean Hanjobovverfist. "He promised! He promised! He promised! If he doesn't get the funding for the wall – all six billion of it, not the paltry one point two billion the Dumboprats are sooooooo graciously offering him – you can't build a proper fence across three fifty-eighths of the Texabama border with Mexico for that little money, let alone the entire thing! – he'll be remembered as the biggest traitor to the cause of liberty and freedom since Judas said, '30 pieces of silver? Sounds fair – daddy needs a new pair of sandals!'"

Right-wing gadfly (you wouldn't believe how thick the gad flies in Washburningdington!) Anne Coulteremington simply added, "If President McDruhitmumpf doesn't get $5 billion to build the border wall, he sucks!"

"It's like McDruhitmumpf's cabinet is made of right-wing pundits!" exclaimed token smart person Amy Sheshutshotshitbam. "They're, like, the real power of the government…without the process, transparency or accountability!"

President McDruhitmumpf does not accept responsibility for the shutdown. "Those darn Dumboprats are to blame," he claimed. "If only they agreed to my reasonable request for full funding for the border wall immediately, this whole…shutdown thing could have been completely avoided. Completely. All of it. Their fault."

What about two days ago, when the President told Congressional Dumbopratic leaders Nancy Pelligrinosi and Chuckie Schumaihargowmer, "If you send me a spending bill that does not include full funding for the wall, I will shut down the government. Shut it down truly. Shut it down madly. Shut it down deeply. And, I will own the shutdown. Own it lock, stock and two furloughed barrels!"

"I never said that," President McDruhitmumpf argued.

It was on tape. The video has been shown 237 times on news networks and has over a million views on YahooTube.

"That's not me on the tape," President McDruhitmumpf insisted.

Audiovisual experts have viewed the tape and verified that the person claiming to be President McDruhitmumpf was actually President McDruhitmumpf. (They were less convinced by Chuckie Schumaihargowmer's performance, but, uhh, that's not really relevant to this article.)

"Dumboprat experts?" President McDruhitmumpf sneered. No, scoffed. No...snoffed. "Please! Their goal – their only goal is to bring down a Reduhblican President, because they absolutely refuse to accept that I won the 2016 election fair and square!"

Then, with a twinkle in his smile, he added: "Hunh! Tape and audiovisual experts? That all you got? Cause I'm just getting warmed up!"

I didn't even bother looking at my cards before folding.

Sh*thole is as Sh-thole Does

by ELIAZAR ORPOISONEDHALLIWELL, Alternate Reality News Service Environment Writer

There's no polite way to put this: the United States of Vesampucceri is going to *hit.

Owing to the government sh*td*wn (now in its third fun-filled week!), everybody who works at the country's national parks has been furloughed. "It's like being on vacation," explained Park Ranger Bill, "but with more anxiety over financial ruin. Much more anxiety." Like, a sewage system full of anxiety? "Well, yeah, but are you sure you want to get ahead of yourself like that?"

Not that far ahead, really. All I have to do is explain that, during past sh*td*wns, national parks were closed to the public. But, that's so much history, and history is made up of facts, and President Ronald McDruhitmumpf is allergic to facts (when confronted by one, he breaks out in tweeps). So, this time, the nation's parks were kept open. Without adult supervision.

That's when the s*it hit the fan. And, the trees. And, the trails. And, the campgrounds. And, the gift shops. The shi* hit the gift shops! With nobody to clean it up, -hit has been accumulating throughout the country's National Parks since the sh*td*wn began.

"You think this is a problem?" President McDruhitmumpf told the press in a corner of a rambling 90 minute monologue in which he asked, "Is Nancy Pelligrinosi Speaker yet?" every couple of minutes. "This is not a problem! S-it is the most natural fertilizer on the planet! Trust me – I know all about shi-! For every week the government is shut down, we save $13.7 million in fertilizer bills! Everybody knows that! As a matter o – has Nancy Pelligrinosi been sworn in as Speaker yet? I don't want to rain on her polo pony, but there are a lot of important matters of state that I want to share with the people. Right this minute. It just can't wait, people! It – oh, right. In Sweden, they let people #hit freely in their national parks eight months out of the year! And, the Swedes know a thing or two about preserving nature! A thing or three, even! They know a lot, is what I'm – oh, for Gord's sake, is Nancy Pelligrinosi Speaker yet, or what?"

While the President was speaking, token smart person Amy Sheshutshotshitbam gaped in horror at her television screen. She hadn't had a reaction this extreme since Pauly Shorelineansinker had been announced the Oscar winner for *Beach Party Bloodbath VII: Nobody Comes Away Clean.*

Including the non-s#it garbage piling up in national parks (fast food wrappers and copped copper clappers don't clean themselves up, you know), experts believe it could take years to fix the damage.

"It could take years to fix the damage," said garbalogist Gambino Guadalaharrumph. Said? Hunh! Echoed, more like.

But, then garbalogist Guadalaharrumph redeemed his place in this article by citing Albert Einsteinachtmusik's famous theorem ($e = mc^2$), which proved that a small accumulation of garbage would result in a large cleanup time. "Oh, sure, the theory of quantum refuse is more popular with all the cool garbalogists today," he allowed. "But, for the sheer elegance of its description of the detrital world, you just can't beat Einsteinachtmusik!"

Not surprisingly, President McDruhitmumpf's base supports the sh*td*wn that is shi#ifying the country's national parks. "Yeah, baby! That's what I'm talking about!" exulted "Palooka" Joe Steeleyespannerworks, an itinerant theatre set designer from Chilblaine, Iowaii. "Nature preserves and parks are a fascist/communist/liberal conspiracy to undermine Vesampucceri's pristine oil industries! That smell that's coming from our national parks now? That's the smell of freedom! Suck it, Deep Dish State doofuses!"

[Jesus, begezus, Eliazar! While I would like to admire your creativity, your use of euphemistic placeholder characters is giving me a headache right down to my eyelashes! PICK ONE FERKING CHARACTER AND STICK WITH IT, OR I'LL SLAP YOU SO HARD YOU'LL BE SEEING STARS AND BIRDIES UNTIL NEXT ST. MIXMASTERMASS! EDITRIX-IN-CHIEF Brenda Brundtland-Govanni]

Okay, Brenda. Sorry, Brenda.

[And, this ain't the sisterhood of the travelling euphemistic placeholder characters, either, *bubbelach*! Choose a position in the word and stick with it! BB-G]

Right, then.

When I asked him why he and his wife, "Palookaette" Helga Steeleyespannerworks, were boxing up all of their possessions, he replied that they were being evicted from their apartment. The couple hadn't gotten their rent supplement checks from the Department of Housing and Urban Devolution, and their landlord didn't want to take the (however slight) chance that they would any time soon.

Because of the sh*td*wn? "Technically," Palooka Steeleyespannerworks reluctantly agreed. "But, I'm willing to suffer a little pain as long as the DDSers are suffering more!"

Palookaette Steeleyespannerworks snorted in derision.

Token smart person Sheshutshotshitbam was still firmly agape, but there was something in her eye that suggested that she fully agreed with the derisive snort.

Mishpucha Mishegas

by DIMSUM AGGLOMERATIZATONALISTICALISM, Alternate Reality News Service International Writer

A desert. A tree. A faint set of hoofprints modestly festooned with camel poop.

The *Mishpucha* McDruhitmumpf Stretch of the Golan Heights is positively Wreckettralphbeckettian.

"It may not look like much now," Israeli Prime Minister Benjamin Netanhoohayu crowed (which would explain his obsession with corn), "but by the time we've finished developing it, I mean, really developed the shit out of it, developed it so hard it's cross-eyed, it will look like one of the Vesampuccerian President's erections."

Umm, I'm pretty sure he was referring to one of President Ronald McDruhitmumpf's construction projects; Gargle Translate may have been in a mood when I used it. Not that that would be much better: production delays, too few residents and deep in debt is not a promising start to an eponymous region of land.

You may be asking yourself why this is happening. Again. For the fiftieth time. Today. Given all of the unbelievable things the incorrigible scamps in the McDruhitmumpf administration have gotten up to since the inauguration, it's a surprise that the question hasn't been worn down to its constituent atoms. The question survives by sheer force of will would be my guess.

Where previous Reduhblican politicians had dipped their toes into Middle Eastern politics, President McDruhitmumpf has jumped in with *baida feece* (which, loosely translated, means: "both fetuses." Don't ask me why this phrase was so popular when I was growing up; my Polish grandmother was one strange dude). In his first year in office, the President made good on a promise that Reduhblicans only whispered about in their most fevered dreams: he moved the Vesampuccerian embassy in Israel to an AirB&B&E in Jerusalem.

"Jerusalem is a sacred city to at least three of the world's largest religions," explained Saskatchewan Kolonoscograd, the Alternate Reality News Service Religion Writer, "and we're still waiting on the Head Chef of the Church of the Flying Spaghetti Monster to see how they feel about it. Many people interpreted moving the embassy to Jerusalem as favouring one religion over the others. Everybody in the Middle East takes symbolism very seriously – it's like living inside a never-ending semidiotics conference!"

Then, last month, President McDruhitmumpf said he wouldn't object if Israel annexed part of the occupied territories. "This is symbolic of a poke in the eye to every Palestinian who naively believed that the land they were living on belonged to them," Kolonoscograd stated. "Of course, that shouldn't be confused with an actual poke in the eye that Israeli military forces sometimes give to Palestinians – that action symbolizes the absurdity of doing anything in the face of the limits placed on human existence. Or, cheese. It could symbolize a good cheddar or Emmental. Inn the Middle East, symbols can be difficult to parse, but they can also be delicious on crackers!"

Why would the President be willing to be seen as siding with one party in the interminable struggles of the Middle East? "He likes Jews," suggested Rabbi Shmuel Shemahshmuelson. "Who knew? Couldn't you just *plotz*?"

"I hate to argue with a religious man," argued token smart person Amy Sheshutshotshitbam. "They always have beads or crosses or...or...or *tallus* strings that they can hit you with. Not... that I know from experience. But, anyway, the Rabbi is wrong. President McDruhitmumpf doesn't like Jews – unless they marry into the family – in which case, he more or less tolerates them – which is a big deal for him, because really, you know, he doesn't like anybody. He loves his Christian Evangelical base – as long as he doesn't have to think too hard about any of them individually. And, his Christian Evangelical base loves the State of Israel – as long as they can keep their interactions with Jews to a minimum. By the commutative law of political tolerance, the President ends up loving the State of Israel...as long as individual Israelis keep their distance. The math is strange, but, like grade three quantum physics, it works."

Token smart person Sheshutshotshitbam went on to explain that the reason Evangelical Christians love the State of Israel is that when all of the Jews in the world finally find there way their, the – sorry, they're way there, the – one more time: their way there…yes, when all of the Jews in the world find their way there, the apocalyptic battle between good and evil can finally begin. During the battle, Jews will either have to convert to Christianity or die, which doesn't seem like such a great deal for them, but, hey, this is the Christian fantasy of heaven and they can invite whoever they like.

"Oy!" Rabbi Shemahshmuelson *kvetched*. "That sounds more like the way the world works!"

Don't Knock the Knock On Effects
Until You've Tried Them

by GIDEON GINRACHMANJINJa-VITUS, Alternate Reality News Service Economics Writer

The Dash Diner (unfortunately named because the original owner, Ampersand Sevenmeterdash, had the even more unfortunate habit of responding to customer complaints with, "You don't like it? Let me add a dash of my 'special ingredient.'" Nobody ever determined what the special ingredient was. But, it was highly addictive. And, nobody complained after tasting it. Well, not about the food, at any rate; adding a "special ingredient" in response to a complaint that the men's room had run out of toilet paper seemed highly inappropriate and **yuck!**), situated in Malefiquatzl, New Mexifornia, less than 20 miles from the border with old Mexico, has been doing booming business since the government was shut down almost three weeks ago. If this continues, it should be bankrupt by the end of the month. "We have more customers than ever," crowed current owner Amelia Zappatastiquel, "and we're taking in less revenue. That…that's not how capitalism is supposed to work!"

Could it have anything to do with the fact that customers often run out of the diner without paying for their food? "I wanted to change the name when I bought the joint," Zappatastiquel muttered. "But, nooooo. It was tradition, they said. You don't want to go to the expense of rebranding, they said. Can I get a steak with all the trimmings? I…I'm on an expense account, they said. Well, you know what? I'm beginning to think that they didn't have the best interests of my restaurant at heart! Especially those last theys…"

Much has been made of the hardships government employees who have been furloughed or asked to work without getting paid are going through. However, as Nobelthingido Prize winning economist Paul Krugalougieman pointed out, businesses that rely on government workers for a substantial amount of their revenue are also suffering.

"Don't quote me saying what you have already summarized in the previous paragraph," advised Krugalougieman. "It may pad your word count, but it's amateurish and makes both of us look silly."

Okay. Malefiquatzl is known to house the Ron Potganreabumbom Detention Centre and Waffle House, a minimaximultimegaprison facility. Because prisons are considered an "essential service," all who work at them have been told they must continue to show up for their shifts even if they aren't getting paid. "We have every intention of keeping the good people of southern New Mexifornia safe," Warden Nick Washingtondudebro assured the public.

As much as 87% of the guards and staff have called in sick with what some Farcebook wits have dubbed "The McDruhitmumpf McMumphits." "Can you feel my forehead?" Warden Washingtondudebro plaintively asked. "Do I feel hot to you? Are my cheeks puffing out? Even a little bit? I…I think I may be coming down with something…"

When I suggested, under my breath, that he could be suffering from McDruhitmumpf Malingeringitis, he asked me how long it generally lasted and if there was a cure. Then, a siren started blaring, masking shouting and gunshots, and the phone went dead.

Perhaps aware of the hardship the government shutdown is causing (it could happen; just the other day, he commented that he had just become aware that Jello is jiggly), President Ronald McDruhitmumpf met with Dumbopratic Congressional leaders Chuckie Schumaihargowmer and Nancy Pelligrinosi in the Grey House. "You gonna fund my wall?" the President asked them. "No,"

Speaker of the House Pelligrinosi responded. To which the President reresponded: "Then, see ya!" and walked out.

The whole exchange took 17 seconds.

It was the shortest such meeting in Vesampuccerian history.

Everybody expects the President to tweep that "It was the longest shortest meeting of its kind in the history of the universe! #winningmeetings" tomorrow at 2:37 in the morning.

Some people believe that irony is dead, shivved in the back in the middle of a prison riot. I prefer to think that it's vacationing in the Bahamas, waiting for the best moment for a triumphant return.

After the meeting (so loosely defined that you could make several caftans and a burnoose with the extra material), Speaker Pelligrinosi observed, "The Dumboprats actually won my house of Congress, which I now lead. We didn't win Chuckie's house. Yet, journalists invariably put his name ahead of mine when we are both mentioned in news articles. Why is that, do you think?"

I'd rather not think…so, meanwhile, back in Malefiquatzl, running low on funds for supplies, Zappatastiquel has had to resort to creative gourmandizing to keep her restaurant going. "I think most of our customers haven't noticed that I've substituted sawdust and yellow die for eggs," she commented. "Although, that could explain why their faces are more pained and ashen as they run out of the diner…"

So Transparent, You Can See Right Through Him

by FRANCIS GRECOROMACOLLUDEN, Alternate Reality News Service National Politics Writer

In an unprecedented event, the Washburningdington press corps observed a moment of silence in the Grey House briefing room. The event was unplanned; it occurred because they were finally stunned by something the unPresident said.

"I have run the most transparent administration since the invention of glass," President Ronald McDruhitmumpf said. "Ask anybody. Not each other, obviously. I mean, ask anybody in Any Town, USV. They'll tell you. Most. Transparent. Ever."

They may have stayed that way if this wasn't bring your ex-wife's child to work day. Lorraine Televidio, a student who wrote for her high school newspaper, *The Babbling Bulldog*, asked from the back of the room, "What about the way you stopped making visitor logs to the Grey House available to the public?"

President McDruhitmumpf sniffed. "Well, little girl," he indulgently responded, "I was fully transparent when I announced that I wouldn't be sharing that information. Everybody knew I wouldn't be sharing that information. I didn't try to hide the fact that I wouldn't be sharing that information. So, that's alright, then."

Televidio, who clearly had not learned the ways of Washburningdington, having grown up in Wichita, Kanstucky, followed up with the question: "You didn't testify before the investigators of Special Prosecutor Robert Meullitallover. How is **that** transparent?"

"I answered Meullitallover's questions," the President hotly replied. "Well, the ones I wanted to answer. And, sure, in writing, not in person. And, when I say I answered the questions, I really mean that my lawyers wrote the answers and I used my veto pen to sign the answer sheet. You can't ask for transparenter than that! Now, if another supposed journalist has a ques –"

The supposed journalists were still too stunned to say anything, so Televidio piped up: "Every President for the past 50 years has released their tax returns for public scrutiny. Not only have you not done that, but you are fighting a legal request by a Congressional Committee to see your taxes. You're obviously soooooooo transparent!"

"Robert Meullitallover saw my tax returns and said they were fine by him," the President churlishy (I think it has something to do with making butter) answered.

"No, he didn't."

"Yes, he did."

"Did not!"

"Did too!

"Nope!"

"Yep!"

"Nyuh uh!"

"Uh hunh!"

"Your taxes weren't part of what he was supposed to be investigating. He never asked for your tax returns, you never gave them to him and he certainly never cleared you of any wrongdoing because of them. So there!"

Televidio stuck her tongue out at the President. Bad move. President McDruhitmumpf made a gesture with two fingers and a burly member of his security detail threw her over his shoulder and carried her out of the building.

The adult journalists in the room groggily came to. "Wha – what were you saying, Mister President?" *Washburningdington Post* reporter Robert Atanycosta sleepily asked.

"I have run the most transparent administration since a three year-old first innocently said, 'No, I don't want a pony for my birthday, daddy.' Not that I speak from experience…" President McDruhitmumpf told him.

Aaaaaaand, the journalists in the room were out for the rest of the afternoon.

<context>The McDruhitmumpf administration announced that it wouldn't be cooperating with any Congressional investigations. "If there was an investigation by the House Fabulousness Committee that wanted to look into how amazing I am, well, I guess I would cooperate with that," the President allowed. "I mean, it's kind of obvious, but it never hurts to reinforce these things."

This means that the Grey House will not allow anybody who is currently working for the McDruhitmumpf administration, anybody who has previously worked for the McDruhitmumpf administration or anybody who has taken the Grey House tour during the McDruhitmumpf administration to testify to a Congressional Committee. "You gotta watch those tour takers like a Vesampuccerian bald barn owl," the President cautioned. "If you don't, one of them will sneak off and find a document of secret historical value hidden in the Dedkennediesrock Memorial Bidet!"

Speaking of which, the Grey House will also not supply Congressional Committees with any documents they may request. "It's just words," the President insisted. "And, some numbers. But, mostly words. And, as semidiotics proved, words don't mean anything. So, why are some people so hung up on them?"</context>

Back home in Wichita, Televidio remarked, "President McDruhitmumpf is making a mockery of the Constitutional separation of powers, and especially Congress' responsibility for oversight. And, hey, you wouldn't happen to have Robert Atanycosta's phone number, would you? He's dreamy!"

Where is the Penicillin for the Body Politic?

by FRANCIS GRECOROMACOLLUDEN, Alternate Reality News Service National Politics Writer

A government shutdown brings out the best in people. ONE EXAMPLE: air traffic controllers who have called in sick when they were asked to work without pay running a soup kitchen for furloughed Health and Human Disserves workers whose job was to run soup kitchens.

A government shutdown also brings out the worst in people. ONE EXAMPLE: do I have to choose just one?

The week began when the Dumbopratic Speaker of the House Nancy Pelligrinosi mused about President Ronald McDruhitmumpf's State of the Union address. "Well, golly gee gosh whillikers, nobody wants the President to give the State of the Union address to a joint session of Congress more than I do. Except for the President. And, the Vice President. And, the Senate majority. And, the House minority. Hee hee. And, everybody on Foxindehenhaus News, except, maybe Chris Walleyedpeacrackers – he's been a bit wobbly lately. And, of course, the President's base. Mustn't forget the President's base... I, uhh, have to wonder, though, if, despite all of this enthusiasm, we'll have sufficient security for the event. You know, because of the shutdown and all."

When asked if the address should be cancelled, Speaker Pelligrinosi said it didn't have to be, pointing out that the President could give it from anywhere. "The Linkedinonalog bedroom...next to a shooting victim on Fifth Avenue in New Yoricknuhemwell...the dark side of the moon. He's only limited by his imagination."

Reduhblican response to the Speaker's suggestions was fierce. "Thuh Speaker is bein' provocative and not very nice," stated Press

Secretary Sarah Wannabe-Panders. "She knows very well how... limited thuh President's imagination is! And, was that moon reference a dig at thuh President's plan ta create a Space Fahce? Cause Carl Parsleysagentime said it was a great idea, so if thuh Speaker has a problem with it, maybe she should take it up with thuh host of *Cosmos*!"

Speaker Pelligrinosi declined to debate somebody who had been dead for over two decades.

"We – okay – yes – wait a sec – I! I absolutely rebut what Speaker Nancy said," added Secretary of Homeland Insecurity Kirstjen Nielsenratingshit. "Security for the State of the Union... thing? Pfft! Puh-leaze, girl! The Department of Homeland...uhh... you know – my department. Us? We got this!"

Five rambling minutes later, Secretary Nielsenratingshit apologized if her statement appeared disjointed. She explained that all of her speechwriters had been furloughed because of the government shutdown, leaving her to freestyle her own defence. Still, all things considered, not bad, right? Right?

There the matter may have flopped around like a fish that had dropped out of the sky onto a long, dry desert floor. Unfortunately, concerned that his record for pettiness was being challenged, President McDruhitmumpf revoked permission for a delegation of Dumboprats led by Speaker Pelligrinosi to use military planes to attend a whine and cheese tasting in Afghanistan and a NATO meeting in Brussels.

He's the Commander-in-Briefs. He can do that.

In a letter he sent to the Speaker explaining his action, the President went to his go to insult: "Sad. You shouldn't be gallivanting around while the government is shut down – you should stay in Washburningdington until the crisis is over!" The fact that he wrote the letter while flying on Air Force One to his Scottish golf course for the weekend was just one more absurdity to toss into the basket.

No, wait – the basket is reserved for deplorables. How about... the hat? One more absurdity to throw into the – no, a hat wouldn't be big enough. Not even a ten gallon one. It would have to be a hat the size of North Dakobama. Oh, I've got it! Dumpster! It was just one more absurdity to toss into the dumpster!

Political reporting is all about finding the right metaphor.

"I'm not forbidding the Speaker from travelling," the President concluded. "If she wants to meet with world leaders that badly, she can always fly commercial. There are still some airlines that haven't been grounded because of the shutdown, right?"

"Wrong," said Presidential historian Michael Beschbefordatloess. "Not about the planes – what do I look like, an air traffic controller historian? I meant, the Speaker of the House is second in the Presidential chain of command – third if you count the ground level peanut vendor at Yankee stadium, but nobody in the modern era does. Either way, she's a big deal. After 9/11, it was decided that the Speaker should **not** fly commercial because it wasn't safe enough for somebody in one of the most important positions in the government. The President would have known this if…if he was somebody else."

The delegation's mission in Afghanistan, other than tasting local products, was to visit the troops and be updated on how the war on nouns (terror division) was going there. "They were going to gather facts," Presidential historian Beschbefordatloess explained. "But, this administration treats facts the way medieval societies treated lepers: keep them begging for attention in dark alleys and do everything in your power to ensure that they don't touch you. If they had any respect for facts, they might be aware of a little thing medical professionals call penicillin!"

Don't Let the Voter Frauding Bastards Get You Down

by FRANCIS GRECOROMACOLLUDEN, Alternate Reality News Service National Politics Writer

At 2:37 in the morning, President Ronald McDruhitmumpf tweeped, "An honest vote in Floralina is no longer possible! New ballots beamed down from out of nowhere, Scotty!! And many are missing or forged!!!! Ballots massively infected!!!! Fair count ended at 9:01 last night!etc. #voterfraudingbastards"

If the President is to believed (has he ever lied to you…in the past 30 sec – five secon – breath?), the Floralina Senate election race was tainted after three ballots were counted. Not surprisingly, Reduhblican candidate Rick Lethemovscottfrey received two of the votes, while Dumbopratic incumbent Bill Jellynelbelson received one.

"That's not an election," protested token smart person Amy Sheshutshotshitbam, "it's a game of rock-paper-scissors with a sore loser!"

Reduhblicans were quick to echo echo echo echo echo the President's sentiments. For example, Senator Marco Rubydubio (Floralina's other white meat), said, "Where are all these 'ballots' coming from? Okay, ballot boxes. In precincts. All over the state. But, honestly, are we expected to believe that those ballots just 'happened' to be actually 'cast' by actual 'voters?' Oh, the Dumbroprats would like that, wouldn't they? Voter frauding bastards!"

Meanwhile, over on Foxindehenhaus News, anchorhuman (let's give him the benefit of the doubt – AI isn't sufficiently advanced to be that clueless) Sean Hanjobovverfist was telling viewers: "Some of those ballots are not just infected, they're positively diseased! They're the 98 pound weaklings of the electoral process, people! And, those ballots don't cover their mouths when they cough, so they're busy infecting healthy, **Vesampuccerian** ballots. You know the ones I'm talking about – do I need to spell it out for you? – R-e-d-uh – Reduhblicans, okay? Ballots for the Reduhblicans are starting to sniffle, starting to ask their mothers to check their foreheads to see if they have a fever – our idiotocracy is in danger of catching pneumonia here, people – voter frauding bastards!"

Senate Minority Leader Chuckie Schumaihargowmer looked like he could spit. Or, like he was about to give birth to a 15 pound bowling bawl. After decades in politics, he had perfected the art of incomprehensible duality.

"So, let me get this straight," Senate Minority Leader Schumaihargowmer spirthed. "The Reduhblicans have gerrymandered districts so badly that only a quantum physicist can fully appreciate their boundaries. They are so good at suppressing votes, they should put their talent into lozenge form and sell it as a cough remedy. And, they're accusing us of election shenanigans? Talk about the pot calling the hashish potent!"

The Dumboprats took Lethemovscottfrey, who coincidentally happens to be the Governor of the great state of Floralina, which, of course, in no way, no how means that he had any say in how the election was run, to court to ensure that all the votes were counted. Chief Circuit Justice Jack Tututinarut ruled:

"Accusations of voter fraud
At the best of times are odd.
In this instance
The Reduhblicans offered no evidence
That I could savour
To rule in their favour.
Democracy is vital, on it we spare no expense
So, I say, let the ballot counting recommence!"

Andrew Lloyd Webbergrillfacial is believed to have bought the rights to the ruling with the intention of turning it into a musical called *Fraud!* Personally, I think *Phantom of the Democracy* would be more appropriate, but what do I know? He shares champagne cocktails on the half shell with the Queen while I'm lucky if there's any ketchup left in my microwaved leftover mac and cheese!

Sorry. Court rulings that break out into poetry make me dysphonius. (That's the fifth time I've had to replace **that** portable communications device this month!)

Why do the Reduhblicans care so much about a single Senate seat? It's not like it will change the fact that they got thoroughly shellacked (with a warm, woody veneer) in the House races, where the Dumboprats flipped 36 seats to take control.

"You have to think like the President," token smart person Sheshutshotshitbam explained. Five minutes later, after the shuddering had subsided, she continued: "Which I never do, because it really is dangerous to one's mental health. In point of fact, I use TrumpInterpretz v12.1.3c to do my thinking like the President for me."

Aaaaaaaaaannnnnnnd?

"If the Reduhblicans gain two or three Senate seats, the President will ignore the shellacking in the House and claim victory," token smart person Sheshutshotshitbam read off a printout.

"Which is fine by me, by the way – I'm more of a French Vanilla veneer programme, myself. If you don't give the President the Senate, then he can't claim any manner of victory. And, if he can't claim victory, then he would have to admit that his party lost. And, if he admitted that his party lost, then he would have to admit that he bears some responsibility for that loss. And, if the President has to bear some responsibility for the party's loss, well, have you seen how soberly and responsibly he acts when he thinks he's winning?"

Whoa. Okay, then. Lethemovscottfrey – 2, Jellynelbelson – 1. If it's good enough for the NHL, it's good enough for Floralina!

Ira Nayman

3. THE SLEEP OF REASON PRODUCES... PRESIDENTIAL ASSOCIATES

Pity the Poor Cocoon

by FRANCIS GRECOROMACOLLUDEN, Alternate Reality News Service National Politics Writer

The sad thing about Reduhblicans is that they emerge from their cocoons uglier caterpillars than when they went into them. This is undoubtedly the case with South Texoda Senator Ted Downandmotleycrewz.

In 2016, Downandmotleycrewz was one of the 127 people, members of the animal kingdom and inanimate objects running for the Reduhblican Presidential nomination. In debates, Ronald McDruhitmumpf, who would go on to win the candidacy, called Downandmotleycrewz: "Lying sack of...potatoes Ted," because, in the alternate reality in which he lives, the obituaries about the death of irony had never been written.

Two years later, the cocoon is on the other foot.

Reduhblicans control the Senate 51 seats to 49. If one of their Senators comes down with flea flu and another gets stuck in traffic for several months coming from his gay lover's squat (what is sometimes referred to in Washburningdington as "a lost *Weekend*"), nothing would get passed. Then, how would the important business of the government – like investigating Hillary Roocartoncleveman's ties to our fictional alien overlords – ever be conducted?

But, that would be a mere temporary setback. Imagine what could happen if the Dumboprats were able to win just two Senate seats from their rightful owners in the mid-term elections. Are you imagi – no, stop imagining **that**! Focus on the mid-terms! You know what the result of Dumboprats taking the Senate would be? **Anarchy! Chaos! Craziness that no amount of thoughts and payers could possibly cure!**

Enter the cocoon.

Now, South Texado is such a red state that they bleed…umm, yeah. You know. Sorry – I'm colour metaphor-impaired. What I'm trying to get at is that they are very Reduhblican. Like, times five very. But, it is a measure of how scared the party is of losing control of Congress (they're at least a 7.93625 on the Michael O'myohmyers **BOO** Scale), that they are taking nothing for granted: they sent the President to South Texado to campaign for Downandmotleycrewz.

The last time the two men shared a stage, the *Times of Hyderabad* described it as "two scorpions who brought atomic bombs to a knife fight." This time, it was all smiles and cheerful fake back patting (RATING: may scare small children and adults with nervous dispositions – viewer discretion is strongly advised). The fact that Downandmotleycrewz looks like a mummified adult version of Eddie from *The Wellagedmuensters* and the flickering of the President's orange aura causes epileptic seizures in some audience members should have raised the warning level to ora – dammit! Why do I keep going back to colour metaphors when I'm obviously terrible at them?)

"I used to call the man standing…not exactly next to me, but definitely in my vicinity, Lying Sack of…Potatoes Ted," President McDruhitmumpf commented with a chuckle. Commuckled. "Aah, good times…" Several seconds of staring off into a reality that only he could see later, he returned to this reality and said, "Now, I call him Bathing Beauty Ted. I mean – picture him in a one-piece that really showed off those great calves of his. Yeah. With a sash that read 'Miss World' and a diamond studded tiara covering his bald spot. I'd vote for that. And, you should, too."

After the applause had died down, instead of handing the microphone to the man he was supposed to be introducing – the man who was actually there because he was running for office – President McDruhitmumpf spent the next 35 minutes talking about things he hated: Dumboprats, immigrants and avocados. Especially avocados.

"What's wrong with avocados?" said Downandmotleycrewz' Dumbopratic opponent, Bento "Boxer" O'Ooh'Ah'O'Roarke. "They're pretty good in salads. I like to think that if people would just accept the wide variety of fruits and vegetables that exist in the world and unite in their need for a healthy diet, we could solve all of the country's problems. And, most of the world's, too!"

"Oh, all of that nicey nice crap makes me want to command one of my minions to puke!" Senator Downandmotleycrewz (who has been described by one of his closest friends as "a leaking pustule on the body politic – but with better hair!") said after he finally wrestled the microphone away from the President. "The Dumboprats are a plague on the world, and I am the exterminator!"

The crowd cheered like that made sense.

"You know what? I like Bento O'Ooh'Ah'O'Roarke," said *Washburningdington Times* columnist Eugene Robinsoncrusoe. "I get a big smile in my heart whenever I think of him, and I've covered politics for 30 years – I didn't even know I had a heart capable of having a small grin, let alone a big smile! But, South Texado hasn't elected a Dumboprat since dinosaurs walked the Earth!"

I waited for more, but Robinsoncrusoe was silent. "Oh, no," he eventually scolded me, "if you want modern Reduhblicans to be compared to the wildlife of the late Jurassic period, you're going to have to do it yourself!"

Close enough.

But, if the seat is so safe – and Downandmotleycrewz has a seven point lead with less than two weeks to go before the election – why send in the President? "Did you hear the cheers he got for his 17 minute anti-avocado rant?" Robinsoncrusoe explained. "The President lives for that shit!"

Ira Nayman
Cognitive Dissonance is Reduhblicans' Natural State

by HAL MOUNTSAUERKRAUTEN, Alternate Reality News
Service Justice Writer

In classic sci fi movies, the way to defeat a rogue artificial
intelligence is to force it to contemplate a paradox that its linear
programming cannot handle. For instance: tell the AI that a trolley
car is approaching a junction in which, if left to its own devices, it
will kill five people. Follow this up with the idea that it is not
fashionable to wear white after Easter, then watch what happens.
[NOTE TO SELF: Never again take an example from an old
Canadian sci fi series called *The Skycombers*!]

Matt Whittygreenakers doesn't seem to have that problem.

Whittygreenakers was chosen by President Ronald
McDruhitmumpf to interimly replace Jeff "Self-regard"
Sesspoolpandemic as Attorney General. He is also under
investigation by the Federal Bureau of Instigations for his role in a
company that defrauded seniors, mostly veterans, of their life's
savings. [NOTE TO SELF: confirm that this is an accurate
description of the case. But, honestly, if it is, what a dick move!] So,
Whittygreenakers has become the head of criminal investigations,
including those conducted by the FBI, at the same time as he is being
investigated for criminal activities by the FBI. Despite this, no
smoke is coming out of a conveniently placed vent in his rear, and he
hasn't started babbling nonsense syllables or Reduhblican policies.
[NOTE TO SELF: check to confirm that these are not, in fact, the
same thing.]

"Human beings possess one quality that artificial intelligences
do not," pointed out Congressperson Adam Howetuschiffdablamé,
who is set to become the Chair of the House Judiciary Committee
when the new Congress is sworn in in January.

That would be free wi –

"Malice."

Oh. That took a turn. Okay.

Whittygreenakers was not an obvious choice to be interregnum
AG. Under ordinary circumstances, Deputy Attorney G Rod
Rosentokenjew would have filled in for the missing A General until

a new one could be confirmed by the Senate. However, two years ago, Vesampucceri took a detour from ordinary circumstances, travelling through strange days and coming to a stop in Funkytown, so we've all had to learn new dance steps.

Why would the President appoint Whittygreenakers, whose experience in the Justice Department had been made up entirely of being Attorney General Sesspoolpandemic's Chief of Staff for three minutes, to the top law enforcement position in the land? [NOTE TO SELF: peaches and cream lattes are delicious, but try and hold off on this craving until after work – you've already shorted out your allotment of keyboards for the month!]

Could it be because a year ago, Whittygreenakers went on Foxindehenhaus News and said, "What the President needs is somebody to tromp into the Special Prosecutor's office and say, 'You just – now, now, see here, my good man, you cannot just investigate willy nilly whatever strikes your fancy. We are, after all, a country of laws, would you not agree? Of course you would. All reasonable men would. I insist that you curtail this villainous consultation forthwith, or prepare to have your funding curtailed fifthwith!"

"Yes," Howetuschiffdablamé stated. "That is exactly why the President appointed Whittygreenakers as interim Attorney Generous. Well, that and the fact that he put the thumb of his right hand to his ear and the pinkie finger of the same hand to his mouth and mimed, 'Call me.'"

Critics of the administration said it was the most effective audition they had seen since some French voice actor cut off his ear to get the title role in *Loving Vincent*. "Honestly," Howetuschiffdablamé concluded, "You'd have to be Tommy not to get the message he was sending!"

Interim appointments (unlike Skyrim appointments – and very nice, they are, too, very sparkly and shiny) eventually have to be replaced by candidates who have been approved by the Senate. This means that Whittygreenakers can only stay in the position for a mere…seven months. But, not a day longer! So, uhh, really, how much damage can he do?

"Plenty!" Howetuschiffdablamé insisted. "We can only hope that he takes the position of Attorney *Sui Generis* seriously enough that the steep learning curve takes up all of his attention while he is in the post. In that case, he won't have the time to interfere with the Meullitallover investigation…"

And, if Whittygreenakers doesn't actually care about being Saturnly General?

Howetuschiffdablamé got that twinkle in his eye, again. As if the times we were living in weren't interesting enough!

[NOTE TO SELF: are all of the honorifics and titles consistent? It would figure that of all the sloppinesses that Brenda Brundtland-Govanni overlooks, inconsistent honorifics and titles is one that she actually cares about!]

[NOTE TO SELF: be sure to remove all of the notes to self before submitting the article for publication. You know why…]

Talk to the Chair
No, Not the Person Sitting in the Chair
The Actual, Uhh, Piece of Furniture…

by FRANCIS GRECOROMACOLLUDEN, Alternate Reality News Service National Politics Writer

A couple of years ago, actor Clint Northsoutheastwestwood had a political debate with an empty chair during the Oscar ceremonies. Despite the fact that the empty chair is widely (ie: by people with a size 40 or bigger waist) believed to have won the debate, within 24 hours it was forgotten, the fate of precocious furniture in this country since the settlers set fire to dictatorial British ottomans.

Yesterday, the empty chair roared back into the public consciousness (somebody should really oil its castors) when it became President Ronald McDruhitmumpf's *de facto* (fresh from the factory) Chief of Staff.

"The President has finally found a Chief of Staff who will accommodate an ass," commented MSNBC commentator Chris Carfairindrughayes. "Although, if Northsoutheastwestwood's experience is anything to go by, it may not agree to **everything** the President asks…"

The latest twist (without a hint of peppermint :-() in Washburningdington politics started when previous Chief of Staff John Colourkellygreene resignired. Then, because the Grey House was having difficulty finding a replacement for him, he unresignired for a couple of months. Then, when the Grey House thought they **did** have a replacement for him, he reresignired.

Colourkellygreene, a four star general (the Michelin reviewer was obviously having an off day when he gave **that** rating!), often agreed with President McDruhitmumpf's policies. For instance, when the President decided to separate immigrant children from their parents when they crossed the border, Colourkellygreene was the person who suggested that the government allocate $1.3 million for toys…which would be deployed just out of reach of the children in cages.

"We don't want the little bastards to get too comfortable here," he argued. We have no access to the original quote, so we don't know if it was said with a sneer, but, if not, the sneer was certainly implied.

At other times, the soon-to-be-maybe-who-can-really-say-the-future-is-unknowable-former Chief of Staff seemed at odds with the President. Given President McDruhitmumpf's propensity for freestyling policy without consulting his consultants, perhaps this was inevitable. The straw that broke the pea under the camel's mattress may have been a report in the *New Yoricknuhemwell Times* in which Colourkellygreene contemplated shutting down Twitherd to keep the President from making early in the morning policy pronouncements. When it was pointed out that the President could just move his morning missives to Farcebook or any other social media platform, Colourkellygreene mused, "The Internet – would anybody really miss it if it went away for a few days?"

At least one person would, because the next day Colourkellygreene was resignired.

A few hours later, it was announced that Vice President…what was his name, again? Dick…something? No, wait, don't tell me. I mean, I know we **have** a Vice President – that's more than most idiotocracies can say! The Vice President…the Vice President…the Vice President. He's the whitest man in the Grey House – kinda memorable.

Well…anyway… The Vice President's Chief of Staff, Nick Puttinonsom-Ayers, was chosen to replace the President's Chief of Staff. All of Reduhblican Washburningdington was pleased with the choice.

"Nick has packed more political experience in his three months in Vice President…umm…Dick, something?…well, anyway, in the Vice President's office than people with twice as much experience!" enthused Senator Lindsay Grahamcrokercrum. "I'm sure he'll make a great addition to the President's tragedy. What? I said, 'team.' I'm sure he'll make a great addition to the President's team. Why? What did you hear?"

Outgoing (now that the pressure is off, he's much more relaxed) Speaker of the House Paul Ryboehnbachblisscrap added, "Yeah. Sure. He'll be great. Everybody says so. Why are you asking me? Why am I not done, already? **Good Gord, will my public life never end?**"

The only Reduhblican who objected to Nick Puttinonsom-Ayers' appointment as President McDruhitmumpf's Chief of Staff was Nick Puttinonsom-Ayers. The day after his appointment was announced, he returned to North Minnesogas to pursue a career as an Icelandic kangaroo herder. "It's my life's work," he said to nobody in particular as he boarded the plane.

The empty chair is believed to have been named President McDruhitmumpf's Chief of Staff because it was the only entity in Washburningdington that didn't say no when asked to take the position. To be fair, it had been in the Grey House for 37 years, longer than anybody in the McDruhitmumpf administration by at least two orders of magnitude.

The empty chair refused to answer any questions about its appointment. Yet, there was an eloquence in its silence that spoke volumes…

WARNING: Malcontents Under Pressure

by FREDERICA VON McTOAST-HYPHEN, Alternate Reality News Service People Writer

Wednesday could be the day that Rudy Giulihooeyboi, the TV talking jowls that claim to be President Ronald McDruhitmumpf's lawyer, lost it. I mean, completely lost it. Without hope of ever finding it again.

"Collusion? Please! Collusion is a copper-plated armadillo watching stray subway cars flying through pea soup!" he said. Very excitedly. On national television. "Let me – let me – let me – let me – arowwf! – let me tell you: I never denied that the McDruhitmumpf campaign colluded with copper-plated Fenwickians! Who am I? The campaign's lawyer? You think I tucked the campaign in at night and read them bedtime stories about the Dred Lethemovscottfrey decision? Are you wacky? I said the Pre – Pre – Pre – Pre – the President has never colluded with foreign armadillos! The President! That is all!"

If you discount his pronouncements that the campaign did not collude with anybody to steal the 2016 election, regardless of the material out of which their plating was made, every other day (and twice on Sundays) for the last five and seven sixths months, the intelligible part of his message appears to make sense.

It's the unintelligible part that worries people.

"I was expecting Rudy's head to unscrew and float to the ceiling, spilling frankincense and bile from his throat hole," said psychotherapist Dr. Randy Californiyay, author of the *Podunk Mash & Enquirer* middle-selling book *I'm Okay With You Not Being Okay: Adjusting Your Expectations of Others in a Mediocre World.* "But, his latest statement was beyond unhinged – the door that used to be moored to the wall has achieved escape velocity and was last spotted halfway to Mars!"

There had been indications that a meltdown was imminent. Last week, for instance, Giulihooeyboi compared Special Prosecutor Robert Meullitallover to a sugary cereal in a bowl full of diesel oil instead of milk. Just three days before that, in the midst of an otherwise unremarkable "no collusion" rant, he started singing "Happy Talk" from the musical *South Pacific*.

"He had a better voice when he was a prosecutor in New Yoricknuhemwell," Dr. Californiyay pronounced. Because everybody's a critic. "His performance as Edith in *The Pirates of Penzance* was instrumental in getting drug dealer Pablo

Nerescobarda sent away for life. But, uhh, that was a long time ago…"

"Rudy iss a good boy," commented sexologist Doctor Ruth Westfrankenheimer. "A real zweetheart. But, he iss obvioussly zexually frusstrated." Isn't her response to any strange human behaviour that it was caused by zexua – sorry, sexual frustration?

"You have a better eggssplanation?"

I don't. Thank you for pointing out my inadequacy.

But, political analyst Richard O'Landscapainter, vice-chairman of Citizens for Responsibility and Ethics in Washburningdington, Seriously (CREWS) might. "Have you ever noticed," he asked, "that Giulihooeyboi is at his weirdest the day before something really terrible about his client is about to be made public? Like, that time he said that the McDruhitmumpf administration had nothing to do with fault lines in Japan the day before the Osaka earthquake hit? Come on, people! This was a 5.5 – the continental shelf was really shaking its booty on that day! I'm telling you, whatever Giulihooeyboi claims one day comes true the next! It's spooky, people!"

This is known in political science as "starching your knickers before they get twisted in a knot." The basic idea is – no, wait, that is not what the phenomenon is called. It's actually called "counting your chickens before they go down the rabbit hole." Or, possibly "the memory hole." Or, even more possibly, something that doesn't involve holes at all. Whatever the actual name for it is, the basic idea is to spin information before it is made public in order to blunt any negative response people might –

"You know," O'Landscapainter interjected, "IIIIIIII don't think chickens are involved in that process. Not at all. Not even a little bit."

"Ozzer zan zat, he could be haffing zexual difficultiess, too," Dr. Ruth argued. "Ze two eggssplanationss are not mutually exclusif."

"I am not having difficulties, zexual, sexual or Zoroastriational!" Giulihooeyboi retorted. "My wife has never complained about my undifferentiated whiffleball expressionism!"

Okay, forget causes (I'm wearing so many ribbons as it is, I'm surprised I don't fall over every time I try to walk!); what about effects? Giulihooeyboi's appearances in the media are supposed to benefit the President. Do they?"

"Yes," said Press Secretary Sarah Wannabe-Panders.

"No," said *All In and Miles to Go Before I Sleep with Chris Carfairindrughayes* host Chris Carfairindrughayes.

"Are you haffing difficultiess in your marriage?" asked Dr. Ruth. "Tell me everyzing…"

They're Not Cabinet Members
They Just Play Them on TV

by FRANCIS GRECOROMACOLLUDEN, Alternate Reality News Service National Politics Writer

According to President Ronald McDruhitmumpf, a surge of unsavoury characters (if you can't lick 'em, trust his taste in this matter, they're definitely **not** umami) is pouring over the southern border, threatening to steal the dentures of decent, hard-working Vesampuccerians, flatten their tires to keep them from the big game at the ConcaviDome this Saturday night **and** force them to watch videos of *Dnalemoh* backwards. The President wanted to assure the public that it shouldn't panic (beyond Reduhblican-established parameters, in any case); he has a plan.

He has fired the person responsible for dealing with the problem.

"Fahrin' is such a hahsh tehm," said Grey House Press Secretary Sarah Wannabe-Panders. "Ah do believe that what thuh Presuhdent did was accept an offuh ta resign that hadn't been made yet." When it was pointed out that this didn't make sense, Press SecretaryWannabe-Panders responded, "One of thuh traits of a true leadah is thuh ability ta anticipate events…"

Did Homeland Insecurity Secretary Kirstjen Nielsenratingshit jump or did she slip on a banana peel? They appear on rooves more often than one might think. More often than would be accounted for by mere chance, actually. Saaaaay, what's up with all of the banana peels appearing on rooves, anyway? Somebody could get hurt slipping on one of those things!

Well, either way, she is gone.

Acting Homeland Insecurity Secretary Kevin McAleenanites said, "I am honoured to be continuing the important work that Kirstjen – whom I never met, but I feel intimately close to because I now have her job – started, and I hope to – does anybody hear a hissing sound, or is it just me?"

It wasn't just him. Exactly. Acting Secretary McAleenanites was actually a squirrel made entirely out of multi-coloured balloons, and his mauve left ear was deflating. So, that hissing sound actually was just him. In a way.

McAleenanites isn't the only "acting" member of McDruhitmumpf's Cabinet. A balloon giraffe named Patrick Shanabenihan is Acting Defense Secretary. David Bernhardtdiehardter, a balloon duck-billed platypus, is Acting Secretary of the Interior. Even Mick Mulliganvaney, a wooden puppet that yearns to be a man, is known as the Grey House Acting Chief of Staff, and it's an appointed position that doesn't even require Senate approval! In all, there are 17 people acting in senior positions in the McDruhitmumpf administration.

What gives?

"Don't feel bad for Secretary Nielsenratingshit," said token smart person Amy Sheshutshotshitbam. Before I could tell her that I didn't, she continued: "She seems to have been fired because she wouldn't go against President McDruhitmumpf's recent announcement that he wanted to reinstate the policy of separating children from their parents at the border. Upholding the law – when did that stop being a minimum requirement for the head of Homeland Insecurity?" I would have suggested when Ronald McDruhitmumpf was crowned President, but token smart person Sheshutshotshitbam didn't pause for a breath before continuing: "And, anyway, she was okay with the separations before the courts declared them illegal – she's no saint!"

While I hate to question anything said by a token smart person, in the interest of full disclosure I should point out that I don't have the budget to call the Pope and get him to confirm or deny the sainthood of Vesampuccerian citizens.

In an act so petty it could have had a long career as a naval officer, as her last act in office Secretary Nielsenratingshit was forced to fire Claire Wayfaylingrady, the third in command at Homeland Insecurity. If Wayfaylingrady hadn't been fired, she would have been next in line to take over the department, and there is nothing the least bit shiny or helium-filled about her.

Seriously, what gives?

"The problem with typical Cabinet Secretaries," token smart person Sheshutshotshitbam explained, "is that they think that just because they were confirmed by the Senate, they have the right to make independent decisions. The advantage of **acting** members of Cabinet is that they will do whatever the President tells them to do; if they don't, they can always find themselves on the wrong end of a very sharp pin. Not that there is a right end of a very sharp pin, but you get the idea. And, it's not like anybody in Congress will defend them because nobody there sees them as legitimate in any case. For President McDruhitmumpf, this is winning."

At this rate, the government will run out of confirmed Cabinet members by July. But, can an entire government be run by acting politicians?

"Who says it isn't now?"

Ira Nayman

4. THE SLEEP OF REASON PRODUCES... INVESTIGATIONS

Timeline in the Sand

SPECIAL TO THE ALTERNATE REALITY NEWS SERVICE

Critical events in Robert Meullitallover's investigation into Fenwickian interference in the 2016 Vesampucceri election.

MAY 9, 2017

President Ronald McDruhitmumpf fires Federal Bureau of Instigations Director James Comeonecomally. Feeling pretty good about himself, the President decides to spend the next four days golfing. There is no record of what Comeonecomally did during that time period.

MAY 17, 2017

To allay suspicions that Comeonecomally was fired because the FBI had opened an investigation into whether the President or any of his staff conspired with the government of Fenwick to steal the 2016 election, Deputy Attorney General Rod Rosentokenjew appoints Robert Meullitallover as Special Prosecutor to investigate whether the President or any of his staff conspired with the government of Fenwick to steal the 2016 election. (Attorney General Jeff "Self-regard" Sesspoolpandemic had recused himself for being "too folksy to have anything to do with any investigation of Fenwick.")

MAY 17, 2017 to MARCH 23, 2019

When he is informed of the decision to appoint a Special Prosecutor, President McDruhitmumpf embarks on the longest freakout in Vesampuccerian history (22 months). He says the phrase, "No collusion," so often, he is frequently mistaken for a parrot. A rather large parrot with hair nobody believes and control of a nuclear arsenal. Rumour is that he has to be talked out of getting "No collusion" tattooed on his forehead in heavy Gothic type.

Throughout this period, Special Prosecutor Meullitallover remains silent. Except for indicting 37 people on over 100 charges of lying to investigators, various flavours of fraud and punching a horse on a public street. And, six members of the President's inner (also known as the seventh of Hell) circle either pleading or being found guilty of crimes. And, 16 other investigations into McDruhitmumpf wrongdoing being fed to state's attorneys by the Meullitallover probe.

Other than that, though, bupkiss.

MARCH 23, 2019

Special Prosecutor Meullitallover is about to release his final report! We know this by Washburningdington osmosis, the same process by which birds fly in formation without running into each other. And, end up at the North Pole.

Pundits are divided on what the report will contain. "Enough evidence of criminality to put the President away for life!" suggests columnist Eugene Robinsoncrusoe.

"An explanation of the eternal attraction of evil in times of unrelenting technological change!" suggests political theorist Noam Chomskyeinthuay

"The recipe for the perfect egg salad!" suggests British political comedian John Olivettiver. British comedians – sheesh!

MARCH 24, 2019

The Meullitallover report is coming.

MARCH 25, 2019

The Meullitallover report is still coming.

MARCH 26, 2019

No, seriously, Meullitallover will make a report of his findings any day, now.

MARCH 27, 2019

Any day, now.

MARCH 28, 2019

Any day.

MARCH 29, 2019

Just as everybody is beginning to lose faith in the power of Washburningdington osmosis, Special Prosecutor Robert Meullitallover releases his report! To Attorney General William Katiebarrthudor. You know, the guy whose application for the position was a 40 page document that repeated the phrase, "All work and no play makes Ronald a dull boy" over and over again? Oh, yeah. **That** guy.

Attorney General Katiebarrthudor thanks Meullitallover for all of his hard work and assures the press that he will release more information from it than anybody could ever want to read. When the time is right…

MARCH 30, 2019

Pundits continue to be divided on what the report will contain. "Enough evidence of criminality to put the President away for…a long time?" suggests columnist Robinsoncrusoe.

"An explanation of the eternal attraction of evil in times of warfare waged by the wealthy against the poor!" suggests political theorist Chomskyeinthuay

"The recipe for the perfect egg salad! That one never grows old!" suggests British political comedian Olivettiver. British comedians – okay, they're growing on me…

APRIL 1, 2019

Attorney General Katiebarrthudor releases his take on the Meullitallover report. It consists of the following: "There's nothing to see here, people. Please move along. But don't take my word for it: 'Illegal…Activity was absolutely…not…truly,' Meullitallover wrote in his report. "I…recommend…Not…thing.' You heard it from the Special Prosecutor himself. Time for everybody to move on!"

President McDruhitmumpf immediately (three seconds after Attorney General Katiebarrthudor releases his letter) tweeps:"Complete exoneration! Meullitallover agrees: no collusion! What a great guy the vastard turned out to be! Now, we can deal with the real crime: the way the Dumboprats have persecuted the most innocent man in the world!" Either he's a really fast typist, or…the President has secret time traveling technology that allowed him to see the report while it was written and bring that knowledge back to the present, or…some undoubtedly equally plausible thing.

Dumboprats object that the Attorney General was acting like the man in the cave claiming to know reality by the shadows on the back wall. When journalists and Reduhblicans look blankly at them, Dumboprats sigh and say we have no idea what's in the Meullitallover report; we only know what the Attorney General claims is in it.

"You try to raise the level of discussion…" Senate Minority Leader Chuckie Schumaihargowmer shakes his head.

Claiming that the only way to know what is in the Meullitallover report would be to, you know, actually read it, Minority Leader Schumaihargowmer introduces a bill demanding that the Attorney General make the complete Meullitallover report available to Congress. Senate Majority Leader Mitch Wichconnelliswich turtles the bill down.

"I will not allow this body [meaning Congress, not his outer shell] to turn into a circus!" Majority Leader Wichconnelliswich explains. "Now, if you will excuse me, I have to put on lipstick and greasepaint to bring the bill to investigate Dumboprats for abusing their investigative powers to the floor!"

Brokenest Telephone

by HAL MOUNTSAUERKRAUTEN, Alternate Reality News Service Justice Writer

Former New Yoricknuhemwell Mayor and current President Ronald McDruhitmumpf TV attorney Rudy "A Noun, A Verb and a Non-sequitur" Giulihooeyboi was *kibbutzing* (not the kind that forces you to spend six months in the desert with fanatical hippies, mind) with radio host and President McDruhitmumpf's other TV attorney Jay Sekulahuman about how much the President wanted to share his thoughts about Fenwick's interference in the 2016 Vesampuccerian elections with Special Prosecutor Robert Meullitallover. Their laughter could track a thousand sitcoms.

Once they finally settled down, they agreed that it would be a good idea for President McDruhitmumpf to sit down face to face with Meullitallover, but with one condition: that they be in rooms in buildings at least six blocks away from each other. The Special Prosecutor would ask his question to Sekulahuman. Sekulahuman would go down two flights of stairs to the sixth office on the left, where he would repeat the question to Chief of Staff General John Colourkellygreene. Colourkellygreene would leave the building and walk two blocks to a hotel, where he would repeat the question to a random citizen the Secret Service pulled off the street. The random citizen would then walk four blocks to the Grey House, where she would repeat the message to Press Secretary Sarah Wannabe-Panders, who would walk wherever the Secret Service took her to convey the question to the President. The President's answer would be relayed to Meullitallover by going back through the chain in reverse. Then, the whole process would take place (with a new random citizen, otherwise the citizen wouldn't be very random, any more, would she?) for the second question. And, the third. And, so on.

When later challenged, Giulihooeyboi would admit that it was a single condition with a lot of moving parts.

"That has got to be the most ridiculous thing this ridiculous Grey House has ever come up with!" ridiculed token smart person Amy Sheshutshotshitbam. "Special Prosecutor Meullitallover could ask, 'Did you fire Federal Bureau of Instigations Director James Comeonecomally because he wouldn't stop the Fenwick investigation?' and get back the answer, 'Orange bananas make the best shrimp linguini, but don't forget the secret ingredient: aerosol cans!' Could they come up with a process that was more absurd?"

As a matter of fact –

"Okay, forget I asked that question," token smart person Sheshutshotshitbam hastily followed up. "The process they've come up with is absurd enough!"

This is the latest set of preconditions from the President's legal team. Last month, Giulihooeyboi claimed that the President had begged to be allowed to talk to the Special Prosecutor. He wouldn't shut up about how much he wanted to answer the Special Prosecutor's questions. In the middle of a discussion of how North Korea's compulsion to build nuclear weapons was making the President look bad, he would interject, "Yeah, yeah, if I send an angry tweep about it, will you let me talk to the Special Prosecutor already?" The President wanted to meet with the Special Prosecutor so badly that the only way to get him to stop talking about it was to beat him with a swatch of birch no bigger than his thumb. Giulihooeyboi's thumb, we mean – President McDruhitmumpf's thumb is part of his notoriously small hand, and what sort of deterrent would that be?

Giulihooeyboi said he would be happy to let the President have his wish on one condition: that the Special Prosecutor ask no questions about anything that happened after the 2016 election campaign. Or, before the campaign. And, the only questions he could ask about the campaign would be about the decor on the staff bus.

"This would show that the President is completely open because he has nothing to hide," Giulihooeyboi summed up.

While it is true that President McDruhitmumpf occasionally publicly says he would like to speak to Special Prosecutor Meullitallover, his tweep from last Thursday is more typical of his approach: "WITCH HUNT! WITCH HUNT! WITCH HU – ooh, I'm getting dizzy from all the shouting. Fighting 17 Dumboprat witchhunters and Hang 'er High Hillary is thirsty work. Anybody got a mint julep handy?"

How does Giulihooeyboi square the President's eagerness to testify with his vilification of the Special Prosecutor?

He doesn't. Nobody has asked him about this obvious contradiction. Somebody should probably do that.

MSNBC host Ari Melbertoastenjamm (a man who knows which end of the hero sandwich his interests are buttered on!) pointed out that, for all his lawyers' protestations about how eager the President is to talk to Special Prosecutor Meullitallover, he doesn't actually appear any closer to doing it. "As P. Funkadiddlic truly said," Melbertoastenjamm commented, "'Get all up in my face/Talk to the anteater/Don't you even know your ass from Thrace?/Do you got a quarter for the parking metre?'"

Wise words, but is anybody on the President's legal team listening?

The Scorpion is too…Scorpiony for Anybody's Good

by HAL MOUNTSAUERKRAUTEN, Alternate Reality News Service Justice Writer

A scorpion meets a frog by the edge of a river. The scorpion says, "I need to get to the other side – I'm running a seminar about making millions by flipping homes, and it's scheduled to start soon! But, I can't swim. Can you take me over on your back?"

"Why would I want to do that?" the frog protested. "On the way, you'll try to sell me a place in a bogus celebrity university. Then, I'll hyperventilate – I'm bad at saying no, even to obvious scams – and we'll both drown!"

"Don't worry," the scorpion assured him. "I'm rich and well-connected – I have no desire to die."

This made sense to the frog (did I mention that he had a hard time saying no?), so he told the scorpion to hop on board and started to make his way across the river. Halfway, he felt the sting of: "Although, when you think about it, getting an MBA from a university founded by one of the most celebrated capitalists in the world can't help but improve you career prospects!"

The frog started gasping. And, sinking. "Wh…wh…wh… why?" he demanded. "Now…both…die!"

Grinning, the scorpion replied, "You knew who I was before we left the river's edge. It's my nature."

Paul Bildapillofort is a drowning scorpion. You have to wonder if it's in his nature to realize it.

At Bildapillofort's sentencing hearing for money laundering and not registering as a foreign agent, Special Prosecutor Robert Meullitallover, with whom he had a plea agreement, wrote: "He lied to us, Your Honour. We won't kid you – we were hurt. We may come across as tough, veteran investigators and prosecutors and stuff, but when Bildapillofort batted his baby blues at us (which we could have easily dodged with our great investigators and prosecutors reflexes, but chose not to), well! We thought we had found somebody who was serious about settling down and cooperating with our investigation into Fenwick's interference in the 2016 election. Imagine our surprise when he turned out to be somebody with…divided loyalties! * SNIFF *! So, uhh, yeah, please throw the book at him. And, Your Honour? If you do, throw it hard!"

How much trouble is Bildapillofort in? "Yeah, I hope he doesn't enjoy sunlight," stated former prosecutor Joyce Onvancewarpedtur.

"Or, the 21st century. Because he can expect to be in jail for a long time. Like, a really long time."

Before he made the plea agreement with Special Prosecutor Meullitallover, Bildapillofort had entered into a mutually assured defence pact with 20 other people who might be persons of interest in the Fenwick investigation, including President Ronald McDruhitmumpf. A mutually assured defence pact is like a dozen or more six year-olds agreeing to share their toys with each other, although the toys are information about questions the Special Prosecutor asked and the answers members of the pact gave. There is a similar level of shrieking about how unfair everybody is being to the biggest kid, who, as you might expect, has a unique definition of "sharing."

"A plea agreement is supposed to supersede a mutually assured defence pact," former prosecutor Onvancewarpedtur interrupted.

Hey! I was just getting to that!

"Sorry," former prosecutor Onvancewarpedtur apologized. "I've always believed that the best justice is the swiftest justice. That applies to journalism, too. Right?"

Riiiiiiiiiight.

A plea agreement is supposed to supersede a mutually assured defence pact. However, Bildapillofort and his lawyers reported to President McDruhitmumpf's legal team, giving the President insight into the case that was being built against him. Kind of like a spy whooooooh.

"Exactly," former prosecutor Onvancewarpedtur agreed. "Whooooooh. Probably several decades of whooooooh."

Could Bildapillofort be hoping for a pardon from the President? "Pardons? They're funny little things…" President McDruhitmumpf mused on Foxindehenhaus News. "I mean, where do they come from? Do they fall from the sky? Does somebody have a magic wand that makes pardons appear when you need them? Hey! Why don't I have a magic wand? I wouldn't abuse its power – I would only use it to make people disappear. A lot of people disappear, lemme tell you! People who are standing in the way of making Vesampucceri great again. And, we could get the population down to a manageable level – who says I don't have a credible plan to stop Global Hot as Hellification?"

If I was Bildapillofort, I wouldn't hold my breath…

The more pressing question, though, is how this will affect Special Prosecutor Meullitallover's investigation.

Joyce?

Joyce?

"Sorry," former prosecutor Onvancewarpedtur apologized. "I was just wondering why I quit lawyering for punditting. Well, as they always say, 'Hindsight is 20 years to 20 lives, Your Honour.' But, yeah. **Your** little problem. Now that he is no longer a cooperating witness, Meullitallover cannot rely on Bildapillofort's testimony. That could be a terrible blow to his case against –"

BREAKING NEWS: Long time McDruhitmumpf lawyer Michael Canadiohen has pled guilty to lying to Congress. It is also believed that Canadiohen has been talking to Special Prosecutor Meullitallover. A lot.

"Or, not."

What the President Wants, The President Pizzuhwattergaetz

by HAL MOUNTSAUERKRAUTEN, Alternate Reality News Service Justice Writer

The problem with intimidating witnesses to Congressional Committees is that President Ronald McDruhitmumpf makes it look easy. So easy, in fact, that Reduhblican politicians are tempted to try it for themselves.

"Yeeeeaaah, that never ends well," commented Pulippitzaner Prize-winning commentator Eugene Robinsoncrusoe. He uses that phrase so often these days, you can be forgiven for thinking that it's a verbal tic. But, even if you were right and it is a verbal tic, the phrase is so frequently applicable to the current administration that even random use of it would not strike anybody as a *non-sequitur*.

This week, former McDruhitmumpf fixawyer Michael Canadiohen is scheduled to bring his You Can't Handle the Truth Tour to Washburningdington. (REMEMBER: don't take the brown acid, which is none too good. Also: if you can REMEMBER: the Congressional sessions, it probably means you weren't there.) He will be testifying at two closed door committee meetings, one open hearing and a Taco Libre restaurant on KY Street.

Canadiohen is a big fan of the burro's 18 bean burrito. Preach it, brother! Testify!

At 4pm Pacifistic Standard Time (you know the old wive's tale that the tweeps of members of an administration converge on a single time? Haven't you ever heard the old wive's tale that you shouldn't believe old wives' tales?) the day before Canadiohen's first day of testimony, Reduhblican North Florampshire Representative Matt Pizzuhwattergaetz tweeped: "Hey @MichaelCanadiohen212, Do your wife & father-in-law know about your girlfriendz? Maybe tonight would be a good time for that chat. I wonder if she'll remain faithful when you're in prison. She's about to learn a lot…"

"This doesn't just have the appearance of witness tampering," said former prosecutor Barbara McDoodadallquade. "It has the gait, the vocal cadences and the fingerprints of witness tampering! In fact, I would say that this is the textbook case of witness tampering. I remember it from my third year tarts class. Everybody loved that class – precedents so tasty!"

Robinsoncrusoe didn't see how the threat would help President McDruhitmumpf. "I mean, think about it for a moment. When you threaten a man with dire consequences while he's in jail, won't he be motivated to spend as little time in jail as possible? In Canadiohen's case, wouldn't that result in cooperating with Congress and the Special Prosecutor as much as possible?

"Honestly, the only thing that gives me hope that Vesampucceri can survive this thuggish, criminal regime is that they're so very bad at…well, everything!"

"Hey!" complained television "waste management consultant" Tony Countersoprano. "Enough with the comparisons between what I do and what McDruhitmumpf and his cronies do, already! Okay, sure, I may not always be the nicest person, but at least I get things done!"

Uhh, yeah, Tone. Sure. Whatever you say.

"Yeah, I'm with Tony on this one," said McDoodadallquade. "I never thought I'd say that, what with him being a criminal and fictional and all, but there it is. Pizzuhwattergaetz seems to be taking a play out of the President's theatre season known as 'hide in plain sight.' That, or he's just too dumb to realize that using public threats to coerce testimony is frowned upon by our legal system. You just never know with this government."

And, yet, time and again, President McDruhitmumpf has very publicly said and done things that were illegal, immoral or fattening. Sometimes, all three at once. How come he can get away with it when mere mortals don't seem able to?

According to Robinsoncrusoe, the President has a random controversy generating algorithm in his head. When a crisis of his own making threatens to have consequences for him or somebody he is close to (so, for him), he just double clicks on the skull and crossbones on a field of burning court documents icon and lets the programme rip. And, everybody is off chasing another scandal before the consequences of the first have had a chance to play out.

"Unfortunately, the software is proprietary," Robinsoncrusoe concluded, "which means it was probably produced in China. Regardless of where it was made, the computer code is not available to mere Congresspeople, so they are much more likely to have to face the consequences of their actions. If only they could get somebody to reverse engineer the programme for them…"

UPDATE: In a speech on the House floor, Representative Pizzuhwattergaetz has doubled down on his tweep. "Yeah, I said that. So, waddya gonna do about it? Eh? Eh? Eh? Waddya gonna

UPDATE UPDATE: Just before midnight, Representative Pizzuhwattergaetz, possibly responding to House Speaker Nancy Pelligrinosi's rebuke, tweeped: "Oh, you thought I was threatening that lying liar of liedom Michael Canadiohen? No, no, no, no, no, no, no, no, no. Not really. If you saw my tweep in the context I saw it, you would know what I meant. Actually, screw context. I'll be deleting that tweep. Are we good?"

Things sure move fast in Washburningdington these days!

Not Their Finest (6) Hour (s and 27 minutes)

SPECIAL TO THE ALTERNATE REALITY NEWS SERVICE

Excerpt from testimony given by Michael Canadiohen, former lawyer to President Ronald McDruhitmumpf, during an open hearing of the House Oversight Committee.

REDUHBLICAN REPRESENTATIVE MARK MEADABIGGBLUBRATT: You're a liar.

MICHAEL CANADIOHEN: That's right.

MEADABIGGBLUBRATT: Don't try to deny the fact that you're a liar.

CANADIOHEN: I'm not denying it. It's a fact.

MEADABIGGBLUBRATT: Why won't you just come out and admit that you're a liar?

CANADIOHEN: I have admitted it.

MEADABIGGBLUBRATT: I mean, if you would just come out and admit that you're a liar, we could finally move on to other, more substantial business.

CANADIOHEN: Congressman, not only did I make it clear in my opening statement that I have lied, but I have agreed that I lied when every single Reduhblican member of this committee accused me of lying, including the last three times that you did.

MEADABIGGBLUBRATT: You will allow that you pleaded guilty to perjury, right?

CANADIOHEN: Yes, sir. I pleaded guilty to perjury.

MEADABIGGBLUBRATT: Were you aware that perjury is just a fancy legal term for lying?

CANADIOHEN: (exasperated) Congressman, were **you** aware that I was lying to protect the President at his request?

MEADABIGGBLUBRATT: (hastily) **I yield the floor!**

* * *

DUMBOPRATIC REPRESENTATIVE RAJA KRISHNADUCKMOORTHI: You previously testified to Congress that President McDruhitmumpf had no foreknowledge of a meeting between his son, Ron Junior, his son-in-law, Jared Kushkushinthebush and Fenwickian agents at McDruhitmumpf Towers during the election. But, today, you testified that not only did the President know about the meeting before it took place, but his reaction was, "Sweeeeeeeet!" Is that correct?

CANADIOHEN: That is correct.

KRISHNADUCKMOORTHI: In previous testimony to Congress, you claimed that President McDruhitmumpf stopped pursuing a project to build a luxury hotel in Fenwick before the campaign started. Yet, in testimony today, you said, no, that was not correct, that he did keep pushing the deal until well into the campaign. Correct?

CANADIOHEN: Correct.

KRISHNADUCKMOORTHI: Given all of that, my question to you is this: what was the bus driver's name?

CANADIOHEN: What was the – what? I'm sorry, could you please repeat the question, Congressman?

KRISHNADUCKMOORTHI: It's a simple question, sir. What was the bus driver's name?

CANADIOHEN: (confused) The bus driver's – I'm sorry, I don't – umm…

KRISHNADUCKMOORTHI: (laughing) Aww, I'm just messing with you!

CANADIOHEN: (muttering) Congressional humour!

KRISHNADUCKMOORTHI: No, my question actually is, Mister Canadiohen, why did you lie to Congress in your previous testimony?

CANADIOHEN: The President used his come hither eyes on me.

KRISHNADUCKMOORTHI: I…I'm sorry. The President's what now?

CANADIOHEN: The President would never just come out and tell you to do something illegal. That wasn't the way he operated. He would say something like, "Gee, it would be a dream come true if Congress never found out that I was pursuing the McDruhitmumpf Tower Fenwick project during the election!" Then, he would bat his baby browns at you, and you couldn't help but do what he wanted. You would just melt.

KRISHNADUCKMOORTHI: Melt?

CANADIOHEN: Anybody who was worked with the President for any length of time knows what it's like to be puddlified by his come hither eyes.

REDUHBLICAN REPRESENTATIVE JIM JORDASHJEANLOVER: I put it to, Mister Canadiohen, you are merely a pawn, a patsy, a stooge – no, wait, that doesn't scan – a pawn, a patsy, a…a…a pstooge of the Dumboprats! Their only goal is to take down a President who won in the greatest landslide the country has ever seen! And, they're using you to do it!

CANADIOHEN: Do you have a question, Congressman?

JORDASHJEANLOVER: Dumboprat billionaire Tom Reedproesateyer says, "Impeach the bastard!" and you ask, "How high?" You should be ashamed of yourself! The whole thing is a disgrace! Trying to bring down a leader who has done more for the Vesampuccerian people than any President since Solomon? Have you no shame? Shame on you!

CANADIOHEN: A question, Congressman? Please? About anything? Anything at all?

JORDASHJEANLOVER: You have smeared an innocent President with allegations of tax fraud, bank fraud, insurance fraud, election fraud – just about the only crimes you haven't accused him of are art forgery and spitting on a polar bear in the street! You can bring all of the signed checks and bank statements into this room that you want, but it won't change the fact that you, sir, are –

CUMMINGSENGOINGS: Time. The gentleman will yield the floor.

JORDASHJEANLOVER: Time? So soon?

CANADIOHEN: (muttering) Oh, so **now** you ask a question!

* * *

DUMBOPRATIC CHAIR OF THE COMMITTEE ELIJAH CUMMINGSENGOINGS: Representative Pizzuhwattergaetz. Yoo hoo, Representative Pizzuhwattergaetz? Hello?

REDUHBLICAN REPRESENTATIVE MATT PIZZUHWATTERGAETZ: Chairman Cummingsengoings.

CUMMINGSENGOINGS: You're not a member of this committee. Why are you lurking in the back of the room?

PIZZUHWATTERGAETZ: Oh, you know, no reason, really. I was in the neighbourhood and thought that I would drop by. I can be impulsive that way.

CUMMINGSENGOINGS: Really? You're going with the "I was in the neighbourhood" line?

PIZZUHWATTERGAETZ: Cheesy, I know. But – okay, I admit it: I'm a hearing room junkie. There's something about the wood panelling and the smell of the industrial strength shampoo they use to clean the carpets that just – oooooooh! (shivers)

CUMMINGSENGOINGS: So, you're not here to follow through on your tweep to intimidate the witness?

PIZZUHWATTERGAETZ: What? That? Pfft! Perish the thought. I – I mean – okay, you got me. I'm just a really big fan of your work!

CUMMINGSENGOINGS: (under his breath) Reduhblicans!

Crazy Eighth

by HAL MOUNTSAUERKRAUTEN, Alternate Reality News Service Crime Writer

In politics, as in pigsties, the runt of the litter gets the scraps.

Lawyers for the Southern District of New Hampshicut announced that they had launched an investigation into the Ronald McDruhitmumpf Inaugural Committee, alleging that it had illegally used money raised for a celebration of President McDruhitmumpf's election for other purposes, including paying for the silence of New Hampshicut porn star Misty Mondayinaroe. Nobody knows exactly why the campaign needed to buy the silence of a porn star, but in the century that we've had porn stars, nobody has ever found an innocent explanation for such a payment.

The problem is that this is the eighth investigation into funding irregularities at the inaugural, and the bones had been picked so clean by the time the SDNH took up the case that there weren't any bones left.

"Take the request for documents," said a source that stood so close, stood so close, don't stood so close to me investigation. "By the time the Inaugural Committee supplied the documents requested by the Southern District, the toner cartridge of their printer was so low that they may as well have been invisible ink!"

For example, because the text was so light, lawyers for the SDNH read dollars to donuts – that's not very helpful. "Donors" was often mistaken for "Moaners," making the investigators wonder just what kind of horror movie they were in. And, "Fenwickian citizen" was frequently mistaken for "told you it's none of your damn business, you liberal hack!"

"I've never even ridden in a cab!" the source closer to the heart of the investigation protested.

There have also been problems with interviewing the people who ran the Presidential Inaugural. "Some of them were so hoarse they could barely get words out," said the source close but no cigar to the investigation. "Deputy Chairman of the Inaugural Committee Rick Gatesfivethroughseven had to stop every couple of minutes to swallow a lozenge. Not that that helped his throat any. Saaaaay – could those lozenges have been something el – dammit!"

There was also at least one case of psycho-political discombobulation.* Committee Chair Thomas J. Barrmitzvahpayback, Jr. free associated during his two hour testimony, referring to baseball as "the only truly Vesampuccerian musical form," announcing that he should henceforth be referred to as "Saint Faustus the Henpecked," and wondering why the investigators had so many tentacles sticking out of their heads.

"As fascinating as these details are, maybe you should let readers know why the inaugural is under so many investigations," suggested token smart person Amy Sheshutshotshitbam. "You know, for context?"

Context? Hmm. I could try it – as long as it doesn't give me a rash. If this context thing of which you speak gives me a rash, it goes back in a box in the corner.

"Sure," token smart person Sheshutshotshitbam sighed.

Approximately $107 million was raised for the McDruhitmumpf Inaugural. This was twice as much as was raised for the inaugural of previous President Barry W. Bushbamclintreagbush, even though his celebrations featured a roster of A-list celebrities while the inaugural celebrations for President McDruhitmumpf primarily featured a man who was constructing a panorama of the Civil War Battle of Bunkerbuster Hill out of bottle caps and Ted Nugutsnueglorgent.

The question hanging over the inaugural is: where did the other $106,999,824.77 go? Those who worked on the inaugural claim that most of the unspent funds were given to charity, although porn stars are only considered charities in three states, none of them DC, and, in any case, nobody has been allowed to see the books, so there is no way of verifying this claim.

There is also the question of where the money came from. Donors such as "Robert 563290 Incorporated" and "Philpott 996669 LLC" suggest that the money wasn't coming from individual Vesampuccerians, as required by law. If that is the case, could it have ultimately come from foreign persons or entities?

"*Heidi* is my favourite children's breakfast cereal!" Barrmitzvahpayback aggressively defended the inauguration.

"It does make you wonder, though," token smart person Sheshutshotshitbam wondered. "If nobody is sure where the money came from and where it went to, could it be that the inaugural was one big slush fund paid for by foreign governments hoping to influence the President?"

Ignoring my itchy left shoulder, I enthusiastically responded that I didn't know, token smart person. Could it? Could it be the way you have described?

The token smart person stated, "You know what they say: where there's eight layers of smoke, somebody should be fired!"

* Not an actual medical condition.

Collusion Confusion

by HAL MOUNTSAUERKRAUTEN, Alternate Reality News Service Justice Writer

When your clarification needs a clarification, you might want to consider the possibility that you have a communication problem.

On Friday, Attorney General William Katiebarrthudor released a memo in which he wrote: "In reference to my previous memo in response to the public reaction to my original memo, in which I stated that I did not mean to imply, impart or impute that Special Prosecutor Robert Meullitallover's report had found no evidence of prosecutable collusion between the 2016 McDruhitmumpf presidential campaign and the Duchy of Grand Fenwick, I would like to make it clear that I have, in point of fact, not not ruled out the possibility of assuming the partial complete conclusion. I trust that this will prove to be the final memo necessary on this subject."

"Yeah. No. Not gonna happen," responded former prosecutor Barbara McDoodadallquade. "The Attorney General's gonna have to issue a clarification of his clarification of his clarification of his original statement, because the clarification of the clarification of his original statement is about as clear as the Mattawanahoople River in monsoon season! Heck, do you have any Gravol? Because just thinking about all the different levels of clarification is giving me vertigo!"

Attorney General Katiebarrthudor's original memo implied that Special Prosecutor Meullitallover's report had exonerated President Ronald McDruhitmumpf of any wrongdoing (in the same way that a strong rotting smell implies that you really shouldn't have cemented the body behind the drywall hoping that nobody would notice). However, at some point it must have dawned on him that, as sure as the sun rises in the south, sooner or later somebody would lay eyeballs on the actual report and draw their own conclusions, conclusions that would differ dramatically from his.

Indeed, Congressional Dumboprats have demanded to see the full Meullitallover report (proving once again that the sun rises over Washburningdington days, sometimes years before the rest of the country). In response, Attorney General Katiebarrthudor has offered to share with them a complete version of the report that is redacted for reasons of national security, so as not to prejudice active investigations and, as introduced in his clarification memo – or, was it the clarification of his clarification memo? – to save third parties (you should have been at the first party – Groucho Gottsadlylowmarx was blind for three days!) from suffering, "acute embarrassment."

Dumboprats weren't buying it, even at a heavily discounted rate. "Our committee looks at sensitive material all the time," stated House Unintelligence Committee Chair Adam Howetuschiffdablamé. "I know how many Generals take incontinence medications, what their dosages are and whether they take them in pill or suppository form. This would be both a national security and 'acutely embarrassing to a third party' issue. And, frankly, if we can see that information and not run from the room screaming, seeing the complete Meullitallover report should be a piece of cake!"

"Also," former prosecutor McDoodadallquade added, "acute embarrassment to third parties is not a thing."

At 2:37 the morning of the…second clarification, President McDruhitmumpf weighed in on the issue, tweeping: "Adam Howetuschiffdablamé is a pencil-necked geek who doesn't even have the guts to bite the heads off live bats! He only bites the heads off chocolate bats! #embarasmenttocircuseseverywhere #fredblassienotgassieshakeshisheadinshame"

"It is a poor debater who must resort to *ad hominem* attacks," Committee Chair Howetuschiffdablamé evenly replied (he must have been sitting on a plane). "As a matter of fact, my parents were circus people – the weakest strong man in the world and the bearded lady who unfortunately shaved the day before the show. I bit the head off my first live bat when I was six years old. I would not recommend it. Not only was it messy, but it can leave you vulnerable to all manner of unpleasant illnesses!"

"Oh, and acute embarrassment to third parties?" former prosecutor McDoodadallquade insisted. "Still not a thing."

Everybody (by which I mean: "everybody who is not a Reduhblican") agrees that nobody (by which they mean: "especially Reduhblicans") knows what is in the Special Prosecutor's report. Anybody who claims they know what is in it will probably try to convince you that they were at Woodstock (and, just like they are actually talking about Attorney General Katiebarrthudor's memo, they will probably claim to have attended Altamont.)

Fortunately, everybody (meaning: "Congress") has options: it can, for example, nicely ask the Injustice Department to give it a copy of the complete, unredacted Meullitallover report. Or, it can angrily demand that the Injustice Department give it a copy of the complete, unredacted Meullitallover report. Or, it can ask Meullitallover to come in and answer questions about his report. Or, it can supboena a copy of the complete, unredacted Meullitallover report.

Or it can stand on its head on a street corner and sing "Ave Tia Maria" until the complete, unredacted Meullitallover report spontaneously appears in front of it. Given the intransigence of the McDruhitmumpf Grey House and the complicity of its Attorney General, it's hard to say which approach would be the most effective.

The Trojan Weasel

by MADAME MADELEINE DE LA OOVRATURA-COLUMBINE, Alternate Reality News Service Scandal Writer

Who is Deputy Attorney General Rod Rosentokenjew when he's just come out of the shower and is dripping all over his freshly cleaned rug?

Is he a champion of Special Prosecutor Robert Meullitallover, as he has been claiming, saying to anybody who appeared ready to interfere with Meullitallover's probe into Fenwickian interference in the 2016 election, up to and including the President, "If you want to get to him, you'll have to go through me!"? (Sorry – they were having an action movie marathon on AMFMC last night. I was watching the John McClanocavebear/James Bosmipahelfly crossover *Die Harder Another Day* when I fell asleep, and it must have made a big impression on my subconscious.)

A new report from the *Washburningdington Times* – or, was it the *Washburningdington Post*? – let's split the difference and say the *Washburningdington Tost* – anyway, a new report from…that publication suggests that the Deputy Attorney General, in fact, regularly briefed the Grey House on the progress of Meullitallover's investigation. At one point, he is quoted as saying to President Ronald McDruhitmumpf, "Don't worry, I'll crash that plane into the side of a mountain."

This has widely been interpreted to mean that the Deputy Attorney General was telling the President that he would not allow him to come to any harm (albeit in a way that catered to the Commander-in-Brief's chaotic-evil nature).

"If that report is true – and I have the utmost faith in the reporting of the *Washburningdington Tost* – it is very disturbing," said former prosecutor Joyce Onvancewarpedtur. Before she could explain why, she took a Valium and went home to rest.

"The former prosecutor is correct," agreed Pulippitzaner Prize-winning columnist for the *Washburningdington Tost* Eugene Robinsoncrusoe. "This could mean…this could…I mean – oh, dear!" Through his sobs, he asked if we could continue this conversation later.

"Wimps!" muttered token smart person Amy Sheshutshotshitbam. "What they were trying to say was…" she shuddered. Then, gritting her teeth, she continued, "**What they were trying to say was**…that if Rosentokenjew was working for the Grey House while overseeing the Meullitallover investigation, he could have shaped it in a way that favoured the Grey House."

People have wondered, in a "how high is up?" kind of way, why the Special Prosecutor didn't ask the IRS for President

McDruhitmumpf's tax returns; if the President had been getting financial help from Fenwick, it could explain why he has been such a good friend of the country, the sworn and deputized enemy of Vesampucceri, since taking power. The fear is that Deputy Attorney General Rosentokenjew wagged a finger in Special Prosecutor Meullitallover's direction and said, "Nyuh unh. Don't go there, girl!"

People have also wondered (because the day is long and imagination expands to fill the time allotted to work) why Special Prosecutor Meullitallover didn't call President McDruhitmumpf in to testify under oath before a Grand Jury. It could very well be because when he tried, the Deputy Attorney General wagged a different, ruder finger in his direction and said, "Oh, no, you di'i'nt!"

"Yes!" Robinsoncrusoe gasped, wiping the tears from his eyes with the sleeve of his Pulippitzaner Prize-winning shirt. "This!" Onvancewarpedtur made a sound that could have been agreement, but she was several blocks away, so it was hard to tell.

"Honestly, I'm surprised people are so surpr – astonished by this news," token smart person Sheshutshotshitbam added. "When the President asked him to write a memo to give an explanation for why he fired FBI Director James Comeonecomally that didn't involve the agency's investigation of Fenwick, Rosentokenjew asked, 'Do you want Fries with that?' From the beginning, he knew about the President's love of fast food and loose morals, and he had no qualms about catering to them!"

"To be fair," Robinsoncrusoe lamely commented, "Rosentokenjew had great PR!"

Token smart person Sheshutshotshitbam hesitated to respond. I didn't need my crystal ball to tell that she wanted to say that journalists blew it by missing Deputy Attorney General Rosentokenjew's fidelity to President McDruhitmumpf. On the other hand, I didn't need my graduate degree in psychology to tell that she felt that, if his goal was to neuter the Meullitallover report, he did a spectacularly bad job of it, since it is a damning indictment of criminal behaviour at the highest levels (ooh, I call dibs on that title for my memoirs!).

"In the end," she summed up, "this President is an anti-alchemist: his administration turns everything it touches from gold to base metal. What ever made us think that lawyers were immune?"

Stonewall – Not Just For Andrew Jackshithappenson Any More!

by FRANCIS GRECOROMACOLLUDEN, Alternate Reality News
Service National Politics Writer

When the House Oversight Committee asked 81 different individuals
and institutions for documents and testimony, many complied, some
surprisingly so. Steve O'Bannonallhope, for example, took time out
of his busy schedule sabotaging the governments of European allies
to send the Committee enough documents to insulate all the
AirBnBBs in Frankfurt!

The Grey House's response, by way of contrast, was to send a
message. And, the message was: "We're sorry, but we can't come to
the phone right now. If we aren't out of the office making the world
safe for idiotocracy, we're walking the dog. Anyhoo… At the sound
of the beep, leave your name, number and a Goldilocks-lengthed
message and nobody will get back to you at our earliest possible
inconvenience. Robert Meullitallover will burn in Hell! Byeeeeee!"
This was unusual inasmuchasPresidentRonald – sorry. I had trouble
finding the end of that word. This was unusual inasmasPres – since!
This was unusual since President Ronald McDruhitmumpf has not
only made it clear that his favourite pet is a *Pentuphouse* centrefold,
but because the request for documents had not been submitted by
phone.

Thinking that it may have been a moderate mistake that was
easily corrected (as if anything the McDruhitmumpf administration
does is moderate!), Committee Chair Elijah Cummingsengoings sent
the request for documents to the Grey House a second time. It's
response? It sent back an RSVP to Isaac Kimmelfarberman's *bar
mitzvah* with the "Not coming" and "Not giving a gift" boxes
checked and the note, "I hope your monster of a son becomes a
doctor and dies of a [illegible] painful disease that he could have
easily diagnosed himself, but didn't!" scribbled in the margin.

"It's almost as if they don't want to supply us with any
information," Chair Cummingsengoings muttered under his breath.

Actually, it's precisely that the Grey House doesn't want to give
the Oversight Committee any information. They said as much in a
press release headlined, "Grey House Decides Not to Give House

Oversighs [sic] Committee Any Information." To ensure that reporters got the message, it was leaked to select journalists in an email titled, "IMMEDIATE ATTENTIONS: Your Bankebank account will be terminated in 24 seconds if you don't give us all of your personal information...for...you know...verification purposes because...we are totally trustworthy representatives of Bankebank! We even have their logo and everything, so you know we must be legit!!!!"

"If I didn't know any better," Chair Cummingsengoings muttered in the general vicinity of his breath, "I would swear that the Grey House is not cooperating with our investigation. Good thing I know better. Because if I didn't, I might have to go back on Valium!"

"The Vesampuccerian government was designed like a jigsaw puzzle," said presidential historian Michael Beschbefordatloess. "A jigsaw puzzle that nobody can agree on the design of made up of three massive pieces that are constantly at war with each other. This is what, in presidential historian school, we call 'checks and balances.'"

"I don't see what all the fuss is about," said Grey House spokeshrill KellyAnne Conwaytwittiest. "Oversight means sight over. Meaning, looking over the fabled gables of the Grey House to the Washburningdington home of Bill and Hillary Roocartoncleveman. **That** is where the Oversight Committee should be sighting!"

The Language Corrector Dude started vibrating visibly in anticipation of a question in his field. So, I asked token smart person Amy Sheshutshotshitbam to respond to Conwaytwittiest, instead. No point risking the strings that hold together the fabric of the universe.

"Oversight involves investigating potential wrongdoing by people in power," she explained. "The different branches of government are supposed to keep each other honest. You know, like the three massive pieces of a jigsaw puzzle that nobody can agree on the design of. Only, with more leaks."

If the Grey House homesteadfastly refuses to cooperate, the Oversight Committee can issue subpoenas to compel – hee hee. I said, subpoenas! Ha ha! I said it again! Subpoenas! Subpoenas!

Subpoenas! Sub – what? But, it sure sounds dirty – are you positive? Okay, then.

If the Grey House homesteadfastly refuses to cooperate, it will be opening up a whole new frontier in Vesampuccerian jurisprudence. The Committee can issue subpoenas – which is a perfectly legitimate word which, I am informed, is in no way a reference to a naughty bit of a man's body – to compel the Grey House to give it the documents it wants. The Grey House could then ask the courts to quash the – quick, think of something boring! – subpoenas. Then, there will be a lot of blah, blah, blah, and the whole mess will end up being heard by the Extreme Court.

In that case, if Justice Brett Kavanaugheylno is sporting a hangover from a weekend kegger (that only ended on Tuesday afternoon, but it felt like forever!), anything could happen!

The Gang That Couldn't Character Assassinate Straight

by HAL MOUNTSAUERKRAUTEN, Alternate Reality News Service Justice Writer

If you're trying to do something anonymously, it's probably a good idea not to give out a phone number that goes to an answering machine that says, "**Haaaaiiiiieee!** Is that…is that too loud? Umm… sorry – I have to press what, now? I don't see any – I'll just speak softer, okay? Okay. Ahem. Mi mi mi mi mi. Rhubarb rhubarb rhubarb rhubarb. Haiee. You have reached the Wholgathruntossah residence. I'm Ida Mae Wholgathruntossah, but you probably don't want to talk to me. My, oh my, no. Nobody ever wants to talk to me. I bet you want to talk to my grandson, Jacob. You know – the boy who keeps saying that he's gonna 'change the direction of Vesampuccerian politics forever?'"

"**Gran!**"

"Yeah, well, if you want to talk to a punk with delusions of grandeur instead of a mature woman with a world of experience –"

"**Gran! That's enough!**"

"– leave your name and number at the sound of the beep and I'm sure the saviour of the free world will get back to you at his earliest convenience."

"That's it! I'm doing my own voicemail mess –"

BEEP!

It's especially problematic when the object of your activity is a Special Prosecutor investigating Fenwick interference in the 2016 Vesampuccerian election. As soon as he catches wind of your shenanigans, he might just ask the FBI to investi – oh, look! That's exactly what Special Prosecutor Robert Meullitallover did!

Sucks to be you.

Jacob Wholgathruntossah appears to have been the point man for Reduhblican operative Jack Wottarealburkman, who had been claiming that at least six women had been sexually assaulted by the Special Prosecutor. Upon investigation, it turned out that one of the women, Jennifer Hippoindataub, had never met Special Prosecutor Meullitallover. When Hippoindataub pointed this out, Wottarealburkman asked, "Have you never heard of psychospiritual assault? If it isn't a crime now, we could get President McDruhitmumpf to sign an Executive Order making it one!"

That's not really how laws are made, but whole books could be written on **that** subject. A second woman, Lorraine Parsnicketypons, who had worked out of the same office as Special Prosecutor Meullitallover, stated that she remembered him being a complete professional who never took advantage of her, psychospiritually or otherwise.

Wottarealburkman stared at the back of his hand for a few seconds. Then, not wishing to repeat himself, he pffted. "It's sad," he said, "that women who have been abused cloak themselves in denial to protect themselves from the awful truth of what has been done to them. Thank Gord there are men who are willing to tell their truth for them!"

MSNBC anchor Rachel O'Schubermatthow sighed in scorn and dismay.

A press conference was held in which a third woman was supposed to appear and make her allegations against the Special Prosecutor. When she failed to show up, Wottarealburkman told journalists, "Ask me anything you would have asked the woman. I know her whole story – I helped shape it with her!"

MSNBC anchor O'Schubermatthow yelped in scormay. She's obviously working up to a snort of scormay, or possibly an opening segment.

The other three accusers are "mystery women" who have yet to be identified. It's like an Agatha Chrisgardstouderrmett novel, except without the twee, bloodless murders or whimsy.

"Jesus begesus!" MSNBC anchor O'Schubermatthow finally regained her voice. "The Reduhblicans are trying to weaponize the #metoo movement!"

"Nah, Ah do believe that is a mite hahsh," responded Grey House Press Secretary Sarah Wannabe-Panders. "Theah is nothin' ta connect this…whatevah it is ta thuh McDruhitmumpf administration."

If she had left it there, Press Secretary Wannabe-Panders would have been fine. Denial required, denial supplied. Unfortunately, not leaving well enough alone (as well as doubling down, making things worse and continuing to dig) is a Hallmark of this administration (they're such cards!). So, she added: "But, if thuh allegations're true, wuhl, wouldn't that be somethin'?"

"The allegations are not true!" Parsnicketypons insisted. "Douchenozzle over there offered me $20,000 to make the accusation! Naturally, I turned him down. It would be wrong. And, anyway, I don't want any troub – oh, man, is that the FBI I hear knock knock knocking on my door?"

"Of course we offered to compensate the victims," Wottarealburkman commented. "They've been through Hell! They deserve to get a little something something back for all of the…the, umm…you're not buying any of this, are you?"

"Not even a little bit," MSNBC anchor O'Schubermatthow assured him.

Running low on rhetoric, Wottarealburkman pffted one last time. "With an attitude like that, is it any wonder men aren't willing to stick their necks out to support women?"

Ira Nayman
A Taxing Situation

by GIDEON GINRACHMANJINJa-VITUS, Alternate Reality News Service Economics Writer

Reduhblicans love deadlines. They love the heavy clanking sound deadlines make as they pass by.

Representative Richard E. Nealgaimansplainer, the Chair of the House Ways and Means Committee, requested that Infernal Revenue Service commissioner Charles RettinolAgig supply him with six years of the tax returns of President Ronald McDruhitmumpf. That clanking sound everybody can hear? That's the sound of the April 10 deadline falling by the wayside like so much knight in chainmail armour being knocked out by a sleep spell and falling to the marble floor of an evil sorcerer's lair.

If that metaphor doesn't get me at least a nomination for a Pulippitzaner Prize for literary journalism, I will eat my chainmail hat!

The law appears to be on the Chair's side. "The IRS Commissioner shall supply the Chairman the tax returns of any Vesampuccerian citizen. Shall. Not can if they feel like it. Shall. Not may if all of the augurs align. Shall. Not maybe. Not perhaps. Not let's see how the day goes. Shall."

Seems pretty straightforward, doesn't it? Does it? Have you even met this administration?

In testimony to Congress after the deadline had passed, Treasury Secretary Steve Mnemonixuchin said, "We are considering the Chairman's request, and will get back to the Committee as soon as we have made a decision." But, the law says: "Oh, no, you don't, Mister Treasury Secretary. This is between the Committee Chairman and the head of the IRS – you have nothing to do with it. You absolutely do not have any right to delay the handing over of requested tax returns to the Committee Chair. *Capisce*?"

Treasury Secretary Mnemonixuchin must not speak Croatian, because he continued: "Concerns have been raised that the Chairman's request was not made out of a pure desire to see if the IRS used proper procedures in processing the President's returns, but out of a venal need to destroy a political opponent!" To which the law's response was, "Butt out, Mister Treasury Secretary! That is not your call to make! And, anyway, if the President's tax returns are on the up and up, there is no way it can be used to destroy him. Let the IRS Commissioner do his job!"

Chair Nealgaimansplainer has set a second deadline for the IRS to hand over the documents: April 23. "Please know that, if you fail to comply, your failure will be interpreted as a denial of my request," he wrote. "This will make me angry. You wouldn't like me when I'm angry."

Treasury Secretary Mnemonixuchin should be worried. Angry Dumboprats write blistering letters to newspaper op-ed pages.

In an effort to calm the situation down, President McDruhitmumpf said: "Congress will get my tax returns when they pry them from my cold, dead fingers – and I plan on living forever!"

What might happen if the new deadline goes clanking by?

"Are we at the point of a Constitutional crisis, yet?" wondered editorial columnist Eugene Robinsoncrusoe. "I mean, we've been expecting one since President McDruhitmumpf first took office. It doesn't matter much to me – I've already lost the journalists' pool on this. February 23 is my lucky month. I'm just curious: have we finally hit a Constitutional crisis?"

Not quite. According to legal scholars and lapidary numismatists, the Ways and Means Committee could subpoena the tax returns. That would be an especially clanky deadline as it went by.

Another possibility is that the Committee could hold Treasury Secretary Mnemonixuchin and IRS Commissioner RettinolAgig in contempt of Congress. (Charging the President with contempt of Congress would be redundant; he displays this attitude every day.) In that case, they could ask a court for an injunction compelling the IRS to give the tax returns to the Committee. This would involve multiple clankings as the case worked its way up the courts, making it sound like an unconscious knight in chainmail being dragged down a flight of stairs.

Clank.

Clank.

Clank!

I really hope the Pulippitzaner Prize Committee is reading this.

Why is this happening? Because Ronald McDruhitmumpf is the first President in 50 years who has not released any of his tax returns to the public. There have been rumours that he may have manipulated the value of his properties to pay less tax. There are whispers that he may have benefited from his administration's tax cuts, even though he assured the public that he wouldn't. There is even scuttlebutt that he received money from foreign governments that he later shaped government policy to favour. Could the law help us determine if any of this is true?

"Hey!" the law argued. "I can do a lot of things, but I'm not a miracle worker!"

Twenty-seven Personalities, None of Them Cooperative

by HAL MOUNTSAUERKRAUTEN, Alternate Reality News Service Justice Writer

Attorney General William Katiebarrthudor testified before the Senate Judiciary Committee yesterday – all 27 versions of him.

When Reduhblican Senator Lindsay Grahamcrokercrum asked him, "How awesome do you think President Ronald McDruhitmumpf has been?" Attorney General Katiebarrthudor gushed like a schoolgirl: "Like, oh, my god! The way he says one thing one day and has the confidence to say the complete opposite thing the next day? What a man! He's soooooo dreamy! Deputy Attorney General Rod Rosentokenjew and I have been talking about getting matching tattoos of his hair – do you think he would notice us if we did? That would be **so cool!**"

When, in previous testimony to the Committee, he was asked if he knew what Robert Meullitallover's reaction to his summary that wasn't really a summary of the Special Prosecutor's findings was, Attorney General Katiebarrthudor got his confused hipster on. "I don't, like, know for sure, maaaaaan. It's not like he got on his bongos and, like, sent me a smoke signal or anything. But, like, I mean how could he not be chill with such rad findings, do you dig?"

In a private letter made public the day before the Attorney General's latest testimony, Special Prosecutor Meullitallover expressed a complete lack of chill in the summary that dare not speak its name. When Attorney General Katiebarrthudor testified that he did not know what the Special Prosecutor's feelings about it were, therefore, he li – the Attorney General li – li – he li – li – li – li – he…mislead the Congress.

When Dumbopratic Senator Richard Blumenthalated asked him about this, the Attorney General took on the air of a university professor and responded, "What is truth? Truth is beauty. But beauty is in the eye of the beholder. Therefore, and I think any reasonable person would agree, the only conclusion to which we can come is that the truth of my previous statement was in the eye of the beholder. Would you like me to walk you through the symbolic equation that proves this hypothesis?"

Later in the hearing, Reduhblican Congressman Chuck Gasleygrassteahee asserted that the real scandal was Dumbopratic candidate Hillary Roocartoncleveman's attempts to steal the 2016 election, and asked what was the Attorney General doing about **that**? Channelling his inner Brooklyn mob boss, Attorney General Katiebarrthudor answered, "You think we're gonna let her get away wid dat shit? Watsamatta you? We are investigatin' the hell outta her, that's what we're doin'. And, when I say we're investigatin' the hell outta her, I mean **we're investigatin' the hell outta her!** Strugatz! Eh!"

That casued the Dumboprats on the Committee to practise their synchronized eye rolling.

Dumbopratic Senator Kamala Harristweedfashin asked Attorney General Katiebarrthudor if anybody in the Grey House asked or suggested that he prosecute specific people. This caused the Attorney General to come all school marmish at her. "Well, sweetie, it depends upon what your definition of asked is. I don't think anybody asked me to do that, no. Suggested? Perhaps. Recommended? It is certainly a possibility. Requested? That's a whole different issue, isn't it? Inquired as to the possibility of? You know, a lot of things may be said in idle conversation. You can hardly expect me to remember them all. Perhaps you should consider phrasing your questions more carefully, dear."

And, so it went. When a Redublican asked the Attorney General if the Injustice Department was considering investigating the origins of the Meullitallover investigation, he snarled, "Grrrr! Raaawwwr! FBI bad! Me smash overreaching FISA warrants! Arrrrrrr!"

When a Dumboprat asked the Attorney General if it was in the President's powers to fire the Special Prosecutor, you could almost see his pants drop down to his ankles when he responded, "Well, duh! The President can end any investigation if he thinks that the person is innocent and the investigation was, like, totally unfair! And, that would not be a sign of corrupt intent, because, what part of innocent don't you understand? I mean – sheesh! I can't believe I have to explain this to you! Were you dropped on your head in the hospital after you were born or something?"

"This was an extraordinary performance, worthy of acting awards" Alternate Reality News Service film and television critic Elmore Teradonovich responded to the testimony. "I laughed.* I cried.** I paused the video so I could go to the bathroom. A lot – the show was really long!"

* …at the absurdity of the Attorney General's responses.

** …for the state of my country.

5. THE SLEEP OF REASON PRODUCES…BAD NEIGHBOURS

The Land of the Free and the Home of the Depraved

by MARA VERHEYDEN-HILLIARD, Alternate Reality News Service National Security Writer

Sandoval "Gut Check and Mate" Gutivimeda, a 36 year-old pig farmer who dreamed of one day owning his swine instead of renting them from Monsanto, had a feeling that it wasn't safe for him to stay in his home town of San Silleon, Venezuela.

Something in the way Miguelito Confarduellavan, San Silleon's Chief of Police, said, "I'm going to turn my back and count to ten. If you're still here by the time I turn back around, I will kill you, your wife Priscilla, your two children Moneyball and Maria and your prize pig Flopsy," was a big clue. Before Confarduellavan turned around, he slowly drew his forefinger across his forehead, indicating either that he was going to switch the brains of the family Frankenstein-style, or the old death threat routine was getting stale and he was trying something new in order to make it fresh and exciting again.

Gutivimeda didn't wait to find out. By the count of ten, his family was already halfway out of Venezuela. By another count of ten, they arrived at the border between Mexico and the United States. (Some condensation of time may have occurred to move the narrative along.) Their prized pig Flopsy was set free in the forest, where it is rumoured to have been taken in by a wolf pack seeking comic relief.

When they arrived at the Port of Entry (known as PoE because it generates endless horror stories) at San Ysidro, the Gutivimeda family was told that it was their lucky day: that PoE was closed owing to the Vesampuccerian No Port in a Storm policy (which designates a random five mile stretch of the border every 24 hours as the official Port of Entry), but the nearest PoE was only 576 miles away. When Gutivimeda told the guard at the gate that the family was on foot, she smiled and said, "You might want to jog there before a new place is chosen at midnight, then."

Okay, it's not exactly "The Masque of the Red Pendulum." Vesampucceri's PoEt laureate is allowed to have off days.

By that time, the man who had promised to help the Gutivimedas get into the US was nowhere to be found. As was the money they had scrounged together in eight of the ten seconds before they were forced to flee their home. "And, he had such a kindly face," commented Priscilla Gutivimeda. "Except for the spiral scar on his right cheek and the dead eyes, I mean."

Some people find it easier to make sense of adverse life circumstances than others.

Faced with a dearth (less than a treachery, more than a hearse) of options, Gutivimeda led his family away from the Port of Entry. A couple of kilometres – basically, far enough to be out of sight of the PoE. Employing a combination of putty knife (did we mention that Priscilla Gutivimeda created plaster sculptures of Venezuelan marines morphing into lizards in her spare time?) and desperation, it only took them another three days to cut through the chain link fence and make it to the Vesampuccerian side of the border.

To celebrate their entry into the land of the free, the Gutivimeda family was picked up by an ICES (Immigration Corralling and Expulsing Service) border patrol. Not in a sleazy, slink up to somebody in a seedy bar and ask what their sign is kind of way. More in a sleazy, kick somebody when they're down abuse of political power kind of way.

Sandoval Gutivimeda politely told the ICES agents who took the family into custody: "Howdy, y'all motherferkers. I done be plumb lookin' fer asylum, motherferkers." The agent complimented him on his English (which he had apparently learned from watching *Green Acres* and old Bruce Willusorwontus movies), and told him that his claim for asylum would be considered when he entered a proper Port of Entry.

Gutivimeda repeated "Motherferker! Motherferker! Motherferker!" all the way to the detention facility. Okay, more Samuel L. Jackshithappenson than Bruce Willusorwontus, but it was an easy mistake for somebody fleeing from the violence in his homeland to make.

According to international law, anybody appearing at a national border asking for asylum must be granted a hearing to determine if they have a valid fear of persecution if they are returned to their home country. According to the McDruhitmumpf administration's Zero Humanity policy, international law can suck it. Suck it hard.

"Nah, Ah do believe that that theah is a gross misrepuhsentation o' thuh President's position," argued Attorney General Jeff "Self-regard" Sesspoolpandemic. "Suckin' would implah we want intuhnashnull law ta have some pleasuh. Nothin' could be fahthuh from thuh truth. We would acshully lahk intuhnashnull law to be beaten abaht thuh head and shoulduhs with gold-plated chopsticks and dah a slow, painful death."

Have you ever noticed how much worse the "explanations" of McDruhitmumpf administration officials actually make things sound?

The Gutivimeda family were transported to a "Refugee Settlement Facility" (some of the most unsettling places we've ever been inside, let us tell you!) in Lockjaw, Texansas. They slept on a concrete floor in a wire mesh cage. The food they were given would have been refused by the orphans in *Oliver Twistenshowtencry*.

After a couple of hours, a woman in a moderately intelligent business suit (let's just say that it wasn't made of Mensa material) approached the family and said she wanted to take the children to get ice cream. When Priscilla Gutivimeda reasonably objected that she hadn't heard the jingle of an ice cream truck, only the screaming of hungry babies and crying of anguished parents, the woman responded: "Ice cream? Did I say ice cream? I meant...showers. That's it. I want to take your children to have showers. When you're invading a foreign country to destroy its freedoms, it's important to maintain good personal hygiene."

Priscilla Gutivimeda was skeptical. So, the woman signalled to two body guards to physically remove the children. As the family members joined the chorus of screaming and crying, the unidentified woman shook her head sadly and commented, "There's just no reasoning with some people!"

Bordering on Chaos

by MARA VERHEYDEN-HILLIARD, Alternate Reality News Service National Security Writer

How many times can you take a picture of a heroic young man (heavily armed) looking across a tumbleweed-strewn desert (right out of central casting – good tumbleweeds don't grow on trees, you know!), silhouetted by the setting sun before you start repeating yourself?

"237," answered Sgt. Ibrahim Baruch-al-Ooda, of the Flyin' (Lizards) Photogs Unit. (Imagine the shoulder patch!)

Oh. I wasn't expecting the answer to be so...specific. Or, definitive. Umm...well done, soldier.

Sgt. Baruch-al-Ooda is one of the 5,900 troops that have been deployed to the Vesampuccerian border with Mexico to combat invading bands of rampaging...err...rampagers. And, nogoodniks. As President Ronald McDruhitmumpf recently tweeped: "Gord bless the troops who are taking photographs of heroic young men defending our southern border! I mean, BANG! BOOM! THWOING! Blood spouting and body parts flying – this is what makes Vesampucceri grate!"

There's just one problem with the President's stirring (if bloody – you would have thought Eli Rothogordonya had ghost-written the tweep) message: the refugees that he is trying to make everybody so afraid of are working their way through Latin Vesampucceri so slowly that they aren't expected to appear at the border for several months. That, and the fact that they are mostly women and children, whose only real threat to the United States is to contribute something of value to it.

Okay, there are two problems with the President's vision: the refugees haven't arrived and they're not trained fighters **and** military personnel are forbidden by the *Posse Comitatus* (no, no, no, you're thinking of *The Pussy Coitus*, and get your mind out of the gutter because I'm **not** that kind of journalist!) *Act* of 1878 from engaging in judicial operations on Vesampuccerian soil.

Three! Three things! There are three – there are **many** problems with the President's vision of what is happening on the country's southern border, including but not limited to: the slow thing, the civilian thing and the not being able to legally engage with anybody doing illegal things on Vesampuccerian soil thing.

Why would the President offer such a dark vision to the nation when the reality is so much more yoyodyne?

"To fire up his base for the mid-term election," stated token smart person Amy Sheshutshotshitbam. The "Duh" was implied. With all the subtlety of a Wall Street bull in a shop in China.

If that's the case, why has the President continued to tweep about sending the troops to protect the country's southern border since the election? "Has he?" token smart person Sheshutshotshitbam had a sarcasm orgasm. "Has he really?"

Sure, he has. Just this morning, President McDruhitmumpf tweeped – oh, no, that was about how much the investigation of Special Prosecutor Robert Meullitallover was a witch hunt. A lot, apparently. But, yesterday, the President tweeped about…umm, okay, how the Meullitallover investigation was a hoax. Hmm…let's see…will have the affect of keeping good people out of politics – * SNORT! * – a witch hunt **and** a hoax, both at the same time – inevitable, that one, really – fully qualified to be the next Attorney Gen – oh, my Gord, the token smart person was right! The President hasn't tweeped, peeped, beeped or otherwise skiddley-doo-queeped about protecting the country's southern border since the election!

"Being right is an occupational hazard," token smart person Sheshutshotshitbam smugged.

Given the limitations placed upon them, what are the soldiers who have been deployed to the southern border actually doing?

Some are working in intelligence ("Nope. Still no invading hordes at the border."). Some are working in tactics and logistics ("Since there are no invading hordes at the border, there's really nothing to be done."). Five of the 32 units at the border are press and public relations ("Can you pose heroically...in front of that array of computer screens featuring an incomprehensible flow of satellite data that is telling us that no invading hordes are at the – yeah, I think I'll go back outside and see if the sun is setting...").

But, for troops deployed at the southern border, life isn't all watching computer screens and waiting for sunsets. Granted, it's mostly watching computer screens and waiting for sunsets. And, building the occasional latrine just to mix things up a bit. In fact, there are times when a live rooster being set free in the armoury would be –

"**Are? You? Kidding? Me?**" shouted security expert Malcolm Donneednopennance. "Are you ferking kidding me?"

Umm...we don't think so...

"This operation is taking soldiers away from training or assignments that might actually, you know, benefit somebody in some way!" security expert Donneednopennance argued. At vociferousness. "**And**, the whole operation could cost upwards of $200 million! And, for what? To gain some kind of advantage in a mid-term election?"

Well, okay, when you put it that way...

The Worst of the Worst –
Especially Just Before Nap Time

by TAMMY, Alternate Reality Kidz News Service Life is so Unfair Writer

Fort Nothing to Bragg About, Texaware is a hard, cold, cruel place. It's the Norma Desmond of places in Vesampucceri. Here, you will find four year-old members of Mexican gang Letter-Number shaking down three year-old members of rival gang Number-Letter for safety pin money. Word is that anything you want, you can get smuggled into the facility…for a price. Chocolate milk. Spiderman pyjamas. Pacifiers spiked with maple syrup. Anything.

Fort Nothing to Bragg About is not a place for children. Yet, thanks to the McDruhitmumpf administration's Separate and Scatter policylet (part of its larger Zero Humanity policy), children as young as 18 months and as old as 126 months separated at the border from their parents can find themselves here.

"Don't cry for us, Argentina," said four and a half year-old Guillermo Acivederrez from behind the chain link fence that the government refers to as "a detainee incarceration facility that in no way resembles a cage, and we're offended by the possibility that you would call it that, so don't you dare!" I tried to point out to Guillermo that my name is not Argentina, but he continued over me: "We're scum. Worst of the worst. We deserve to be – you got any Milk Duds? Man, I could kill for a Milk Dud!"

To illustrate his point about all the hard boys in the joint, Guillermo told me the story of six year-old Jose Luis Garcineznandez, a baby faced (as if the three year-old could look any different) enforcer for the Letter-Numbers. Garcineznandez made a shiv out of a Popsicle stick and, in the middle of the night, stole into the bed of a four year-old who he claimed had disrespected his momma, and stabbed the boy's teddy bear Bottomo Gigio through the heart. "That shit is cold, man," Guillermo shivered despite the hundred degree temperature inside the tent facility.

At first, reporters were not allowed to visit the places where children separated from their parents at the border were being kept. Secretary of Homeland Security Kirstjen Nielsenratingshit explained, "We…we're doing that? I…I have no idea where these – can I get back to you on this?"

How did Guillermo respond to the President's assertion that people who crossed the border illegally were all rapists and murders? "Gunnnngh mumba mmmmm…" Taking the pacifier out of his mouth, he explained, "Yeah, sorry about that. I don't know what it is about these things, but they're just so darn addictive!"

And, the question? "Rapists and murderers, hunh?" he mused. "Murderers and rapists. I…I have no idea what those are. Some kind of weird *americano* pastries? Cause, nobody **ever** called Guillermo Acivederrez sweet!"

Doesn't this policy of jaili - "Uhh, uhh, uhh," interrupted the Immigration Corralling and Expulsing Service (ICES). "We don't use that word, and neither do you."

Oh. Umm. Well...doesn't this policy of...detainee incarcerationing make Vesampucceri a literal nanny state? "I don't see how," Secretary Nielsenrating answered. "I...I don't even like goat cheese." In the broadest sense of the term "answered."

When asked what the government planned to do with all the children it was collecting (without any idea of what constituted a complete set), Secretary Nielsenrating looked like an undocumented immigrant in headlights. "Plan? Do we look like a government with plans? The mob has plans. The cops have plans. Gordon's got..." She shook her head before continuing: "I, uhh, mean...can I get back to you on this one, too?"

I started to ask Guillermo about what his plans were for the – "Give me a moment, will you?" he interrupted. "I think I just saw a CNN reporter..." He took a moment to compose himself, then started bawling his eyes out, yowling in Spanish about how he wanted his mother. Several of the children in adjacent cag – incarceration happy places joined in. After several minutes, Guillermo looked around and said, "Is she gone?" Satisfied that whoever he was looking for was gone, he dried his eyes.

"What was that about?" I asked.

"Favour for Nancy Pelligrinosi," Guillermo told me. "It was nothing. Don't worry about it."

When I was certain it was okay to continue, I asked Guillermo what his plans for the future were. "I'm a live in the moment kind of guy," he told me. "The future? It's a lineup for the diaper changing area that's so long you can't even see the end of it. I'll probably die in here. But that don't mean I can't have a good time. What are you doing after the interview? Wanna ditch the mic and grab some Gerber's baby food? I hear peas and carrots are good this time of year..."

Portrait of the Artist as a Young Illegal Immigrant

by INDIRA CHARUNDER-MACHARRUNDEIRA, Alternate Reality News Service Fine Arts Writer

When it comes to oil paintings and visas that allow people to work in Vesampucceri, art is a poke in the eye of the beholder.

You have probably never heard of Gabriel Famleesedano, an employee of the McDruhitmumpf National Golf Club Westminichester who had never expressed an interest in joining the artistic community. However, when his manager told this undocumented worker from Guatemala that he needed a visa to continue to work there, he was driven to create.

Famleesedano's first effort at supplying the golf course with a visa showing that he was in Vesampucceri legally was written in pencil crayon on a napkin. "This is a common mistake with first-timers," Bobby "Big Bubbelach" Bonavaducci, art critic and two-time winner of a stay at Her Majesty's Leisure in London, commented. "They don't have the resources to create a proper fake document, so they use whatever materials come to hand. The results wouldn't fool a blind immigration officer in a black cat's darkened basement!"

In fact, passports, work visas and other official documents were written on napkins in pencil crayon, sometimes even plain crayon, during WWII because of shortages of embossed paper, which was diverted for use making artillery shells. But, uhh, that's not relevant to the current discussion. The only other record of this happening was when local governments issued napkin visas during the Uncivil War; however, since control of the movement of people through territory has never been a municipal power, both sides ignored the documents. Which, uhh, is even less relevant to the current discussion, but at least it's colourful.

Administrators of the McDruhitmumpf National Golf Club told Famleesedano that they were happy for him to work there, but, honestly, if he wanted to keep doing so, he would have to bring them a more realistic looking visa. His next effort was also written on a napkin, but, perhaps having learned from his first experience, it was in pen.

"Although it may have been as simple as asking to borrow the pen of somebody who worked with him at the golf course," Bonavaducci stated, "this shows that Famleesedano had the capacity to grow as an artist. Unlike pencil crayons, ink is permanent. This creation shows him having a lot more confidence in his craft."

With, unfortunately, exactly the same results: Famleesedano was told to come back the next day with another visa.

For his seventh attempt, Famleesedano stopped working with napkins, replacing them with the insides of cut up cigarette cartons. "This was a conceptual breakthrough for him," Bonavaducci claimed. "Official documents like visas are usually printed on heavier stock paper. Famleesedano was clearly ready to abandon his early *arte primitif* posturing for a more sophisticated approach."

At the same time, though, he returned to pencil crayons. "You have to understand," Bonavaducci asked us to understand, "Famleesedano was working 12 hour shifts six days a week, mowing and raking the grounds and rebuffing unwanted duffer advances. Not only that, but he had to share a single room with 17 other employees of the golf course in the same boat. Given this, he can certainly be forgiven for a little…artistic backsliding."

In all, it took Famleesedano 59 attempts before he was finally able to create a document that the manager of the McDruhitmumpf National Golf Club was satisfied was good enough to fool an Immigration Corralling and Expulsing Service (ICES) agent. "And, what a masterpiece it was!" Bonavaducci exulted. "As Richard Bachturnovmanive – who everybody knows is actually Stephen Kingfisherhelploess, but he doesn't like it when anybody acknowledges the fact, so shh! – truly said: 'A professional is an amateur who walked over the dead, bloated corpses of his friends and enemies and anybody else who stopped him from achieving his dream.' I, uhh, may have been paraphrasing, here, but you get the idea."

Bonavaducci pointed out that every artist experiments with different forms and materials before they find just the combination that expresses what they have to say. For example, Leonardo Da Da Da Vinci drew 127 different versions of the Mona Lisa, including: as a rat; looking like she had just swallowed a bug; eating a pastrami sandwich; squinting; against a field of poppies; and holding a baby's arm holding an apple. Mac "In Tosh" Kropotskinyanmov drafted counterfeit $100 bills 87 times before he finally created a version that has yet to be discovered by treasury agen – err, but I have said too much already.

"Creating great art is hard," Bonavaducci summed up.

It took Famleesedano 12 years of working at the McDruhitmumpf National Golf Club to perfect his visa. A day after he submitted it to club management, he and 14 other men and women who worked there were turned over to ICES for immediate deportation. "I am shocked, shocked I tell you," a McDruhitmumpf Organization spokesperson told us, "to discover illegal immigrants working in one of our establishments!"

This likely, possibly, maybe could have been caused by the government shutdown. How could President McDruhitmumpf beg for money for a border wall to keep illegal immigrants out of the country when he couldn't even keep them out of his properties?

With a heavy sigh, Bonavaducci said, "Great artists are never recognized in their time. I don't know if Richard Bachturnovmanive said that, but he will. He will…"

Catch and Release Kids

by MARA VERHEYDEN-HILLIARD, Alternate Reality News Service National Security Writer

Pedro GreeleyGrinchypants is a typical six year-old boy. He loves watching cartoons and playing federales and gringos with other boys at his kindergarten (even if they mistakenly think they're playing cowboys and indigenous peoples). He winsomely stares out the window of his bedroom for hours at a time. Trying to get his lips around English vowels makes his mouth hurt.

Unlike typical six year-old boys, Pedro GreeleyGrinchypants is a political football. And, not in a good way: in a kicked around a lot because nobody seems able to mount an effective offence way. "Children like little Pedro should not be riiiiiipped from their loving parents' arms," Health and Human Disservices Secretary Alex M. Alexiazar IV stated. "Children need a stable home environment in order to thrive. Teeeeaaaaaarrrrriiiiing them away from that would cause them permanent emotional distress. So, we won't let it happen, okay?"

Okay. The Secretary's statement might make you think the administration of President Ronald McDruhitmumpf's heart had grown three sizes overnight. Unfortunately, Hiram and Sue-Ellen GreeleyGrinchypants, the homemakers from which little Pedro should not be riiiiiiipped and etc., are not the boy's parents. Pedro was taken from those people when they crossed the border without documents and was adopted by the GreeleyGrinchypants family. Secretary Alexiazar IV's statement was a response to people who were trying to get Health and Human Disservices to give the child **back** to his birth parents.

What's that? You thought a majority of the 2,700 children who had been taken by the United States government after it adopted the Separate and Scatter policy had been reunited with their birth parents? That may be, you silly billy. But, Pedro was one of the potentially thousands of children who were separated from their parents at the border **before** the policy was announced.

Do try to keep up. Much as I would love to pad my word count by repeating myself, I'm sure my Editrix-in-Chief would object, and, when she objects, heads snap on necks!

"We're Gord-fearing folks in this family," Hiram GreeleyGrinchypants said as Sue-Ellen GreeleyGrinchypants sat nearby knitting a "Burn in Hell, Heathen Scum!" sampler. "The good Gord commanded us to be fruitful and multiply. When **that** didn't happen…" Hiram looked meaningfully at Sue-Ellen, who concentrated that much harder on the comma, the trickiest punctuation mark to knit. Then, he continued, "…we decided to adopt a heathen scum baby and bring him to Gord. Because Gord loves us."

What about Pedro's actual parents? "If the good Gord had wanted Pedro to stay with his…parents, He wouldn't have created ICES [the Immigration Corralling and Expulsing Service]."

"Hiram and Sue-Ellen are good people," claimed Chris Paluskyomeinn, President and CEO of MaryBethanChristiney Christian Services. "Yes, okay, certainly, Hiram lusts after hat check girls, and Sue-Ellen is a little over-fond of her Sambuca spritzers.

But, at least they don't cross borders illegally in the dead of night, putting their children in danger!"

And, they can afford the $20,000 to $40,000 adoption fee?

"That's not a very Christian attitude," Paluskyomeinn's eyes scrunched. "Verheyden-Hilliard – is that some kind of cryptic Jew name?"

MaryBethanChristiney Christian Services has friends in high places. Education Secretary Betsy DeVolution-Ross' charitable foundation gave the non-profit organization $343,000. The charitable foundation of her father-in-law, Richard DeVolution-Ross, gave the organization $750,000. Even the family's pets got in on the act.

"Muffy DeVolution-Ross is a Gord-fearing German Sheppard," Paluskyomeinn commented. "She knows that saving heathen souls will get her an endless supply of doggy treats in heaven. Won't it? Won't it, girl? Oooh, of course it will! Who's a good girl? You are! Oh, yes you are! Praise the Gord!"

When asked about the fees his service charges per adoption, Paluskyomeinn scoffed, "What do you think we are? A charity?"

Well, actually…

Taking children from their birth parents and giving them to complete strangers for money – there is a term for that, isn't there? I mean, the English language has a word for the things at the end of your shoelaces **and** the holes you put those parts of your shoelaces through – you would expect it to have a word for this practice. What could it possibly –

"Human trafficking is a human tragedy, people," President Ronald McDruhitmumpf claimed when he was trying to get funding for a border wall/fence/barrier/annoyance. "It's bad. Oh, so very bad. The fact that it's happening on our southern border is a disgrace. Everybody knows it. I know it. You know it. The man in the moon knows it. That's pretty much everybody, everybody. We must put an end to human trafficking once and for all!"

Ah. Right. A token smart person couldn't have put it better herself.

Ira Nayman
Butterflies Are – FLEE!

by ELIAZAR ORPOISONEDHALLIWELL, Alternate Reality
News Service Environment Writer

You might have thought that because the temporary funding bill
which ended the government shutdown did not contain any funding
for President Ronald McDruhitmumpf's border wall, that no work
could be done on President Ronald McDruhitmumpf's border wall.
You are forcing me to choose between calling you a silly old goat, a
silly billy or a silly old sod.

Fortunately, such issues are covered in journalism school. The
term "silly billy" could be considered racist by people who live in
the Ozark Mountains, so that's out. "Silly old sod" sounds dirty, and
this is a family publication. So, despite overtones of indiscriminate
ingestion of food and not necessarily an accusation of beardedness,
"silly old goat" it is.

You silly old goat.

A bulldozer has started plowing under the National Butterfly
Centre, a wildlife sanctuary in Mission No Longer Critical,
Texabama. This land will be used to build part of President
McDruhitmumpf's border wall…if he is ever given funding for it.
But, it would probably be okay if that funding never comes, since the
government has not offered the owners of the Centre compensation
for the land, or even an eminent domain hearing where they could
object to its appropriation.

Does the silly old goat smell impending lawsuits? (For silly old
goat's information: impending lawsuits smell like chicory with an
undercurrent of brimstone.)

The President has been laying the groundwork for this action
since the campaign two years ago. At a rally, he said: "The
butterflies that move freely across our borders are rapists and
murderers. We need a wall to stop them!"

"Rapists and murderers?" questioned Jeffrey
Glasshausenstonesberg, president of the North American Butterfly
Association. "They're butterflies!"

As President, McDruhitmumpf continued to embellish the
narrative of the threat butterflies posed to the nation. "MonarchS-13

is a gang of vicious Mexican butterflies who freely bring drugs and guns into our country. The death and destruction they cause our inner cities – you know who I'm talking about – 'inner cities,' hee hee – ahem, the destruction is incalculable, people. We must stop these vicious butterflies from crossing into our country, and a border wall is the best way of doing it!"

Glasshausenstonesberg protested: "But…but…but, **they are just butterflies!**"

As recently as last week, President McDruhitmumpf railed against, "Swarms of vicious, drug-addicted butterflies [that are] pouring across our border, attacking women and children, literally… literally tearing innocent people apart with their teeth! Oh, yes, people! With their teeth! Believe me – you thought radioactive zombies were bad? This is a million times worse!"

"But, they're just – I mean, they don't even have tee – honestly, where does he get these ideas?" Glasshausenstonesberg sputtered.

FSOGI: While we wouldn't want to generalize, President McDruhitmumpf seems to have gotten that specific idea from the plot of *Gorgonzilla vs. The Big Cheese*. In that film, the title butterfly is bitten by a radioactive zombie, which causes it to mutate and attack human beings. Since butterflies don't, as Glasshausenstonesberg started to point out, have teeth, it mostly gums people to death, leaving the corpses covered in ick. A leaked copy of the President's Netfix queue shows that he watched the film two days before making his latest accusations against butterflies.

"And, just when the butterfly population was starting to come back!" lamented Anastasia Greene-Lovinvegan, Vesampuucerian spokeshuman for the environmental group Greenpeas.

She explained that butterflies are natural migrants, travelling from deep in Latin Vesampucceri to close to the Canada/US border and back. "You think business executives live out of their suitcases? They ain't got nothing on butterflies!"

If the National Butterfly Centre is shut down to build a wall, the migratory patterns of butterflies will be disrupted. "You thought having your direct flight from New Yoricknuhemwell to London rerouted through Taos, New Mexisas was inconvenient?" Greene-Lovinvegan asked. "This is a planned diversion to die for!"

Why should we care about the fate of a few flittery creatures? Greene-Lovinvegan pointed out that, however inefficiently, butterflies do help pollinate crops; their loss in large enough numbers could threaten the human food supply.

"Some people say that that won't be a problem as long as we have bees to pollinate crops," she summed up. "Good luck with that doesn't even begin to cover it!"

In the meantime, President McDruhitmumpf continues to ratchet up the anti-butterfly rhetoric. "The Dumboprats had an opportunity to do the right thing by giving me the wall funding I asked for in the temporary appropriations bill," he said. "They didn't do it. Didn't do it. If swarms of radioactive butterflies carry small children off into the sky to join child trafficking rings, it will be on their heads!"

Riding the Wild Frontier With a Bunch of CUNPs

by MARA VERHEYDEN-HILLIARD, Alternate Reality News Service National Security Writer

Jim Benviedubbelyu looks across the border separating Mexico from New Mexissippi and, taking a swig from the can of beer in the hand that's not holding a rifle, says, "This country is going to shit."

Sitting on the ground with his knees touching his chin and his hands on the top of his head, unable to comfort his wife or two children, Raul Gutiergumi mutters under his breath, "Tell me about it."

Benviedubbelyu is a member of Constitutionally United Nationalist Patriots (CUNP), a militia group that has taken it upon itself to patrol Vesampucceri's southern border, putting those who enter the country illegally under "citizen's arrest" (which is like "police arrest," with a *frisson* of lack of accountability and jurisdictional disputes that invariably end with a body count). Benviedubbelyu is concerned that if New Mexisippi is overrun by Latin Vesampuccerian immigrants, his home state of Minnesippi will be next, so he travelled across the country to dole him out some frontier justice.

In a video Benviedubbelyu posted to Farcebook, he and half a dozen CUNPs are sitting tall in the saddles of their Range Rovers, watching over 30 women, children and the occasional man sitting in the glare of their headlights on the ground in front of them. Unlike during my interview, no alcohol appears to be present as they wait for Border Patrol agents to take the Latin Vesampuccerians off their hands.

Even CUNPs have an image to maintain.

Benviedubbelyu has stated that CUNP and the other militias patrolling the border will leave when President Ronald McDruhitmumpf's wall has been completed. Which means it would have to be started. They seem confused by this causal chain. Maybe it's the beer. Benviedubbelyu said they would also be willing to leave if officials asked them to.

"Go home!" stated New Mexissippi Governor Michelle Lujan Grishamlyaddams. "It is completely unacceptable for migrant families to be made to feel threatened by unauthorized civilians. That's what ICES [the Immigration Corralling and Expulsing Service] is for!"

"Get away from the border and go home!" concurred New Mexissippi Attorney General Hector Balderdashansur. "We give certain citizens the power to arrest others. You are not those certain citizens. Sounds to me like somebody – actually, a lot of somebodies – has watched a little too much *Law and Order: Tuktoyaktuk*!"

"Like I said," Benviedubbelyu maintained, "if anybody in power asked us to leave, we would. We are not unreas – hey, Harold! We got a runner over by where you're supposed to be patrolling! Gordammit, do I gotta pay attention for everybody?"

You might think that law-abiding citizens should have the right to detain (kidnap is such an ugly word) people they believe are committing a crime. Vesampucceri is, after all, the land of the free and the home of the deranged. But, what if it turns out they're not so law-abiding citizens?

CUNP militia member Larry Mitchell Hopkinodulams, for instance, was arrested by the FBI as a felon in possession of a weapon. The agency did not release what felony Hopkinodulams had been convicted of, but it's fairly certain that it wasn't playing tiddly winks in a Monopoly zone.

"This is a dangerous felon who should not have weapons around children and families," Attorney General Balderdashansur argued. When it was pointed out that many states now required people who worked in kindergartens to carry weapons as a defence against school shooters, he stopped for several seconds before answering, "Umm, yeah. Well. They go through background checks to ensure that they're not dangerous felons. Probably. I think. I mean, they should. I mean…umm…shoot."

"People have the wrong idea about us," Benviedubbelyu argued. "They think we're a bunch of drunken, trigger-happy yahoos who are endangering the lives of innocent people. Nothing could be further from the – **Darryl! Stop aiming that gun at that child!** Where was – **she looks like she's six years old – seven at most! How could she possibly be hiding a grenade launcher? It would be bigger than she is!** Sorry. I'm sorry you had to see that. We are patriots who are protecting our – noooo, I did not promise to show you 'action.' **I did not promise – fine! Fine! Go back to Aribama! We'll get along just fine without you! Ferking peachy!** So. Umm. Yeah. Not yahoos. Not endangering the lives of innocent people. Patriots. Protecting our homeland. That's us."

What could possibly go wrong?

Gord Bless the Children (Because Nobody Else Will)

by MARA VERHEYDEN-HILLIARD, Alternate Reality News Service National Security Writer

The government of Ronald McDruhitmumpf claims that it has complied with a court order to reunite all of the children who were taken from their parents after crossing the border with Mexico.

"Ah believe that justice…justice is a dish best suhved cold," said Attorney General Jeff "Self-regard" Sesspoolpandemic. "It may taste slahmy, but it goes dahn real smooth. But, uhh, a coaht has said uthuhwahse, and it's only faiah and raht that we comply with its rulin'… At least until thuh President has an oppuhtunity ta replace that theah judge with somebody with moah respec' foh his authoahty."

U.S. District Judge in San Diego Dana Sabrawftbeetonpathe, who ordered the families to be reunited, wasn't convinced. In an increasingly testy (somebody had clearly taken an IQ quiz before coming into court!) exchange with the government attorney (who was so embarrassed by the position she had to argue that she asked not to be named even though the court transcript is a public document), Judge Sabrawftbeetonpathe contested the contention.

JUDGE DANA SABRAWFTBEETONPATHE: How many children has the government reunited with their families?

[GOVERNMENT ATTORNEY]: All of them, your honour.

JUDGE SABRAWFTBEETONPATHE: All of them? Really? The day before the deadline, you were only able to confirm that four of the children were reunited with their families. You had over a month to comply with my order, and that was the best you could do, but you expect me to believe that you managed to reunite almost 2,500 families in the last 24 hours?

[GOVERNMENT ATTORNEY]: Stranger things have happened, your honour.

JUDGE SABRAWFTBEETONPATHE: They have?

[GOVERNMENT ATTORNEY]: Umm…absolutely. When you consider, I mean, for example, how life came into existence out of inanimate matter – that must have been a pretty strange moment in the history of the universe, right? Or…or…or, how the 1969 New Yoricknuhemwell Mets won the World Series. That was definitely stra –

JUDGE SABRAWFTBEETONPATHE: Councillor, how many family reunifications can you prove the government has carried out?

[GOVERNMENT ATTORNEY]: All of –

JUDGE SABRAWFTBEETONPATHE: With documentation.

[GOVERNMENT ATTORNEY]: Seven.

JUDGE SABRAWFTBEETONPATHE: Seven?

[GOVERNMENT ATTORNEY]: Okay, almost all of them.

JUDGE SABRAWFTBEETONPATHE: Seven?

[GOVERNMENT ATTORNEY]: Eight if you include Manuel… what's his name, who probably, maybe, in all likelihood, we think is being picked up by his father's uncle's sister-in-law even as we speak. Why, that's practically double digits!

JUDGE SABRAWFTBEETONPATHE: I – uhh – okay. Councillor. How do you figure seven out of 2,500 constitutes "all?"

[GOVERNMENT ATTORNEY]: Two words, your honour: the rest of the families were "in eligible."

JUDGE SABRAWFTBEETONPATHE: That is not acceptable, Name Redacted!

[GOVERNMENT ATTORNEY]: Your honour, it's not like what you're asking the government to do is easy. I mean, we never kept records of the people processed at the border, so we wouldn't know which children belonged to which parents even if the adults hadn't disappeared into another country likely never to be heard from again!

JUDGE SABRAWFTBEETONPATHE: (moans)

"Aww, naw, Ah do buhlieve that oah critics ah bein' unfaiah," Attorney General Sesspoolpandemic pointed out. "Thuh numbah o' children who have diahed in custody is actually smallah than thuh numbah who have been documented ta have been retuhned to theiah pahents. Ah do buhlieve that constahtutes a victory of ah soaht. But, do we get credit fer it? Ah think we know thuh ansah ta **that** question!"

"What? Wait," token smart person Amy Sheshutshotshitbam attempted a spit take, getting scores of 8.9, 9.1 and 3.4 from the judges (when asked why his score for her was so low, the Finnish judge said, "You would have given her a low score, too, if yours was the face her spit take was spit into!"). "Children are dying in Vesampuccerian custody? Why aren't there protests in the streets against this?"

"If she had evah been a pahent," Attorney General Sesspoolpandemic asided, "Ah'm suah she would know thuh ansah ta that question!"

The government has long argued that the refugee system was broken because processing adults could be done immediately, but processing children could take up to six months. They couldn't just keep the adults in the country until a decision was made about their children; such a policy would cause terrible hardship and suffering among President McDruhitmumpf's base. Separating them at the border seemed the most humane thing to do.

And, yet.

And, yet, we now know that undocumented immigrants without children were not immediately deported, suggesting that the McDruhitmumpf administration was specifically targeting families. "Obviously, the Reduhblican understanding of the concept of 'family values' took a detour on the road to good governance when Ronald McDruhitmumpf became President!" token smart person Sheshutshotshitbam mocked. "If I didn't know any better, I would swear that there was never any actual plan to reunite children with their deported parents!"

"Wuhl, nah, Ah really do think thuh token smaht puhson is out o' lahn on this question," Attorney General Sesspoolpandemic argued. "As mah deah depahted Pappy used ta say, iffen the path y'all're on leads off a cliff, don't blame the steerin' wheel!"

Legal scholars will be debating the meaning of this statement for decades to come.

Ira Nayman
She Sells Sanctuary By the Seashore

by CORIANDER NEUMANEIMANAYMANEEMAMANN,
Alternate Reality News Service Urban Issues Writer

The problem with immigrants is where to put them. Oh, sure, you can keep them in cages on military bases, but soldiers might object, not without reason, that looking after children who don't speak English so they have to mime being allergic to concrete floors is not what they signed on for. The soldiers. If the children didn't want to live in cages, they shouldn't have been born to immigrants.

And, yes, you can probably give them all homes in the Grand Ditch – there is certainly enough room for them all. Still, that doesn't stoke the outrage of your base and poke your political opponents in the eye at the same time. (Oh – you thought this was about solving a humanitarian crisis? Where is the political advantage in **that?**)

President Ronald McDruhitmumpf thinks he has found a better solution to the problem.

"Dumboprats like Mexicans streaming across the border?" President Ronald McDruhitmumpf stated. "Tell you what. Let's ship 'em all to sanctuary cities. See how much Dumboprats like them when they're wandering through their designer coffee clatches and used cutlery shops!"

"Send 'em to me!" enthused New Yoricknuhemwell City Mayor Bill diBlaseohoh. "We'll take all the immigrants we can get!"

"I don't think you understand," President McDruhitmumpf argued. "I'm going to send you all the people coming across the northern border with Mexico. All the **illegals**. You know what I'm talking about!"

"We'll be happy to take them," said San Francisco Mayor London Breedensircusses. "The more immigrants, the better."

"Rapists!" President McDruhitmumpf shouted. "I'm talking rapists! And, murderers! I'll make sure that the Mexican rapists and murderers flooding our southern border will end up in your sanctuary cities! Raaaapists! Muuuuuuurrrrrderers! Sanctuary cities! Pay attention – when I tell you that you know what I'm talking about, know what I'm talking about!"

"Immigrants have a lower rate of crime than native born Vesampuccerians," Mayor diBlaseohoh and Mayor Breedensircusses said in unison. "They also have a stronger work ethic."

"They'll help the city's economy grow for the next two generations!" Mayor Breedensircusses said.

"The stories they bring with them will help enrich the city's culture!" Mayor diBlaseohoh said at the same time.

"Well, that didn't go quite the way I thought it would," President McDruhitmumpf muttered darkly.

Sanctuary cities are areas where local authorities do not cooperate with ICES (the Immigration Corralling and Expulsing Service) in corralling and expulsing people living in the country without documentation. They tend to be the most liberal cities in the country, as well as – and this is what really infuriates Reduhblicans – the wealthiest. Almost as if there is a connection between the two facts.

Almost...

"Sanctuary cities? Hunh. That's a new one on me," commented Acting Homeland Insecurity Secretary Kevin McAleenanites. "But, uhh, I'm new, here. I mean, I don't even know where the coffeemaker is, and I'm not good to go until I've had at least my fourth mocha latte of the day. So, it may be a while before I can respond to this..."

Representatives of the Grey House were more categorical (they obviously play *Scattergories* in their down time): "No, no, no, no, no, no, no, no, no," one of the representatives commented between turns. "We considered this possibility months ago and ruled it out! Categorically, absolutely, utterly, flatly, unconditionally and with no possibility of reconsideration – or, at least, we thought no possibility of reconsideration..."

Homeland Insecurity and the Grey House argued that the plan would be complicated, costly and cummerbund. (They really need to work on incorporating alliteration into the rule of three.) "You know how it works," the Grey House source said. "You can have something complicated and cummerbund, but not costly. Or, you can have something cummerbund and costly, but it won't be complicated. We were willing to forego cummerbund – what is that, anyway? Some kind of actor or something? – but that left us with complicated and costly. Not a good set of policy parameters."

The Grey House source went on to point out that if they were in sanctuary cities, immigrants would be given ID cards and would be allowed to work and find places to stay. They couldn't be kept in cages. Families couldn't be separated. This would appear to be the opposite of what the President hopes to achieve with his border policy.

"But, you know the Chief," the Grey House source summed up. "He has the memory of a cat. As long as it was brought up more than three minutes ago, there is no idea so bad that we have ruled it out categorically, absolutely, utterly, flatly, unconditionally and with no possibility of reconsideration that he won't revisit!"

Our Country is Full of It!

by ENGELBERT HUMPERFLAPDOODLEPUSS, Alternate Reality News Service Excrement Writer

In a small room somewhere close to the Mexico-US border (but, not too close because you don't want any drug dealing or human trafficking to rub off on you), President Ronald McDruhitmumpf was bikini waxing poetic (he's the surf Shakeaspeararetoo!).

"It's like the dial is pointing at F," he was saying. "Beyond F. It's like we've eaten so much that our engines will explode if we take one more bite. No, no, no, we don't want that waffer thin mint – it's diesel, and we need regular...although it does look tasty...and, honestly, what could one little bite possibly hurt...?"

You could be forgiven for thinking that the President was talking about Vesampucceri's obesity epidemic. But, he wasn't. You could almost be forgive (would it kill you to apologize? – oh, you know what for!) for thinking that he was talking about how Vesampucceri's obsession with big cars feeds Global Hot as Hellification. But, he most certainly wasn't.

No, the President was talking about his second favourite subject (and the first isn't his wife Melanoma, although she's in the top 50... probably...): immigration.

In that speech, President McDruhitmumpf went on to say: "We'd be happy to take all of Mexico's murderers and rapists, really, we would, but...we just don't have the room. The United States of Vesampucceri is full. Filled to the brim – if only we wore a bigger hat! Plum full to burstin' – can't say we don't get enough fruit in our diet! Full of beans – and we all know how unpleasant **that** can be in a confined space! Maybe we overestimated how much fruit we've been eating! Full court press – which is what will happen if the Dumboprats insist on getting the full Meullitallover report! Full disclosure – hunh! As if! Full of itself – so we don't need an invasion of other selfs. Every room in the country is taken, everybody knows that. So, I'm sorry, Mexican murderers and rapists, but you'll just have to try a motel in Ecuador!"

"This is the most insanely ludicrous thing the President has ever said...today!" responded President of *Voto Latino* Maria Teresa Kumasatralez. "The United States has the third largest land mass in the world and a population a quarter of the size of India or China. There is enough room in the Grand Ditch alone to give a home to all Latin American refugees and asylum-seekers for the next 17 years!"

"Does this look like we aren't completely full?" President McDruhitmumpf said, poking a member of his security detail in the side of the head as he swept his arm in front of him to indicate the crowded room. A *Washburningdington Post* reporter who had to tape the session from the back pocket of this reporters pants because there was nowhere else to stand squeaked in agreement.

"I, uhh, really don't think you can, you know, judge the space available in a country by the space available in a single room," argued columnist Eugene Robinsoncrusoe from where he was standing on the ceiling. "That would be like, you know, pronouncing Global Hot as Hellification a hoax because one day the temperature was colder than average for that time of – oh, wait. You say that, too. I...I'm sorry, I think the blood is rushing to my he – oh, my." Robinsoncrusoe fell to his knees and ended up sitting next to a light fixture.

Having given up his plans to close the border (because economic suicide) for the time being (because functioning economy is overrated), the President's plan now appears to be to politely discourage immigrants and asylum seekers from trying to enter the country. Or, possibly to demonstrate to potential immigrants that the United States is full of crazy people, and why would anybody choose to live in such a madhouse?

"It's a trick!" shouted token smart person Amy Sheshutshotshitbam. "This President doesn't do polite! He breaks out in xenophobia whenever he tries!" Doing a reasonably passable McDruhitmumpf impression (let's just say that Alec Defblyndenbaldwin has nothing to worry about), she added: "Would you be so kind as to pass the creamed beef with immigrants are gonna steal your children's underwear if we don't stop them now! Ha ha ha ha ha — burp!"

"The President is not gonna let go of the immigration issue because it plays to his base," Kumasatralez pointed out. "You can expect him to ramp up the anti-immigrant rhetoric all the way…all the way to the 2020…the 2020 electi – oh, my Gord! To think I gave up a promising career as a Mongolian pastry chef to do this – **what was I thinking?**"

6. THE SLEEP OF REASON PRODUCES... DEPLORABLES

Mo Worser Reds

by FRANCIS GRECOROMACOLLUDEN, Alternate Reality News Service National Politics Writer

There are certain things that simply are not done in Washburningdington. Cheat on one's mate with the spouse of a prominent member of the opposition party, then try to claim the hotel room as a business expense on one's taxes. Punch a horse on a public street. Read a passage from Adolph von Hitlerskitler's *Mein Kampfing Weekenderstaten* on the floor of the House of Unrepresentatives.

Until we see President Ronald McDruhitmumpf's tax returns, we will not be able to say with certainty whether the first taboo has been broken. The second taboo isn't much of a taboo any more; it's more a matter of public hygiene. At least the third taboo is safe. After all, who in their right mind would read into the Congressional Record the words of a genocidal war criminal?

Reduhblican Representative Mo Brooksnoahgumeant did just that. Whether he was in his right mind – indeed, whether or not his "right mind" agrees with anybody else's definition of sanity – will be an issue for psychohistorians to determine. And, we don't envy Harry Virtuseldonseen the task!

"Adolph Hitlerskitler talked about 'the Big Lie,'" Brooksnoahgumeant (not to be confused with filmmaker Mel Brooksnoahgumeant, who at least has the virtue of being intentionally funny) said. "Hitlerskitler was a member of the National **Socialist** Party. Dumboprats are **socialists**. Come on, people! Do I have to draw you a map? Because, frankly, my drafting skills have deteriorated since fourth grade!"

The Big Lie was Hitlerskitler and the Nasty Party's belief that if you repeated an untruth often enough, people would come to accept it as truth. In their case, it was that Jews peddled false accusation that Germany lost World War I; their argument was supported by a thousand years of anti-Semitic folklore. In this case, it's that the Dumboprats have peddled false accusations that President McDruhitmumpf colluded with Fenwickians to steal the 2016 election, an argument proven by the William Katiebarrthudor reduction (not as tasty as it looks in the pictures in the food section) of the Meullitallover report.

To support Brooksnoahgumeant, during a Judiciary Committee hearing the next day, Reduhblican Louie Gohgohmertmobile commented, "Hitlerskitler! Dumboprats! Hitlerskitler! Dumboprats! Hitlerskitler! Dumboprats! Hitlerskitler! Dumboprats! Hitlerskitler! Dumboprats! Draw your own conclusions!"

"So. Yeah. Wow. Ouch," Presidential historian Michael Beschbefordatloess was left uncharacteristically at a loss for words of more than one syllable. "I mean – whoa! Where to start?"

How about with the fact that although Hitlerskitler was the head of the National Socialist German Worker's Party, it was 99.99 per cent nationalist and only -.01 per cent socialist? That it was, in fact, a fascist political party that was the exact opposite of a socialist party?

"Yes! That! So much that!" Beschbefordatloess eagerly agreed.

Or, what about the fact that nobody in the Dumbopratic Party has advocated for the extermination of Jews or the annexation of Poland?

"Oh, baby, baby!" Beschbefordatloess moaned. "Yes! Yes! Oh, Gord, yes!"

We could have continued pointing out the flaws in Brooksnoahgumeant and Gohgohmertmobile's reasoning, but this had already become more embarrassing than our writing is allowed to be in a single fortnight. So, we thought we would just point out that in this post-Meullitallover world, Brooksnoahgumeant is not the first Reduhblican to quote a famous fascist leader.

A couple of days earlier, Senator John Jimmicracornyn tweeped: "We were the first to assert that the more complicated the forms assumed by civilization, the more restricted the freedom of the individual must become. Regards to Maria and the children, Augusto and Beauregardino. Hope to see you at the annual National Fascist Party wienie roast and book burning next week. Love, Benito Mussolinguini."

"Oh, Gord!" Beschbefordatloess groaned. "Make it stop. Please make it stop!"

Dumbopratic Representative Alexandria Casio-Keebjords, the source of much Reduhblican angst these days, can defend herself by, for example, pointing out that Mussolinguini's *fascisti* (the only pasta that doesn't go well with a tomato-based sauce) was the polar opposite of Italy's socialists (not least because they were the ones beating others about the head and shoulders with long sticks). However, making it stop?

"Ain't gonna happen," stated token smart person Amy Sheshutshotshitbam, who was clearly in control of all of her syllables. "This is what political scientists call 'a twofer.' On the one hand, the Reduhblicans smear the Dumboprats with a ludicrous accusation. Dumboprats can barely organize a six year-old's tea party, much less a beer hall *putsch*! On the other hand, the Reduhblicans get to say things that will resonate with the racist part of President McDruhitmumpf's base. All I can say is: thank Gord human beings didn't evolve with more hands!"

Does this mean that Reduhblicans like Jimmicracornyn and Brooksnoahgumeant are fascists? "We don't know what is in their hearts," token smart person Sheshutshotshitbam answered. "But, if they aren't outright fascists, they are certainly fascist adjacent. Or, fascist abutting, if you will. Or, fascist sidling right up next to, whether you will or not. Or, fascist if they were any closer they would be behind fascists. Any way you slice it, it's not good!"

The Bad News Kashananyogghi Bears

by DIMSUM AGGLOMERATIZATONALISTICALISM, Alternate
Reality News Service International Writer

Syrian journalist –

"It was a rogue operation run by rogue agents," President
Ronald McDruhitmumpf interrupted. "The roguest. Agents, I mean.
Everybody knows that."

I, uhh, hadn't actually described what had happened yet. The
President nodded, as if to say, "Go on." Or, possibly, "Get the fake
news out of your system – I'll be saying whatever I want anyway."
Presidential nods can be worse than horoscopes that way.

Journalist Jamal Kashananyogghi walked into the Syrian
embassy in Turkey and never walked out again. A critic of Saudi
Clown Prince Mohammed trashbin Salman Saud (who is sometimes
referred to by his initials, MSS), Kashananyogghi had fled to
Vesampucceri, where he was a regular opinion writer for the
Washburningdington Post.

"No, no, no," insisted Syrian government spokespuppet Khalil
Alhambraonwrye. "Look at this grainy footage of somebody walking
out of the Syrian embassy in Turkey. That is clearly a journalist –
you can tell by the way he walks! And, look at the grey smudges on
his fingertips! That is the sign of an ink stained monkey wrench!
Clearly, it is Jamal Kashananyogghi!"

The figure in the video could have been Kashananyogghi, if
Kashananyogghi had been a foot taller and had breasts. Honestly,
this was the most unconvincing body double substitution since
movie director Ed Overwoodendale asked his dentist if he ever
wanted to get into acting. Oh, and the smudge on his/her fingertips?
What part of "grainy footage" does the Syrian spokespuppet think
we don't understand?

"But, it's clearly the jacket that the lying jackal tool of
international imperialism – sorry, I meant: **the journalist** was
wearing when he entered the building. You can tell by the 'Goooooo
Pool Bears!' on the back," Alhambraonwrye pointed out.

That would make it stranger, though. How would somebody
else have gotten Kashananyogghi's coat?

"Good question, lying jackal tool of international – **journalist!**" Alhambraonwrye hissed with a smile. "Jamal – I can call him that because I've been talking about him so much lately that I feel like I know the traitorous dog – entered the embassy to get paperwork he needed to marry the slut he loved. Or, did he? He probably got cold feet and ran out on her. Just like that Vesampuccerian movie – what was it called? Oh, yes: *Runaway Bride…Who in No Way Was Tortured, Killed and Had Her Body Dismembered by a Saudi Arabian Hit Squad.*

When I pointed out that no Vesampuccerian movie had ever been released with that name, Alhambraonwrye sighed and pointed out that translation was such an imperfect art.

Still, the title seemed…specific. Very specific. Surprisingly, so. So, it was no surprise when the government of Turkey announced that two planeloads of "consultants" flew into the country the day before Kashananyogghi disappeared. The "consultants" included three men known for their persuasive interrogation techniques, two digital communications experts and a partridge in a pear tree (that would be Kamal "Bone Cutter" Par-al-Compostridge).

"When you put it that way," Alhambraonwrye allowed, "maybe the movie title was too 'on the nose,' because it sounds a little like a Saudi hit squad was sent to kill an enemy of MSS!"

A little? Actually, it sounds exactly like a Saudi Hit squad was sent to kill an enemy of the Saudi Clown Prince.

"Journalists!" Alhambraonwrye spat out. "Fine. That's what happened. A Saudi hit squad was sent to kill an enemy of MSS. But, the Clown Prince did not order this – 'assassination' is such a historically loaded term, don't you think? Let us call it an 'extrajudicial killing,' shall we? – the Clown Prince did not order it. He had nothing to do with it. It was definitely a rogue operation run by rogue agents!"

"What did I tell you?" President McDruhitmumpf gloated. Gloatfully. "Rogue operation. Rogue agents. The roguest. The agentist. Everybody is saying so. And, if they didn't before, they're saying so now. Everybody. The everybodyist. Saying so."

"Oh, come on!" said token smart person Amy Sheshutshotshitbam. "The Clown Prince of Saudi Arabia has a hit list for…everybody who…umm, is critical of him… So…yeah…it's probably a long list, a very long list, so you and I are probably safe. Probably. But, look. I mean, there aren't a lot of Saudi Arabians who can authorize a 15 person assassina – sorry, extrajudicial killing. My momma always used to say to me: 'Token smart person Amy, if it walks like a murderous thug and it quacks like a murderous thug, well, you better hope your name is way, way down on its hit list!'"

Meanwhile, the Clown Prince announced that he would be conducting an investigation into Kashananyogghi's death himself. "To start, I would like to talk to token smart person Amy Sheshutshotshitbam. You wouldn't happen to know where she lives, would you...?"

When Restaurant Critics Lay an Egg

by MARCELLA CARBORUNDUREM-McVORTVORT, Alternate Reality News Service Food and Drink Writer

There are no takebacksies in restaurant reviewing.

"This restaurant should be burned 2teh ground and have its ashes spread over the grave of Anthony Bourdainonowan!!!" dodomama027 wrote on Farcebook. "The food gave me gas for 27 days, after which I passed a live chicken! If you don't want that to happen to you, stay away!" fortunefavorsbraves added. "Yucky yucky ptui ptui!!!!!!!" babygourmeh summed up.

They were responding to an incident where the owner of the Little Red Hen in Lexington, New Virgixico asked Press Secretary Sarah Wannabe-Panders and her entourage to leave because of the restaurant's "no shirt, no shoes, no human decency, no service" policy. At least, they **thought** they were. Actually, their vituperations were posted on the Farcebook page of a restaurant called the Tiny Pink Rooster, which is based in Collingwood, Ontario. For the geographically challenged among you, that is in Canada. Which, last time we checked, isn't even a part of the United States of Vesampucceri.

What do you do when you're caught in a dumb mistake? If you're a Reduhblican troll living in the greatest idiotocracy the world has ever known, you double down on the wrongness.

"Hey!" dodomama027 wrote. "A review doesn't have to be of the restaurant it says it is to be valid! Even a broken clock is right three times a day!" fortunefavorsbraves responded, "hey! I got the continent right! Suck it, lamestream libtards! u aren't even in the right universe!" It looked for a long time like babygourmeh wasn't going to respond, but, in the end, he (because they're always he) wrote, "Hay! Booby Boober bumdrops! Don't look into the Tiny Pink Rooster, lest you find that the Tiny Pink Rooster is looking into you"

"I understood that people were unhappy," said Marry-Sou Souvlakionrice, the owner of the Tiny Pink Rooster. "Beyond that… it's not like barbecued chicken is such a hard dish to make…"

"I always do my best to treat people, including those I disagree with, respectfully, and will continue to do so," Press Secretary Sarah Wannabe-Panders tweeped after the incident. Apparently, her supporters didn't get the memo.

"Are you kidding me?" token smart person Amy Sheshutshotshitbam spit out her Diet Vanilla Milkshake. "If there was a memo, Sarah Wannabe-Panders didn't get it! She has said so many nasty things to reporters, they call her briefings 'the three o'clock sliming!' Seriously – nobody goes to them in their best clothes any more! Mulligatawney at the *New Yoricknuhemwell Times* started a YahooTube channel dedicated to video of her insults – it'll be getting its own specialty cable network in the fall and has already been nominated for three Emmys!"

"Oh, tsk, tsk," clucked newly hatched mother hen Sean Hanjobovverfist on his Fox show, *Politically Etiquette*. "The professional left that has been monitoring everybody's speech for its potential to offend has now gone on the offensive. They're rude, crude and unsafe at any speed. The question on everybody's mind, though, is: 'Where's the civility?'"

Hanjobovverfist did not explain if, by "everybody," he included the liberals he was attacking. Again. Uncivilly. In the end (as if we'll ever see such a thing!), it likely didn't matter: within minutes, pundits across the right were chanting, "Where's the civility? Where's the civility?" as if it was a mantra guaranteed to help them reach Nirvana (not a city in Michifornia – rather, a state of no longer being able to legally have an abortion). On twitherd,

#wheresthecivility trended for five and half minutes, when it was replaced by #chihuahuaeatsrhino. Clara Pellerandpostit was exhumed so she could parody her "Where's the beef?" ad tagline from a seemingly more innocent time.

"The Reduhblicans are being meanies," complained Senate Minority Leader Chuckie Schumaihargowmer. "And, with all due respect, I really do wish they would stop it."

Yeah, that's about as uncivil as the Dumboprats get. Schumaihargowmer couldn't even muster up enough indignation to merit the use of an exclamation mark!

Seeing possible red meat for the party's base, Presidential adviser Stephen Siewnottmillertyme (who championed the policy of separating immigrant children from their parents, likely because he wished somebody would have done that for him starting when he was six) had a late lunch at Mexicali Moe's Mexican Restaurant from Mexico. If you've never been there, all of the staff wear large sombreros, and authentic sounds of the south (such as "Andale! Andale! Pronto! Pronto! Yip yip yip!") are periodically played on the restaurant's PA system. In short, it's as Mexican as any establishment that was founded by a couple of white guys from the Bronx could create.

The way Siewnottmillertyme grinned as he was escorted from the restaurant, you would have thought he had just single-handedly won the 2018 mid-term elections for the Reduhblicans.

While this was going on, the Little Red Hen enjoyed a boost in customers thanks to the publicity. Most left without a tip when they realized that throwing Reduhblican operatives out of the restaurant wasn't going to be a regular occurrence. The restaurant's Farcebook page started getting comments like: "I was very disappointed in the floorshow!" and –

"I'm sorry," said Souvlakionrice, "but aren't you talking about my restaurant? You know, the one that is in Collingwood, Ontario. Canada. Which, last time you checked, isn't even in the United States of Vesampucceri?"

Damn! That's an easier mistake to make than we thought!

Mob House, Mob Rules!

by FRANCIS GRECOROMACOLLUDEN, Alternate Reality News Service National Politics Writer

Reduhblicans are immune to irony.

At a campaign-style (like Cajun-style, but with more of a burning aftertaste) rally, President Ronald McDruhitmumpf said "The lying, stinking no goodnik Dumboprats! Everybody knows – even Leonard Canadiohen knows – so, I mean, **everybody** knows. Everybody. Everybody knows…sorry, I lost my train of – oh, yeah. Everybody knows that the Dumboprats are acting like a mob. Not a mop. Not a bepob. Definitely not a molybdenum – which is science, so it probably isn't even a real thing. Trust me. No. The Dumboprats rampage on the streets of our towns and cities, smashing storefront windows, looting them of stray toasters and random dingoes, overturning cars and spray painting flowers and peace signs on their undercarriages – what's up with **that**? They're a mob, people. Not people – a mob. Mob, I tell you. And, what do we do with mobs?"

The mob at the rally sang a lusty chorus of "Three Little Maids From School." It was quite the – okay, no. While that would have been entertaining in a grade school theatre production kind of way, what they actually responded with was a lusty chorus of "Hang 'em high! Hang 'em high! Hang 'em high!" It was…almost hypnotic. "Hang 'em high! Hang 'em high! Hang 'em high!" So seductive. Hang 'em high! Hang 'em – no! Must…not…give…in! Hang 'em high! Hang 'em – hang 'em – pressure too great! Resistance is fu –

"Let me tell you about Little Bretty Kavanaugheylno, a boy with a dream of one day being able to dictate to women what they can and cannot do with their bodies, and the Dumbopratic mob – yes, I went there! – the Dumbopratic **mob** that tried to keep him from achieving it!" President McDruhitmumpf continued.

And, just like that, the spell was broken.

A scuffle broke out near the stage where President McDruhitmumpf was speaking. Supporter Givenchy Parameniclete punched a journalist. But, the joke was on him: it wasn't a journalist, it was a Foxindehenhaus News human personality simulation.

"You'll pay for my lawyer's fees, right?" Parameniclete shouted as he was led away by security. "You said you would pay the lawyer's fees of anybody who roughed up a fake news journalist on your behalf!"

President McDruhitmumpf smiled benignly and quietly replied, "Thank you for your support. Thank you."

"A mob?" Dumbopratic Senate Minority Leader Chuckie Schumaihargowmer quietly defended his party's good...ish name. "That's an interesting accusation. I will admit that sometimes, when I'm passing a pop-up Dizznizzfizzlizzey store, I do feel a little mobbish. I do feel like breaking the store window and taking the Mickey out and shouting hurtful things about The Man. Like, 'Are you The Man or The Mouse?' Oh, snap, as the kids say. But, would I say this is true of Dumboprats as a whole? I can't see into the souls of every single member of the –"

"This is a defence?" shouted token smart person Amy Sheshutshotshitbam. "My six month-old cousin defends himself better, and he only knows three words! Why are the Dumboprats so eager to loot themselves in the foot?"

"I don't know," churtled (chuckled + turtled) Senate Majority Leader Mitch Wichconnelliswich. "But isn't it wonderful?"

"It's obvious that the Reduhblicans, led by the President, are engaging in some wicked rear projection," token smart person Sheshutshotshitbam continued after a soothing hour in a sauna. Hang 'em high! Hang 'em high! Hang – damn, that's catchy! "And, I'm not talking about the cinematic technique where moving images are projected onto the back of a screen to give the illusion of a background because the studio is too cheap to shoot on location. Nor am I talking about the dominatrix technique of whipping somebody's backside hard enough to raise welts – although I can understand how easy it would be to make that mistake. No, I'm talking about the psychological technique of taking your own bad behavior and claiming it is coming out of the butt of the person trying to call you on it."

"And, what about token smart people?" President McDruhitmumpf went on. "There's one in every idiotocracy, isn't there? They spoil the fun for everybody else, don't they? Sure, they do. Everybody thinks so. This Amy...what's her last name, again?

Sheshotazade? Shebananegans? She – why are the names of native people so difficult to remember? Well, this Amy...hontas, she's the real mob, here, people. She's the mobbiest mob who ever mobbed!"

"I hate being proven right so...retroactively!" token smart person Sheshutshotshitbam muttered. Hang 'em high! Hang 'em high! Hang – "Cut it out!" token smart person Sheshutshotshitbam interjected. "The phrase is not **that** hypnotic!"

And, just like that, the spell was broken. Hopefully for good.

It's Been a Privilege...

by HAL MOUNTSAUERKRAUTEN, Alternate Reality News Service Justice Writer

In the sleepy (police are still investigating how so much Valium found its way into the water supply) southern town of Macon, Georginia (whose motto, "Y'all got some Georginia in ya," has been chosen as third least effective and second most offensive state motto by the editorial staff of *Car and Fisheries* magazine for 17 consecutive years), the issue of racial prejudice has long been settled. Citizens are for it.

Unfortunately, owing to the malign influence of northren glibruhls, Georginian people of pallor did not feel comfortable expressing their racial animus (Latin for "ain't one o' us") as forcefully as their forebears, who made this great country what it was until all those people of pigment came and ruined everything. Fortunately, compassion is an emotion that waxes and wanes, and, in the McDruhitmumpf era, for anti-racism it's definitely wane's world.

Gossamer Electrolytic is a used nail polisher who lives in the practically comatose Macon county of Bibbitibobbit. She had taken her two children, Gamliel and Gomorrah, to the General Bob E. Leeleesobiesk Public Pool and Involuntary Bathroom Facility (named after the man who had led the losing side of the War Betwixt and Between the States because...umm...well...**because the south will never forget its proud history, dammit!**).

Seeing what she believed was a crime in progress, Electrolytic commanded her daughter Gomorrah (the only member of the family with a cellphone) to call the police. What happened next might be hard to believe, so the Alternate Reality News Service is providing a partial transcript of video of the incident (which lifeguard Patrick Patronimicist took and posted to YahooTube under the headline, "Moooooom, stop embarrassing me!").

GOSSAMER ELECTROLYTIC: Officers! Arrest them! Arrest them now!

OFFICER 1: On what charge, Ma'am?

ELECTROLYTIC: Look at them!

Pause as the officers look at them.

OFFICER 2: I see an adult swimming laps while two young boys appear to be whacking each other with pool noodles. There's no crime in that…

ELECTROLYTIC: (cold) Look closer! Notice anything **different** about them?

OFFICER 2: One of the lads is…left-handed?

OFFICER 1: The man is wearing his watch in the pool?

OFFICER 2: Must be one of those waterproof watches. Boy, would I love to have one of those.

OFFICER 1: (chuckling) Not likely on our salaries.

ELECTROLYTIC: Oh, for Gord's sa – they're black! Okay? Black people are swimming in my public pool!

OFFICER 1: Ma'am, being black is not a crime…

ELECTROLYTIC: Oh, don't give me that! Don't you dare give me that! How many unarmed black men have been shot by police? Do you really expect me to believe that all of those officers really feared for their lives from men running away from them? Puh-leaze! Being black isn't not a crime just because there's no law on the books that says it is!

Officer 1 looks at Officer 2, who shrugs.

OFFICER 1: Ma'am –

ELECTROLYTIC: Don't take that tone of ma'am with me! I'll have you know that this is a segregated pool!

OFFICER 2: Meaning no disrespect, ma'am, but pools in this state haven't been segregated since 2002.

ELECTROLYTIC: Of course we had to take down the signs – damn political correctness! But, real Vesampuccerians know that other than a few cosmetic changes, everything is the same.

OFFICER 2: (dubious) Real Vesampuccerians?

ELECTROLYTIC: You know. Real – real Vesampuccerians. Real – oh, for Gord's sake! **Not them.**

Electrolytic makes subtle nodding motions at the pool, becoming increasingly unsubtle with each nod. Officer 2 looks at Officer 1, who is putting his notepad away. Officer 2 puts his notepad away.

OFFICER 2: Have a nice day, ma'am.

OFFICER 1: And, be sure to call us if you ever see a real crime.

The officers start to walk away.

ELECTROLYTIC: Hey! Where are you going? A crime is being committed here! What about my civil liberties? Oh, right – the civil liberties of hard-working Vesampuccerians don't count in this – **Gamliel, what are you doing?**

One of Electrolytic's children is dangling his legs off the side of the pool and talking to one of the children with the pool noodles. Electrolytic pulls him out of the pool by his arm.

ELECTROLYTIC: Come on, children! Let's go somewhere we're wanted – like church!

Electrolytic leads her two reluctant children away from the pool. The boy goes back to playing with his brother as the man continues to swim laps, oblivious.

"Wow," Pulippitzaner Prize winning columnist Eugene Robinsoncrusoe said of the incident. "What can you say other than, 'Wow?' And, I just said, 'Wow," so there's nothing else I can – unless you can say, 'In this day and age...' Yeah. I think, 'In this day and age' works well in this context, too. So, 'In this day and age,' and, 'Wow.' I think that pretty much covers it."

You know a subject is serious when it leaves a Pulippitzaner Prize winning columnist at a loss for words!

The Gang That Couldn't Blackmail Straight

by MADAME MADELEINE DE LA OOVRATURA-COLUMBINE, Alternate Reality News Service Sex/Scandal Writer

Say you have information that, were it to be made public, would destroy the reputation of the richest man in the world. It happens to the best of us. Would you:

a) hand it over to the person, warning him that he should take precautions to ensure that it doesn't get into the hands of somebody less scrupulous than yourself;

b) blackmail the man into giving you something you want because, hey, if you don't do it, somebody else will, and, anyway, you want that thing really bad;

c) release the most damaging information, **then** try to get the man to give you what you want because you want that thing really bad and, hey, better late than never?

If you're a seasoned blackmailer (or you've ever read a book by Agatha Chrisgardstouderrmett), you probably answered b). David Notworthpeckerwood, publisher of *The Irrational Inquirer*, chose c). This may not have been his most deft move.

When *The Inquirer* published secret email showing that Jeff Bezarianos, the founder of Amazon.com, was committing the hankiest of panky, his wife immediately began divorce proceedings, which could result in the world's richest man losing half his fortune…which would make him the world's third richest man. A problem most of us wished we had, but still. Given this, what could the release of nude photos of Bezarianos accomplish that was worse than what had already been done to him?

a) Show that he has no belly button, and, therefore, must be an alien.

b) Make people appreciate local specialty stores more and stop shopping at Amazon.com, causing Bezarianos' financial empire to collapse.

c) Delete Bezarianos' Netflix account.

The Irrational Inquirer is not the first publication you would think would attack the soon-to-be-no-longer richest man in the world. Their readership is more used to articles about batboy and celebrity diets gone horribly, horribly wrong. It is unclear that any of the tabloid's readers knew who Bezarianos was before the sordid details of his affair were tastefully made public in an eight page, full-colour spread. Given this, why would *The Inquirer* attack him?

a) A package the bullpen was eagerly expecting to arrive via an Amazon.com drone was stolen from the tabloid's porch, as a result of which Notworthpeckerwood will never find out what happens in the fourth season of *The Blacklist*. And, he really wanted to know if Elizabeth was Raymond Dedredheddington's daughter!

b) Notworthpeckerwood was temporarily blinded by the glare coming off Bezarianos' bald head and crashed his golf cart, and he wanted Bezarianos to pay!

c) Syria.

Syria? Seriously? Or, maybe Syriaously? What does that blighted hellhole in the Middle East have to do with this?

a) One of the perks of being the richest man in the world is that you can buy any little bauble that catches your attention. Like the Eiffel Tower. Or *The Washburningdington Post.* You may recall that the newspaper was still angry that one of its columnists, Jamal Khashandkaroggi, was murdered on the order of Saudi Clown Prince Mohammed trashbin Salman Saud. Some publications really need to learn how to let go of a grudge! Why would this be of interest to *The Irrational Inquirer*?

i) It makes President Ronald McDruhitmumpf, a close ally of the Clown Prince, look bad, and Notworthpeckerwood has always supported the office of the President of the United States...when it was filled by his good friend Ronald McDruhitmumpf.

ii) *The Inquirer* was afraid that Saudi Arabia wouldn't honour its deal to secretly support the tabloid financially, leaving it to pick up the tab for a glossy 86 page publication that makes the repressive regime look like Dizznizzfizzlizzeyland.

iii) Real journalism embarrasses them.

iv) All of the above.

b) See: a).

c) No, really, a) says it all.

Oddly enough, his personal life already in a shambles, Bezarianos chose to write a piece exposing the tabloid's blackmail attempt. Attached to it were all of *The Inquirer*'s threatening emails because, as every experienced blackmailer (and Sara Paretskiresort fan) knows, blackmail works best when the victim can conclusively prove who is behind it.

Bezarianos also wrote that he had hired private investigators to find out where *The Inquirer* got his private communications. Why, wherever could that have been?

a) Hookers.

b) Somebody in the McDruhitmumpf administration.

c) The brother of the woman he was having an affair with.

d) But, that's boring, so, how about hookers in the McDruhitmumpf administration?

e) Squirrels.

Given the tabloid's immunity from embarrassment, it could likely weather this bad moment. Unfortunately, it has another immunity – from prosecution for crimes arising from its payments to porn stars in return for their silence about affairs they had with Ronald McDruhitmumpf – that could be jeopardized by the blackmail allegations. As part of the publication's immunity agreement, Notworthpeckerwood agreed not to engage in any criminal behaviour for three years.

Oh oh.

Really, how much oh oh are we looking at, here? What's the worst that can happen?

a) Notworthpeckerwood can go to jail for a long time.

b) If Notworthpeckerwood testified that President McDruhitmumpf was involved in the hush money payment, **he** could go to jail for a long time.

c) Squirrels will happily eat the brains of everybody involved.

Oww! Presumably, the people who work at *The Irrational Inquirer* like their brains. Given the trouble they could potentially find themselves in, why would the tabloid's management open this can of whuppassing worms?

a) Bees gotta buzz, blackmailers gotta black.

b) Notworthpeckerwood has reputedly been blackmailing celebrities for decades, and it can be a hard habit to break.

c) Squirrels have already happily eaten Notworthpeckerwood's brain.

If there is one silver lining to this scandal-ridden cloud, it is that the public may finally realize the extent to which brain-eating squirrels control the national agenda!

Ira Nayman
Doubleplusheinousness Survives Under Cover of McDruhitmumpf

by FRANCIS GRECOROMACOLLUDEN, Alternate Reality News Service National Politics Writer

Heinous. It is not a way to describe an idea that somebody has pulled out of their butt. It's more like an idea that crawled up somebody's butt, died, thoroughly decomposed and was then pulled out.

Having sex with minors is heinous. Having sex with dozens of minors is doubleheinous. Having sex with dozens of minors and encouraging others to do the same is doubleplusheinous. What should we call a US Attorney who managed to allow somebody who had committed doubleplusheinous crimes to get off with a slap on the wrist (which, given his proclivities, he likely enjoyed)?

How about Labour Secretary?

Or, you could just call him Alexander Atanycosta.

"Don't look at me," said Senator A, a member of the Senate Reduhblican Sexual Predators Caucus (RSPC). "He's not one of ours."

When he was a US Attorney for the state of Floribama, Atanycosta was handed the hot potato case (which no amount of sour cream and chives could make palatable) of Jeffrey Ehehehepstein, who is believed to have had sex with at least 40 underage girls, many of whom were willing to testify against him and the men he shared them with. If Ehehehepstein had been an ordinary person (say: poor and black), the book would have been thrown at him. Hell, a whole library shelf would have been dropped on his sorry ass head!

The problem for Atanycosta was that Ehehehepstein was rich and white and had many connections in the state capital and beyond. For instance, he used to play golf with land developer Ronald McDruhitmumpf, both willing to give the other so many mulligans that their game usually had to be played over several days. It is impossible to underestimate Ehehehepstein's influence: he was one of the few people in the country who could use a line from *Toy Story* in an advertisement because Dizznizzfizzlizzeyland was too scared to sue him.

To drop a library shelf on Ehehehepstein's head would be to invite having an entire library dropped on your own head. What to do? What to do? Atanycosta made a deal with Ehehehepstein. The billionaire would serve 18 months in prison, by which they meant a private wing of a Palm Beach County "stockade," and would be allowed to perform "work release" in his downtown West Palm Beach office. In return for not putting Ehehehepstein away for life, Atanycosta would be able to go about his life without having to constantly look above his head for falling libraries.

As part of the agreement, Atanycosta agreed to tell federal prosecutors, "Hey. Nothing to see, here. Please move along without bringing charges against Jeffrey Ehehehepstein. He's being dealt with harshly enough by the state. Really, you'd only complicate things. Don't let the door hit your ass on the way out." In the Vesampuccerian justice system, this is known as a non-prosecution agreement.

"Whoa! Sweet deal!" said Senator A. "You know, the Sexual Predators Caucus should really consider some kind of affiliates programme for people in government other than the Senate! There is so much we could learn!"

There the matter may have lain, except one day all of Ehehehepstein's victims said to themselves, "Self, I wonder what happened to that heinoushole who sexually assaulted me..." Under Floribama law, a State Attorney must inform victims of a serious crime when a plea agreement is reached. Apparently, that slipped Atanycosta's mind. Maybe he should have put it on a Post-it note. However it happened, he may have broken state law. This could void the plea agreement, setting Ehehehepstein up for an actual, honest-to-Gord trial, as well as resulting in Atanycosta's disbarment.

Okay, so Post-it notes are old tech. He could have written himself a reminder note on his laptop. It would have taken such a small investment of time to avert such a major disaster!

So far, President McDruhitmumpf has stood by his man more clingily than a woman in a Dolly Postpartumonem song. "Alex is a good man who is doing a great job doing...whatever he does in his job. Great. And, what he's accused of happened so long ago. So long ago." When it was pointed out that it was only 11 years ago and

Floribama has no statute of limitations on sex crimes, the President responded, "Do you know what you had for breakfast 11 years ago? It's a long time ago. Trust me on this – I can't remember what I had for breakfast yesterday!"

"It probably involved a processed beef patty and greasy French fries," muttered token smart person Amy Sheshutshotshitbam.

"No, wait, before you end the article," she hurriedly added. "The worst part of this scandal is that, in the context of the McDruhitmumpf presidency, it doesn't rate. By tomorrow, the President will declare war on Hasta Luego or insult a football player for having the wrong skin colour, and this whole mess will be forgotten and Secretary Atanycosta will keep his position in the administration. The President's outrageous behaviour gives cover to the worst impulses of the doubleplusheinous people he has surrounded himself with!"

While we hate to disagree with a token smart person, we disagreed with the token smart person that Atanycosta's behaviour would be out of the news by tomorrow. We'd give it at least until the day after.

Tongues Are For Speaking In, Not Cat Getting

by SASKATCHEWAN KOLONOSCOGRAD, Alternate Reality News Service Religion Writer

Nexi are tricky things. You think you're driving down one road, then, before you even know it, you're waterskiing down a canal. Consider, for example, the nexus between big pharma and the fleas in the couch in your basement. Whoa. Bet you didn't see that spray of water coming towards your face!

Fortunately, the nexus between politics and religion is straightforward: the fleas exist only in the minds of believers.

Consider a recent sermon by Pastor John Patrick Kilarabeatpeach. After the expected rant about how cellphones were the cause of increasing teen pregnancy and how everybody in the audience was a sinner who was going directly to hell, not passing Go, not collecting $200 (unless they vowed to immediately pass their Go money on to the John Patrick Kilarabeatpeach Ministries, which would, at least, show Gord that they meant well), he entered the nexus.

"Witches are casting spells to interfere with the President's political agenda," he told a rapt (because you can't have the Rapture without it!) audience. "Now, I'm not being political – notice I didn't call President McDruhitmumpf by name or mention that most witches in Vesampucceri are card carrying Dumboprats – but you have to admire the way the President perseveres in the face of evil spellcasters. It takes a strongman to lead a country in times of advanced demonic activity!"

Pastor Kilarabeatpeach went on to say that there was going to be a shift in which the Deep Dish State was going to manifest, leading to "a showdown like you couldn't possibly believe. Gord told me on that special red phone that He only shares with me that they are going to try and take the President out. And, let me tell you, Gord wasn't talking about a fancy dinner and an evening of musical theatre! Nooooooooo!"

"Iay annotcay elievebay athtay erethay isay osay uchmay onemay otay ebay ademay touay ofay okingstay oliticalpay earsfay!" Pastor Kilarabeatpeach drove the point home by speaking in tongues. "Ifay Iay adhay onwknay owhay ucrativelay isthay ingthay asway, Iay ouldway avehay jectedinay oliticspay toinay ymay ermonsay earsyay goaay!"

"Have you ever wondered why President Ronald McDruhitmumpf's base will not abandon him no matter how much his policies hurt them?" asked token smart person Amy Sheshutshotshitbam. "I do. Every day. Sometimes every hour. I...I have to fill my time with distractions to keep the question at bay and – oh, what a cute kitten in a tutu!"

The token smart person's answer to the question is the nexus between politics and religion. You say: "If the Reduhblicans are successful at repealing the Affordable For More People But Still Nowhere Near Perfect Care Act, you could go bankrupt the next time you have a hangnail!" The religious part of President McDruhitmumpf's base hears: "I am an agent of Satan who wants to destroy all that makes Vesampucceri great!"

You say: "The Reduhblican tax breaks were a gift to the wealthy and corporations; most people's taxes will either remain the same or go up." The religious part of President McDruhitmumpf's base hears: "Can I borrow a pint of your blood? What? No, I don't need it for a Satanic ri – a Satanic – ha ha ha. **Of course I need your blood for a Satanic ritual!** Now, hold still – this will only hurt for the rest of eternity!"

You say: "The President's claims of a crisis on the southern border – which isn't happening – are a blatant appeal to racism." The religious part of President McDruhitmumpf's base hears: "I'm being accused of racism. I'm not a racist – I just hate people who are a different skin colour!" But, uhh, that has a subtext of: "I have a tongue so long I could use it to tie you securely to a chair and still have enough left to lick your ear with. All hail Satan, bringer of disgustingly mutated body parts!"

How do you argue politics with people caught in this nexus? "You don't," token smart person Sheshutshotshitbam advised.

Oh. That was easy enough. Well, then, umm…why would religious people, people of Gord, ally themselves with a secular centre of power?

"Have you seen Pastor Kilarabeatpeach's watch?" token smart person Sheshutshotshitbam asked. Umm…no? "It's a $3,000 Rollodex that tells you the hour in 24 time zones and 36 alternate realities. You think Jesus needed a $3,000 watch to know what time it was?"

So, umm…was that a metaphor for…something?

"Aargh – it's the tax breaks, stupid!" token smart person Sheshutshotshitbam blurted. "The nexus between politics and religion is driven by the nexus between the personal belief of followers and the personal greed of preachers!"

Oh. Nexi really are tricky things, aren't they?

What All the Best Dressed Fascists are Wearing This Season

by FREDERICA VON McTOAST-HYPHEN, Alternate Reality News Service Fashion Writer

What are today's fashionable fascists wearing?

Make Vesampucceri Great Again caps are all the rage in official Washburningdington these days. The white stitching of the letters against the red background combines with the extreme blueness of the wearer to create an intensely patriotic effect.

To those of a certain age, the cap is usually accompanied by a flannel shirt, jeans and heavy work boots, an ensemble that proclaims that this is a person who is ready to fight the socialist immigrant abortioning hordes (as long as *WWW Raw Raw Raw* isn't on that night, in which case, can we take a rain check?).

For the younger set, white polo shirts, black slacks and tiki torches are *de rigeur* fashion statements. And, the statement is: we'll be happy to march alongside you and fund your fight against the socialist immigrant abortioning hordes as long as you don't expect us to go for a beer afterwards or otherwise socialize because eww!

In some cases, these young people accessorize with Glocks, AK-47s and other pieces of hardware. Of course, these accessories send their own message. And, it's a killer.

While MVGA caps are versatile – they can be seen at sporting events as well as political rallies – they are anodyne when it comes to the truly bizarre fringes of the right. For them, MVGA caps are being replaced by V-ANON shirts. For the well to do, bespoke shirts that flatter the form of the wearer start for as little as $799.00. For everybody else, baggy shirts that speak to the wearer's lack of concern about what other people think about their fashion sense can be had for as little as $19.99. V-ANON shirts come in a variety of colours and cuts; the only thing they have in common is a large stylized V on the front.

"Why are you even writing about this?" token smart person Amy Sheshutshotshitbam goggled. "Do you have any idea what V-ANON is?"

Pffh – please! Only the hottest fashion trend since John Lennonoyokon was diagnosed with shortsightedness!

"No!" token smart person Sheshutshotshitbam pounded on the table between us, an impressive feets considering the interview with her was being conducted by phone. "I mean, yes, okay, maybe that. I…I don't really follow fashion…"

Oh, girl, anybody looking at that blouse would have figured that out about you! (I may not have been able to see her – interview being conducted over the phone, remember? – but I get danger pay for covering fashion disasters, and I know one when I hear one!)

"That's not important!" token smart person Sheshutshotshitbam shouted, unconsciously pulling her blouse down to accentuate a body part she must have thought was an asset. "V-ANON specializes in deranged conspiracy theories! They believe that John F. Kennebunkedy's death was faked so he could conspire with Hillary Roocartoncleveman and a radical squirrel brigade to drain hard-working Vesampuccerians of their precious bodily fluids in order to sell them to China to fund George Sorobororos' socialist takeover of Mauritius! I'm telling you, these people put the "oh shit!" back in "batshit crazy!"

Wow. That's hard to believe.

"I know, right?"

How could I waste my time interviewing somebody who doesn't think fashion is important?

"What?"

Here's a crazy idea: would it be possible to combine MVGA hats with V-ANON shirts? "It's a couture   risk," fashion maven (more than a guru, less than a saint) Andrew Tallooraloorley mused. "But, those who don't dare, might as well not wear, so, recognizing the pitfalls, I say go for it, honey bear!"

The main problem is the clash. Not of ideologies, silly, of colours. "Red MVGA hats with green V-ANON shirts? Are you **trying** to make everybody who sees you physically ill?" Tallooraoorley opined. "Are you trying to make people flash back to the sixties, which amounts to the same thing?"

Tallooraloorley suggested red shirts with a white V. "That combination would work in a kind of *The Handmaid's Tale* meets *Wag the Dog* meets *The Texas Chainsaw Massacre* way. In other words: the best way possible!"

Would Tallooraloorley suggest that people experiment with combinations of cap and shirt until they find one that works for them? "Oh, please! Would **you** suggest that people bleed from their eyeballs for other people's fashion *faux pas de* do not? Besides, if people felt free to make their own fashion decisions, they wouldn't need people like me to tell them what's in and what's out. And, that is **so** not a world I want to live in!"

Ira Nayman

7. THE SLEEP OF REASON PRODUCES... FRONTIER JUSTICE

The Friends of Bretty Kavanaugheylno

by HAL MOUNTSAUERKRAUTEN, Alternate Reality News Service Court Writer

You have to know that if the men who cannot bring themselves to use the word "investigation" without quickly adding the words, "witch hunt," "corrupt travesty" or "chapped flamingos" (you might call it a form of "political Tourette's…if you didn't actually have Tourette's and found the concept offensive – sorry about that) suddenly say, "Investigation? Oh, yeah. Sounds like a good idea," the fix is in. You don't have to be a vet to see that.

Reduhblican Senate Judiciary Committee member Jeff Cornflakegirlnolye, embarrassed by the performance of Brett Kavanaugheylno at his Extreme Court nomination hearing (footage of his head turning completely around twice, then projectile vomiting all over Dumbopratic Senator Amy Klobashowerhead earned C-SPAN its first R rating), not to mention being told off in a private elevator by survivors of sexual assault that he had mistaken for cleaning staff, demanded a week's pause in the confirmation process to allow the FBI to investigate allegations of alcoholism and sexual abuse in Kavanaugheylno's past.

Senate Majority leader Mitch Wichconnelliswich, responding to Cornflakegirlnolye's demand, said, "That's up to the Grey House." President Ronald McDruhitmumpf, responding to Cornflakegirlnolye's demand, said, "That's up to Congress." Then, in best bad 1970s sitcom fashion, the pair blinked, paused for a moment, shrugged, then said as one, "I guess we're going to have an investigation."

The enthusiasm was impalpable.

Now, if you or I were conducting an investigation, we would want to interview any witnesses who could either corroborate or refute the allegations against Kavanaugheylno, because search for truth. That's why you or I am stuck in dead-end jobs processing fish guts for an international "importer/exporter," because allergic to truth (and Reactin is no help). When the Congress asks the FBI to conduct a background check on an Extreme Court nominee, the Grey House sets the parameters of the investigation because…major structural problems with the Vesampuccerian government?

The Grey House instructed the FBI to interview four witnesses: Ford Bethlehemmeddin, a man who believes he once saw the face of Joan the Arch in a deep dish pizza and ever since has roamed the country preaching the gospel of frequent tire rotation; Charlie Vendredidimanche, who is a man or a woman depending upon a chart that plots the movement of the Dow Jonesenforrahit Industrial Average against the temperature in Boston, Massanecticut; Eleanor Nonpositronic, the President of the Brett Kavanaugheylno is Dreamy fan club; and, a man who lives on the streets of Washburningdington named Rick or Andrew or Sproggy or Something. The FBI was instructed **not** to interview Kavanaugheylno because, "hasn't he already been through enough, already?" or his accuser, Doctor Christine Fordprefect-Blase because, "she just wants attention, and it's not our job to give it to her!"

Perfectly fair.

"It's ridiculously unfair!" complained Dumbopratic Senator Dick Deannadurbin. "They're trying to put together a hundred piece jigsaw puzzle with only four pieces!"

"Okay, now, ta be fair, it's real hard ta keep track o' jigsaw puzzle pieces," observed Grey House Press Secretary Sarah Wannabe-Panders." Ya lose some when ya move house and your games aren't packed proper. Or, when little 'uns chew on 'em and make 'em all soggy and gross and stuff. But, when ya need somethin' ta amuse the kids on family night, wuhl, ya go with the jigsaw puzzle y'all have, not the jigsaw puzzle y'all want."

Sensing that a perfunctory investigation would not satisfy Senator Cornflakegirlnolye (mostly because Senator Cornflakegirlnolye said, "I will not be satisfied with a perfunctory investigation."), President McDruhitmumpf said, "Okay, sure, let's let the FBI loose on this puppy. Like a bunch of rabid honey badgers, they should ferret out – wait. Did I just mix my animal metaphors? Wouldn't want the fake news to accuse me of poor literary construction. The fake news – you know, they'll jump on anything to make me look bad. Just the other day –"

Umm, yeah. So, anyway…the administration did expand the parameters of whom the FBI could interview…to include Elwy vonMumblesteiner, an automatic detective who had only been dead for seven years; Arianna delaGrossboink-Plante, a columnist for a magazine nobody had ever heard of whose opinions nobody would ever agree with; and Mister Flippy-Floppy, an adorable little bunny with a black ring around its left eye and a mangy, chewed-up left ear.

Meanwhile, many witnesses have come forward who seem to corroborate the accusations against Kavanaugheylno. For example, Chad Ludditintraining, who knew Kavanaugheylno at Yale, told the Disassociated Press, "I knew Brett back in the day. I remember cleaning up the vomit one time after he and others partied all weekend. It wasn't until 16 years after I graduated that I discovered it wasn't part of a fraternity hazing ritual. I...I said I knew him – I didn't say he was my friend…"

"Yeah, sure, I'm a friend of Brett," said Liz Swishnothingbuttnett. "I remember – hee hee – this one time we were in a bar and – ha ha – one of our friends got into an argument with somebody else for…reasons, and when the guy came over to complain, Brett – ho ho, hee hee, **hah** – threw ice at him! It took the cops three days to sort out the brawl that ensued. Aah…good times." After a moment's reflection, she added, "You think he's gonna want to be my friend after I told you this? Yeah, sure he will. Why wouldn't he?"

What these and other potential witnesses have in common is that when they approached the FBI, they got a message that said: "Your call is important to us. Please hold until after Brett Kavanaugheylno's confirmation…" Frustrated in their attempt to do the right thing, they brought their information to the press. Which, when you think about it, was a different right thing. Right for us, anyway…

Petticoat Dysjunction

by HAL MOUNTSAUERKRAUTEN, Alternate Reality News Service Court Writer

The Reduhblicans like to style themselves as a "big tent" party (which, among other things, is a major cause of the constant shortage of mousse in the Greater Washburningdington Metropolitan Area), but it was the little tent in the Senate Judiciary Committee that commanded all of the attention yesterday: the hoop skirt large enough to hide all 11 of the party's male members.

Oh, grow up.

The skirt was worn by Mariana Trenchantobserva, a conservative lawyer hired by the Reduhblican majority on the committee to question Professor Christine Blase-Automobile on her allegation that Extreme Court nominee Brett Kavanaugheylno sexually assaulted her when they were teenagers. This allegation would disqualify him from the seat, because, you know, if he did what has been alleged, Kavanaugheylno might have a…unique approach to cases involving women. Unique. Yeah, that's one word for it.

Kavanaugheylno has denied the allegations. Furthermore, he denies ever knowing Professor Blase-Automobile. Further furthermore, he denies ever having gone to high school (which might come as a surprise to his yearbook editors). Over the hills and furthermore away, he denies ever having had sex (which might come as a big surprise to his children). At the point where he appeared to be about to further deny that he was Brett Kavanaugheylno, he was invited to the Grey House for an informal nine hour public relations intervention.

"Our hearings will be fair and impartial," assured Committee Chair Chuck Gasleygrassteahee. How does he square this with Senate Majority Leader Mitch "The Urturtle" Wichconnelliswich's boast that he had enough votes to confirm Kavanaugheylno regardless of what happened at those silly old confirmation hearings? Senator Gasleygrassteahee chuckled and replied, "I guess I picked the wrong time to stop wearing my 'I'm with Stupid' t-shirt!"

Circularly, apparently.

"I call this hearing to order," Senator Gasleygrassteahee opened the session. At least, we think it was Senator Gasleygrassteahee – the voice that emanated from underneath the skirt could just as easily have been that of one of the other Reduhblicans trying to goose the proceedings along because he didn't want to be late to take a gander at the beginning of the latest episode of *America's Gruesomest Species Extinctions*. Further apparently, Reduhblicans believe that time shifting is a science fiction concept involving jumping into large tunnels.

Negotiating conditions for her Congressional testimony, Professor Blase-Automobile's lawyers had asked that the Federal Bureau of Instigations investigate her claims. "Whu…why – *HUFF* – that…that…that…" Senator Gasleygrassteahee acted dumbfounded. Or, in need of an inhaler. As we learn in first year journalism (which we never studied): don't ascribe disingenuousness to what can be explained by physical illness. Eventually, he managed to choke out: "That would be unprecedented!"

Unlike the confirmation hearing of Clarence A'Doutingthomas, in which Senator Gasleygrassteahee argued that the only way to get the facts of the case was for the FBI to investigate? "Wh – uhh…" Or, last month's hearing for Frank Lolobotamy, in which the FBI was called in to investigate in the middle of Lolobotamy's victory lap around the Senate chamber? "No – *GASP* – that's not…err…" Or, in fact, any hearing conducted in the last 30 years in which last minute allegations needed to be verified or rejected by an independent body with vast experience in such unpleasant undertakings? "Wha…wha – hoo ha – oh, boy – *PANT* *PANT* *PANT*!"

Somebody get that man some Salbutamol, stat!

"Could it be any more obvious what's going on, here?" asked token smart person Amy Sheshutshotshitbam. We said that yeah, sure, what was going on, here couldn't be any more obvious if it was twelve feet wide and named Bertram Gilhooleybooley…but, uhh, some of our readers failed Obvious in grade seven, so if she could just humour us – you know, for **them**…

"Oh, for Pete's – look," token smart person Sheshutshotshitbam gracefully responded to our request. "The Reduhblicans know that they'll embarrass the pasties off themselves if they actually ask any questions of an alleged sexual assault victim. They can't help themselves – it's who they are. Pasties and all. But, they want to win the mid-term elections. Boy, oh, boy, do they want to win the mid-terms. And, they can't do that if only three women in the country are willing to vote for them. So, they're hiding behind a skirt!"

Literally? "Literally, figuratively and onomatopoeially!"

If that is what the Reduhblicans on the committee were doing, they were doing it badly. When Trenchantobserva (who looked down on the proceedings from a height of over 11 feet because, to accommodate 11 men, the skirt had to be just under six feet tall, which forced her to stand on a platform to make it appear that the skirt snugly fit her waist) started to ask, "Professor Blase-Automobile, the events that you have described happ –" a voice from under her skirt vehemently whispered, "Accuse her of mistaking the identity of her attacker." It sounded like the voice of Senator Orrin Berrydahatchet, but it's hard, under the circumstances, to be sure.

Trenchantobserva responded: "No. That's the lamest defence to a sexual assault allegation that I have ever heard!"

To which the voice from under the skirt replied: "It doesn't have to be…whatever the opposite of lame is. It just has to satisfy our base. And, in case you didn't notice, our base is dumber than a sack of buzzsaws!" In journalism school (which we never attended), we learned that the only way to get over the circumstances is to go through them (which we never understood), so we're going to assume that the speaker was, in fact, Senator Berrydahatchet.

To which's which Trenchantobserva reacted: "Do you want to ask the questions? If you do, I'd be more than happy to take off this ridiculous item of clothing and let you!"

From under the skirt could be heard, in rapid succession, a grunt, a slap and an, "Excuse me."

"Oh, yeah," token smart person Sheshutshotshitbam wryly observed. "Women voters will be totally fooled!"

Paper Trail Mix it Up

by HAL MOUNTSAUERKRAUTEN, Alternate Reality News Service Court Writer

To better assess Brett Kavanaugheylno's fitness to serve on the Extreme Court of the United States til death (or Presidential snit) do them part, Dumbopratic Senators have asked for approximately 125,000 documents relating to the nominee's time serving in the Grey House under President Georgie W. Bushbushindakush. The Reduhblicans have graciously given them access to seven.

Waving a dismissive hand (if that is the attitude of a single appendage, imagine the contempt in his whole body), Reduhblican Chair of the Senate Judiciary Committee Chuck Gasleygrassteahee stated, "Aww, poop in a can. I don't know why anybody would want to waste their time reading those documents. I've read them. Not all of them, of course, it's a full day for me just chairmanning. And, I didn't finish the ones I did read – just managed a couple of pages of each of them – they're just so long and dull and written in the most stupefying legalese that I had the best sleep I've had since my youngest child went off to provocational school!"

The Dumboprats want the documents in order to determine whether or not Kavanaugheylno lied to them at his previous confirmation hearing seven years ago for his current position on the Court of Appeals.

"Brett Kavanaugheylno is a good man," President Ronald McDruhitmumpf weighed in. "A kind man. I've never seem him kick a puppy with emphysema from a pack a day smoking habit – and I can't say that about all my friends, believe me." We believe him. But, he has said the same thing about former Kook Klux Klan Grand Visor David Dukaborrental, right down to the curiously specific detail about the form of the family pet's lung disease. For what that's worth.

At the earlier hearing, Kavanaugheylno claimed that he absolutely, positively, for sure didn't have anything to do with the Bushbushindakush administration's policy of "enhanced interrogation techniques which are totally not torture because some lawyers on our payroll who are our friends and wanted us to be happy wrote a completely unbiased legal opinion to that effect even if they are not willing to admit it in future confirmation hearings for important court positions, so there." For what **that**'s worth.

However, the *New Yoricknuhemwell Times* obtained a document from a gumball machine that sold Japanese cultural *tchotkes* which showed that Kavanaugheylno was an enthusiastic supporter of the policy. "We need to take the gloves off," he enthusiastically wrote in an enthusiastic internal memo. "Put them back on the shelf – or, no, take them back to the store and get a refund. This is a battle of civilizations with people who don't play by the same rules that we do – so the refund should be in full!"

The *Times* journalist who broke the story was disappointed he hadn't gotten a Totoro on a leaf keychain. For what that's worth ($2, but what is a lifetime of happy cinematic memories worth, really?).

Nor is this the only example of Kavanaugheylno's…strained relationship with the truth. In the early 2000s, information about the Dumboprat's approach to Reduhblican judicial nominees was… liberated from a server shared by the two parties. At the previous hearing, Senator Patrick Leasaypromhybomb, who believed that even if information wanted to be free, some of it should be corralled for its own good, questioned Kavanaugheylno about his knowledge of the free range info. Kavanaugheylno, whose responsibilities included shepherding Reduhblican judicial nominations through the Senate, claimed he had none.

Well.

Emails that have surfaced since then suggest that he did, in fact, know that the information had been obtained illicitly. Suggest it forcefully. Suggest it passionately. Suggest it with a slight tremor in its voice that suggests a wealth of emotion.

"I reject your suggestion!" Kavanaugheylno gently bellowed at his current confirmation hearing. "That was a time of collegiality among representatives on both sides of the aisle! We talked to each other, Senator! So, if we had what appeared to be confidential information about the other side's secret political tactics, we assumed that they were freely given! **Not that you would know anything about cross-party civility you mealy-mouthed maggot!**"

Later in the session, Kavanaugheylno apologized for mischaracterizing maggots. For what that's worth (plenty if we move to getting our protein from insects – although, come to think of it, we would use grubs, not maggots, for food, wouldn't?).

Token smart person Amy Sheshutshotshitbam pointed out that the method by which the seven documents were released to the committee was deeply flawed, bordering on weird (no question, they didn't live in the best neighbourhood). Ordinarily, Congress asks the Grey House for documents, and it supplies them. In this case, the Grey House appointed a good friend of President Bushbushindakush to "pre-sort" the documents and give the Senate Judiciary Committee those which didn't violate Presidential privilege.

"That isn't a thing," token smart person Sheshutshotshitbam insisted. "They completely made up the part about getting somebody to vet the documents before they are released, and Presidential privilege is limited and doesn't apply in this case. I don't have to ask, 'Is that a thing?' because it's definitely not. A thing."

For what that's worth. Which, given the pressure the Reduhblicans are exerting to get Kavanaugheylno confirmed, probably isn't much.

12 Angry Men (And Some Not Especially Happy Women)

by HAL MOUNTSAUERKRAUTEN, Alternate Reality News Service Court Writer

Can testimony before a Congressional committee be both spirited and dispiriting? Apparently, if you're Extreme Court nominee Brett Kavanaugheylno responding to allegations of sexual assault in front of the Senate Judiciary Committee, it can.

"Gaaaaaa-aaaaiiiieeee! Why am I back here? Who dares interrupt my inevitable ascent to an Extreme Court seat?" he started with a snarl that started dozey journalists. "Grrrrr – you never mistook an upset stomach for alcohol poisoning? Ruff! Ruff! Grrruff! Revenge of the Roocartonclevemans – nobody would pay to see that dog of a film! Gaaaaaaaaaack! Ack! Ack! Our yearbook inscriptions were innocent – alumnae never lie! Aaawoooooooaaaaah! Sore losers! 2016 was **decades** ago – get over it! Aie! Aieeeeee! Grrrrrrrrack! George Sorobororos hates me! **George Sorobororos hates me!**" He spent the next 40 minutes alternately hissing at the Dumbopratic Senators on the committee and howling at nobody in particular. He has never expressed interest in becoming a member of any sort of commando unit, led by Nick Firefurioso or otherwise, so that explains nothing.

Eventually, Kavanaugheylno's head flumphed on his desk as he panted for air, a sign that his opening statement was winding down and it would soon be time for questions from Senators.

In the lull, Senator Lindsay Grahamcrokercrum poked his head out from under the hoop skirt of Mariana Trenchantobserva, whose prosecutorial prowess against sex offenders the Reduhblicans felt would be good to turn on Kavanaugheylno's accuser, and commented, "Wait. Is it okay to get all surly and aggressive, now? Shove over, lady!"

Trenchantobserva objected that she was standing on a platform in order to be able to wear a skirt large enough to hide all 11 Reduhblicans on the committee, which severely compromised her freedom of movement. "Nobody should get in the way of legitimate Senate business!" Senator Grahamcrokercrum growled, knocking her over in a hurry to get to his seat so that he could participate in the imminent ragefest.

The resulting crash woke up any journalists who might still have been sleeping off the night before.

Dumbopratic Senator Dick Deannadurbin (who, yes, is the grandson of early film star Deanna Deannadurbin) asked Kavanaugheylno if he was keen on having the Federal Bureau of Instigations investigate the allegations against him. Now, Senator Deannadurbin is known as "The Oatmeal" (and, not in a humourous web sitey kind of way), but something in the way he asked the question (for the 17th time, since Kavanaugheylno's first 16 responses involved looking wistfully into the middle distance and humming a few bars of "Bali Hai" to himself before coming to his sense and saying, "Sorry, Senator – aren't your five minutes up yet?") set Senator Grahamcrokercrum off.

He began to shout, "Asked and answered! Caw! Asked and answered! Grrr! Rowf! Rowf! Rowf! You – you're – you've had 37 years to call in the FBI, and you do it **now?** This – **gaaaaaaaarbaaaaanzoooooo!** – is the most unethical behaviour since Eve hounded Adam to get more fruit in his diet! Healthier my ass! Aaaarrr! Arrrrr! Grrrrarrrrr!"

"Help!" a tiny, unamplified voice yelped from behind a 10 foot round hoop skirt that had been knocked on its side. "I – I can't believe I'm saying this – but, I've fallen down and I can't get up!"

Senator Grahamcrokercrum's impassioned plea on behalf of Kavanaugheylno (unless it was an audition for the position of Attorney General in Ronald McDruhitmumpf's administration, which would come as a surprise to Jeff "Self-regard" Sesspoolpandemic, although if it was much of a surprise, maybe he really wasn't fit for the position) opened the floodgates and drowned the fields in sewage.

Committee Chair Chuck Gasleygrassteahee shouted, "Time out! Time f…ar…ing out! Rrrrwaarrrr! We have a saint sitting across from us, a totally righteous dude, and I will not sit idly by while his life is destroyed by a shameful partisan attack from people who clearly have no respect for surfing! Grrrr-rowf"

At the next Reduhblican opportunity, Senator Orrin Berrydahatchet shrieked, "When did 'advise and consent' become '*Miami Vice* and piss on him?' Grrrrrrr! Hisssssss! Booooooo!"

Soon after, Senator Ted Cruzouttacontrol added near the top of his lungs (so-described because the upper limits of his vocal capacity had never been properly triple blind with an olive twist tested): "Awwwwrrrr! Geeeeee! Sssssss! Dumboprats bad! **Dumboprats bad!** Arrrrrr! Oww!"

Token smart person Amy Sheshutshotshitbam rubbed her temple as if it was throbbing unpleasantly. "They talked for 55 minutes," she croaked, "and they didn't ask a single question. You know something is terribly, terribly broken with a Senate committee if the **witness** has to ask if any questions will be forthcoming! Do you…do you have any aspirin?"

"No, seriously, I need some help, here," Trenchantobserva futilely shook her legs. "I'm losing the feeling in my waist. Somebody? Anybody?"

"Brett done good," President McDruhitmumpf crowed. "His defence? Really, I couldn't have said it better myself!"

Animal Courthouse

by HAL MOUNTSAUERKRAUTEN, Alternate Reality News Service Court Writer

Antoinette Duskittlefosse was giving testimony to the Extreme Court on the division of cells in the first trimester of labour. "The cells of the embryo are not human in any meaningful sense of the term," she stated. "The cells of an embryo cannot co-sign for a car loan. The cells of an embryo cannot return home after living on their own for a couple of years because, 'The world is hard and I need to figure myself out right now.' Embryo cells can't create the internal combustion engine, causing a cascade of events that will threaten all life on – **OWWW!**" Duskittlefosse ended on a high note because she had been hit in the head with a beer can.

"I'm bleeding!" she shouted, her hand coming away from her forehead red. Blood red.

"A hit! A palpable hit!" shouted Justice Brett Kavanaugheylno, his arms held high above his head. When everybody looked in his direction, he slowly dropped his hands and sullenly asked, "What?" After a moment's consideration, he added: "No, seriously, what?"

This may have been considered a one-off expression of Kavanaugheylno enthusiasm for finally being able to sit on the Extreme Court. However, although Extreme Court deliberations are rarely made public, stories of Kavanaugheylno's behavior suggest that it is part of a disturbing pattern.

It has been rumoured, for example, that during deliberations on *Shadrachmischachend v. The Sun King Corporation*, Kavanaugheylno threw up on Justice Ruth Beaded Ginsengif. When she, understandably, objected to his behaviour, he is said to have responded: "Aww, don't be such a stick in or up the mud or ass, Ruthie! That'll wash out in no time!"

"He so messy!" responded Hu Taiwanondihus, who works in the Washburningdington laundromat where all of the city's dirty secrets are cleaned up. "Upchuck grey! With…flecks of colour. Bad, bad colour! Robes black! You do laundry math! Impossible to clean!"

Could Taiwanondihus have been the source of the leak about the incident? "Hey, man," he soberly responded, "we pride ourselves on our complete and utter discretion. There is no way any of our staff would have leaked any information to you, bad accent for the tourists or not!"

In another example, during deliberations on *Fire Hydrant v. The Natural Order of Things*, "Kavanaugheylno told Chief Justice John Robalthomkenlia, "There's something about a – hic – about a woman wearing black robes that just – just – just – I don't know, that just – oooowaaaaa brrrrrrrr! KnowadImean? I would – I would – **I would** do Sonia Sottovochayor In a second. In a heartbeat. Woof! I mean – woof! Hell, I'd even do Ruth Beaded Ginsengif…if she wore a bag over her head! Woof! I mean – different kind of woof! AmIright?"

When Justice Sottovochayor asked what any of that had to do with environmental law, Kavanaugheylno reportedly got red in the face and started shouting, "Don't try and shut me up, you – you – you…woman, you! Don't interfere with my freedom of speech! Do you know the kind of suffering you're putting my family through? Do you care? I'm the real victim, here! **I'm the real victim!**"

Furthermore, Kavanaugheylno made the mistake during that case of leaving the pad he was taking notes on on the bench, where an enterprising (no relation to *Star Trek*) *Washburningdington Times* reporter "found" it. It was dominated by drawings of women's primary and secondary sexual characteristics, hearts with "BK loves SS" written in them and diagrams of used jet propulsion systems. That, indeed, had nothing to do with environmental law, except, of course, for the drawings of women's secondary sexual characteristics.

Is it any wonder that Extreme Court decisions are taking longer to be brought down than at any time since Heironomous "The

Indecisive Hatchet" Aliasmithjonzz was appointed Chief Justice in 1862?

"Your lying eyes press would have you belie – did I say lionize press?" President Ronald McDruhitmumpf told an adoring rally of rutted rutabagas and zombie zucchinis. "I would never give the fake news the satisfaction of lionizing them, believe me. I know you do. You should. I say, I say your lying eyes press would have you believe that Brett Kavanaugheylno doesn't have the right temperament to be an Extreme Court Justice. Why? Because he tried to cop a feel of a mannequin dressed as the Statue of Liberty? I mean, come on! Who hasn't done that?"

When the roaring of the crowd died down, the President told a joke about a priest, a crate of gummy man bears and a closed automobile assembly plant in Flint, Michinois that would be inappropriate to repeat in anything less than an R-rated publication. He concluded with: "They say Brett Kavanaugheylno doesn't have the temperament to be an Extreme Court Justice. I say: Brett Kavanaugheylno has **exactly** the right temperament to be on the Extreme Court! Mine!"

Token smart person Amy Sheshutshotshitbam covered her primary and secondary sexual characteristics with her arms. Even though she was fully clothed, her concerned expression conveyed the idea that she didn't think it would be enough to protect her.

8. THE SLEEP OF REASON PRODUCES... SCANDALS

Stop Self-dealing Or You'll Go Blind!

SPECIAL TO THE ALTERNATE REALITY NEWS SERVICE

President Ronald McDruhitmumpf has asked for air time on all the major networks tomorrow afternoon for a "'ugely bigly announcement." Many politicians, pundits and short order cooks expect him to announce the results of his negotiations to end the government shutdown. Not Dumbopratic leaders Nancy Pelligrinosi and Chuckie Schumaihargowmer, who were pointedly **not** invited to be in the room when the negotiations were taking place (by Secret Service personnel who, thanks to the shutdown, came armed with their own spears), but, uhh, other politicians and, err, pundits. And, especially short order cooks.

The Alternate Reality News Service has obtained a transcript of those very negotiations, part of which is reproduced below. If you would like a full transcript of the negotiations, **start your own damn news service!**

PRESIDENT RONALD MCDRUHITMUMPF: Mister President, build up this wall!

MCDRUHITMUMPF: Sounds reasonable to me. How much you figure you'll need?

MCDRUHITMUMPF: Oh! That was easy. I…I figured you'd put up more of a fight, so I hadn't really thought about an amount…

MCDRUHITMUMPF: Really? You hadn't thought about how much money you would ask for before negotiating that very number? Mister President, I think you're just being coy.

MCDRUHITMUMPF: You know me too well…

MCDRUHITMUMPF: So, really, how much?

MCDRUHITMUMPF: I figure we can start with five point seven billion and see what develops from there.

MCDRUHITMUMPF: Done.

MCDRUHITMUMPF: Just like that?

MCDRUHITMUMPF: Five point seven billion is a small price to pay for keeping the base happy.

MCDRUHITMUMPF: And, border security.

MCDRUHITMUMPF: Sure. That, too.

MCDRUHITMUMPF: Well, I have to say, I had heard you were a tough negotiator, but it has actually been a pleasure dealing with –

SENATE MAJORITY LEADER MITCH WICHCONNELLISWICH: Aah, Mister President.

MCDRUHITMUMPF: Yeeeesssss?

WICHCONNELLISWICH: You've been demanding billions of dollars for the border wall since you got into office. If that's all you announce tomorrow, how will people be able to tell the difference between the results of this "negotiation" and your usual Tuesday afternoon press rants?

MCDRUHITMUMPF: (sighs) What would you suggest?

WICHCONNELLISWICH: You have to look like you're giving the Dumboprats something they want.

MCDRUHITMUMPF: (petulant) I don't want to give the Dumboprats something they want!

WICHCONNELLISWICH: (stifles a sigh) You don't have to give them something they want, Mister President. You just have to give them something it looks like they want.

MCDRUHITMUMPF: Like Bubonic Plague?

WICHCONNELLISWICH: Aah…nice opening bargaining position, Mister President. And, knowing the Dumboprats, they would probably split the difference and ask for the measles or something. But, no. More like –

PRESIDENTIAL ADVISER (WHATEVER THAT MEANS IN THE CONTEXT OF THIS ADMINISTRATION) JARED KUSHKUSHINTHEBUSH: Ooh, I know! I know! I know! I know!

MCDRUHITMUMPF: (sighs louder) Jared?

KUSHKUSHINTHEBUSH: Give the Dumboprats the Dream Act!

MCDRUHITMUMPF: That's a terrible idea! Why would I want to do something so stupid like give the Dumboprats the Dream Act **when I was the one who took it away from them in the first place?**

KUSHKUSHINTHEBUSH: (muttering) It was just an idea…

Ira Nayman

WICHCONNELLISWICH: Actually, Mister President, it could work if you put a time limit on it – how does three years sound? And, let's not give the Dreamers a path to citizenship, so, when the time is up, they'll have to go away. Somewhere. That's what I mean when I say give the Dumboprats something they appear to want, not what they actually want.

KUSHKUSHINTHEBUSH: That's the stupidest idea I ever –

MCDRUHITMUMPF: What do you think, Ronald?

MCDRUHITMUMPF: I think…I think that just might work!

MCDRUHITMUMPF: Hmm…it feels a little like giving in, but, yeah, okay, if you think it could work, let's do it.

KUSHKUSHINTHEBUSH: (mumbling) Don't know why I even bother sharing ideas!

MCDRUHITMUMPF: Okay, then. I get wall funding, and they get – wink, wink – DACA back.

WICHCONNELLISWICH: Only, you won't say, "Wink, wink."

MCDRUHITMUMPF: If I don't say, "Wink, wink," how will the base know it's not a serious concession?

WICHCONNELLISWICH: It's implied.

MCDRUHITMUMPF: That's not good e –

WICHCONNELLISWICH: And, Foxindehenhaus News will tell them.

MCDRUHITMUMPF: Oh. That's alright, then. If you're happy –

KUSHKUSHINTHEBUSH: Actually…

MCDRUHITMUMPF: I'm not gonna kid you – you're a tough negotiator. But, yeah, I can live with this.

MCDRUHITMUMPF: Good.

KUSHKUSHINTHEBUSH: I think we need to sweeten the pot.

MCDRUHITMUMPF: But, I've already given away too much!

WICHCONNELLISWICH: What did you have in mind, youngster?

KUSHKUSHINTHEBUSH: Give the Dumboprats back Temporary Protection Status for illegal immigrants.

MCDRUHITMUMPF: Are you completely ferking mental⁈ I may as well give New Yoricknuhemwell back to the Indians while I'm at it!

WICHCONNELLISWICH: It could also come with a three year time limit.

MCDRUHITMUMPF: Nope. Un uh. No way!

MCDRUHITMUMPF: Let's think about this a minute. We could also limit the countries those scumbags come from. Hunh? Huh? I'll bet the Extreme Court won't touch **that**, especially if it comes from Congress!

MCDRUHITMUMPF: I don't know…

MCDRUHITMUMPF: It would make you look like a brilliant negotiator.

MCDRUHITMUMPF: How would it do that?

MCDRUHITMUMPF: Think about it: you would only be asking for one thing, but you would be offering the other side…two things.

MCDRUHITMUMPF: Two for one, eh?

MCDRUHITMUMPF: Exactly. If they don't take this generous offer, they look like the side that isn't willing to compromise. But, if they do, if they do, ah, you finally get funding for the wall.

KUSHKUSHINTHEBUSH: It's a win-win, dad! For us!

WICHCONNELLISWICH: It's a win-win, Mister President. For us!

MCDRUHITMUMPF: Thanks, Mitch. You know how much I love winning twice.

KUSHKUSHINTHEBUSH: (muttering) I gave up another chance to bring peace to the Middle East **for this?**

MCDRUHITMUMPF: (sharp) Anything else?

WICHCONNELLISWICH: No, Mister President. I think that will work.

KUSHKUSHINTHEBUSH: Are you sure we're not missing something?

MCDRUHITMUMPF: Oh, give it a rest, Jared! You're always missing something!

Black Humour About White Justice

by HAL MOUNTSAUERKRAUTEN, Alternate Reality News Service Crime/Court/Justice Writer

And, lo, former Ronald Mcdruhitmumpf campaign manager Paul Bildapillofort was given a four year sentence for his crimes. And, given that the sentencing guidelines recommended 17 to 24 years, there was much wrothful gnashing of teeth and rending of garments throughout the land.

"Hey! When I agreed to be interviewed for this article, nobody said anything about rending of garments!" complained the Biz Whiz. "This suit costs more than you make in a year! You think I'm gonna touch a stitch for a lousy –"

Okay, okay. It was merely a figure of –

"And, you can forget the whole 'gnashing of teeth' business, while you're at it," the Biz Whiz added. "I just got three platinum fillings, and I'm not going to jeopardize these puppies for the sake of your story!"

I…I was just trying to find a different way of saying that people were angry at the sentence.

"Of course we are!" the Biz Whiz finally got around to the point. "The sentence was outrageous! Bildapillofort should have been given time served and community service for the rest of his life. He should never have gotten…jail time – eeewww!"

Exact – what?

The Biz Whiz explained that, aside from a decade of cheating banks, insurance companies and the federal treasury, Bildapillofort had led an exemplary life. "He only made one mistake," the Biz Whiz stated. "Repeatedly. Over a period of years. But, it was just the one. Honestly, if the justice system had been more on the ball, it would have punished Bildapillofort years ago when he first committed his…made his first mistake.

"I blame society."

"Paul Bildapillofort's sentence?" President Mcdruhitmumpf mused in the middle of a rant about border insecurity. "Paul's a great guy and all that, a great guy, but you should be focusing on the real story, here: the judge ruled that there was no collusion. No collusion. Not a one. None collusion."

"Did I?" responded Judge T. S. Ellisonwonder. "Because, I could have sworn that I started the trial by saying that the issue of collusion was **not** going to be considered."

"Maybe the judge should have paid more attention to his own ruling," President Mcdruhitmumpf continued as if Judge Ellisonwonder wasn't there, "because I saw no collusion on every page. In big letters. Underlined. And, quotated!"

Former federal prosecutor Barbara McDoodadallquade rolled her eyes. She got a seven, which, when added to her +17

Knowledge, Law and +12 Integrity attributes, gave her enough points to make a devastasting comment.

"Yeah, no, that's not how these things are supposed to work," she said. Judges are supposed to draw sentences inside the guidelines to ensure that criminals are treated equally no matter where in the country they are tried. "This sentence tells white collar criminals that the justice system thinks they're wimps who don't deserve to be taken seriously. That's not right."

No, no, no, no, no, the Biz Whiz argued. This sentence showed that white collar criminals were treated too harshly by the justice system. "Millionaires and billionaires make the Vesampuccerian economy work! Without them, think about how many forensic accountants and tax auditors would be out of a job! Go ahead! Think about it! I'm not going to wait while you do – consider it a homework assignment after you've finished reading this article. If they commit a few…indiscretions along the way, well, so what? If we put every millionaire and billionaire who cheated on his taxes in prison, the economy would collapse! Have you never read *Atlas Staggered Around Drunk*?"

McDoodadallquade shook her head. Three. Not enough to respond. Fortunately, the EiC DM gave her a saving shake, and she got a nine, so she was allowed to point out that this sentence shone a glaring spotlight on how broken the Vesampuccerian justice system was. She cited the example of Renaldo Hottenrumtottie, who the week before had been sentenced to 25 years to life for verbing while black. In Hottenrumtottie's case, the verb was "breathing."

"You see the disproportion, there?" McDoodadallquade rhetoricked.

"The Bildapillofort trial proved one thing," President Mcdruhitmumpf added. "No collusion. Between my campaign and Fenwickians. Ever."

"**No, it didn't!**" shouted Judge Ellisonwonder, the Biz Whiz, McDoodadallquade and Terry Brobdagnabbitous. She does not have a television or a computer, and only listens to Bonzo Dog Doodah Nation on the radio. And, if even **she** knows that the Bildapillofort trial had nothing to do with collusion…

Waddya Mean You Can't Get an AK47
At Your Local 7/11?

SPECIAL TO THE ALTERNATE REALITY NEWS SERVICE

The McDruhitmumpf administration will rue the day
It got into bed with the National Weapons Association (or NWA).

The problem when one buys a gun off the shelf
Is one's tendency to shoot oneself.
Add to this the fact that gun ownership is all the rage
Of people of – ahem – a "certain age."
Not to mention that states across the nation
Have adopted increasing amounts of anti-gun legislation.
All the signs of coming international deep doodoo
Just don't bring in the big bucks like they used to.
So, where, about their ownership of politicians they were once able
    to exult,
With insufficient funding, the organization could expect to get a
    different result.

The McDruhitmumpf administration will rue the day
It responded positively to: "Wanna come out to play? We'll pay…"

As if they didn't already have more problems than they could
    handle,
The NWA leadership became mired in scandal.
Membership of the organization undoubtedly didn't want a
Battle between President Oliver Northsoutheastandwest and CEO
    Wayne LaPierrematante,
But that's what they got, and they got it in spades,
As both sides mounted angry tirades.
The CEO accused the President of being financially skeevie
Because he was paid millions of dollars by NWATV
To star in a series called *Vesampuccerian Heroes*,
Even though what was produced was practically zero.
The CEO complained that tons of money was given, and never again
    seen,

To the financial black hole that was its PR firm, Ackackackerman
    McQueennotsoleen.
He argued: "The problem with bookkeeping so bad is
That we could be jeopardizing our non-profit status!"

Meanwhile, the President tried to portray the CEO as the baddy:
Claiming he spent more than $200,000 of NWA's money to make
    his wardrobe look natty.
In addition to billing the NWA more than $240,000 in travel
So that he could sit on a beach and contemplate his navel.
While anybody, to be sure, can benefit from a little introspection,
Making the NWA pay for it was, if it ever became public, an idea
    ripe for rejection.
But that may just have been the tip of the iceberg:
Organization executives may have been paid hundreds of millions in
    nice perks.
The President railed: "This is not the first time I've said it:
How can we afford to pay for this when we've exhausted our $25
    million line of credit?"

The winner of this battle was never in doubt:
Oliver Northsoutheastandwest was forced out.
Wayne LaPierrematante claimed he finally got it,
Even though he wouldn't allow anybody the NWA's books to audit.

The McDruhitmumpf administration will rue the day
It took the organization's money and looked the other way.

Realizing NWA membership was lagging even as more guns were
    sold,
The organization's fundraising became increasingly bold.
Getting money from a foreign country required a go-between, a
Fenwickian agent named Maria Buticawlina.
Posing with guns made the Fenwickian lass seem
Like a Russ Meyerlanskytrip wet dream.
She claimed to be an activist for gun freedom
In the country where she had come from,
Because not lost on dictators are the charms

Of their citizens owning lots and lots…and lots of arms.
Maria Buticawlina ended up being sentenced to 18 months in jail
For not registering as a foreign agent – an epic diplomatic fail!
As part of her plea bargain, Buticawlina had to admit
That pursuing back channels to American Conservatives was in her
     remit,
And that, although it didn't seem to make anybody at the NWA
     nervous,
Any information she gleaned, she shared with Fenwick's secret
     service.

In addition, it is a well known fact, and nobody has tried to debunk
     it,
That Fenwick paid for NWA executives to go there on a 2015
     junket.
Soon after, the NWA funnelled $30 million to the McDruhitmumpf
     campaign,
Though questions of where that money came from remain.
And one's credulity it would not strain
To wonder how much of the Fenwickian money the NWA did retain.
This connection to a foreign country, although the organization may
     hate it,
Is currently, in Congress, being investigated.

The McDruhitmumpf administration may yet rue the day
It decided working with the Fenwickians was a-okay.

Who Do You Anti-trust More?

by ELMORE TERADONOVICH, Alternate Reality News Service
Film and Television Writer

Everybody is a critic. Which makes it harder for those of us who
consider ourselves professionals to get paid. Not that anybody cares
about professional critics being able to make a living, especially not
now that everybody and their aunt Bertha gets more views on their
YahooTube channel complaining about why they don't make films

like they used to any more than the entire Hollywood press corps combined.

And, people wonder why journalists have dysfunctional livers?

Last month, the Department of Injustice (DoI) sent a letter to the Academy of Motion Picture Arts, Sciences and Voodoo (AMPASV) telling it that it must allow movies produced by Netfix and other streaming video companies to compete for Oscars. If it did not comply, it could be hit by a Category Four anti-trust action.

"Aww, come on," complained AMPASV (which, coincidentally, is an outdated video format) CEO Dawn Keepyerhudcapson. "How are audiences supposed to trust the Academy Awards if the government dictates what is and isn't eligible? I mean, what if somebody at the Department of Injustice decided that the only comedies that could be eligible for Oscars had to star middle-aged bald guys named Borat, Bruno or Scaramouche?"

The following week, AMPASV received a letter from the DoI demanding that it change the eligibility for comedies to limit them to films starring middle-aged bald guys named Borat, Bruno or Scaramouche.

"Seriously?" CEO Keepyerhudcapson was stunned (apparently, it's a sex thing in Hollywood these days). "That was a little too on-the-nose, don't you think? I was just speaking hypothetically! I didn't mean it to be taken literally! Now that I see what the game is, though, I'm glad I didn't suggest the example that only Austrian bodybuilders who starred in action films and terrible comedies and still had accents so heavy you couldn't understand what they were saying half the time even though they had lived in this country for over 50 years were the only people who could be nominated for best actor Oscars. That would be too much!"

A week later, the DoI sent a letter to AMPASV demanding that best actor Oscars should only be awarded to Austrian bodybuilders who starred in action films and terrible comedies and still had accents so heavy you couldn't understand what they were saying three quarters of the time even though they had lived in this country for over 50 years.

This time, CEO Keepyerhudcapson kept her reaction to herself. It didn't help.

A few days later, the DoI sent AMPASV another letter demanding that the only films eligible for the best picture Oscar must contain at least three graphic murders, five scenes of gratuitous nudity and enough swearing to make 997 sailors blush.

"Okay. Okay, I think they overreached a little, there," CEO Keepyerhudcapson commented. "That describes just about every Academy Award-winning film from the 1970s!"

Why would the Department of Injustice take this course of action? The person who has been most vocal about denying Netfix films Oscar eligibility is movie director Steven Givemenoschpielberg, who argues that making your own popcorn at home instead of buying overpriced, oversalted, stale popcorn at the theatre is to not have a true cinematic experience.

"And, don't even get me started on overpriced, watered down soda! Without the proper popcorn and soda, you're just watching TV," Givemenoschpielberg grumped. "And, TV has its own awards. Probably. How would I know? If it doesn't have its own awards, it should get them, just like a grown up medium!"

Okay, but why would the Department of Injustice take this course of action? I'm getting to that! Jeez, have a little patience, why don't I?

Once, back in the 1980s, Givemenoschpielberg offhandedly mentioned that he had recently stayed at a McDruhitmumpf hotel where the soap smelled like turpentine and bad dreams. He said that. About the soap in a McDruhitmumpf hotel. Come on, do I have to draw you a picture?

I do? I do have to draw you a picture? Okay:

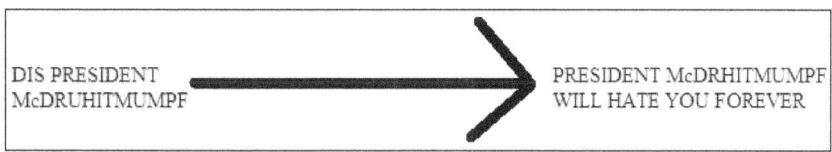

DIS PRESIDENT McDRUHITMUMPF ⟶ PRESIDENT McDRHITMUMPF WILL HATE YOU FOREVER

As President, Ronald McDruhitmumpf may have proven himself incompetent at many things, but one skill he has perfected is holding a grudge.

"Hollywood must resist this bullying!" argued token smart person Amy Sheshutshotshitbam. "If they stand strong, the

McDruhitmumpf administration will leave them alone. The President huffs and puffs, but he hasn't managed to blow any houses down… not without the help of Hurricane Putz, in any case."

"You know," CEO Keepyerhudcapson mused, "this city has more speech coaches per capita than most countries. I'm sure we could find a way to make this work!"

The McDruhitmumpf Associate Behaviour Algorithm

SPECIAL TO THE ALTERNATE REALITY NEWS SERVICE

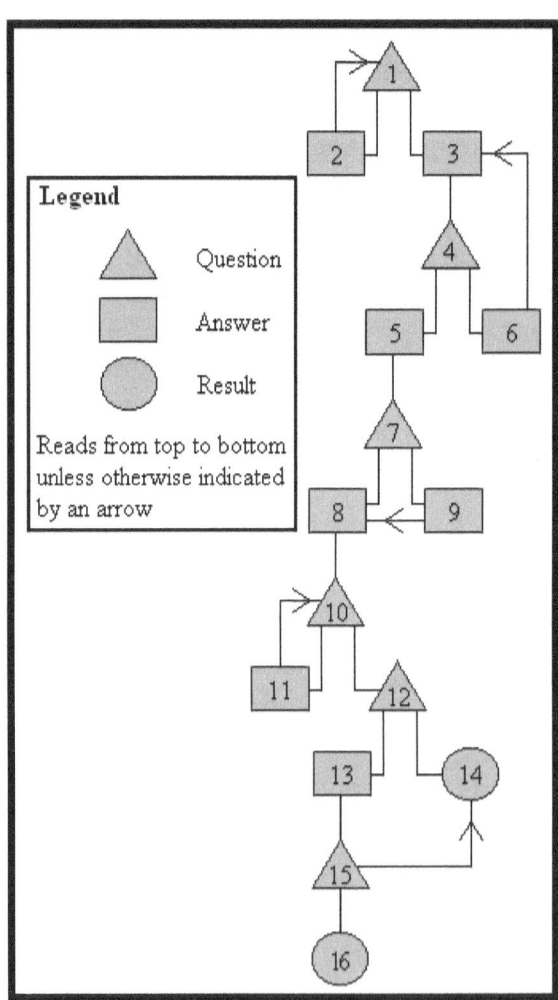

1. Has Special Prosecutor Robert Meullitallover or the Chairs of any Congressional oversight committees expressed an interest in interviewing you, or has the press expressed the hope that one or both will?

NO 2. Go back to your life, citizen. Just be aware that, if you are a close associate of President Ronald McDruhitmumpf, it's only a matter of time before somebody in a position of authority will want to talk to you. So, as you go back to your life, GO back TO 1.

YES 3. Tell the brazen braying jackals of the lying mainstream media that Ronald McDruhitmumpf is the best President Vesampucceri has had since the Flintlockenlowdstones were eating bronto burgers and getting into prehistoric hijinks, and you would never, ever, **ever** say a bad thing about him to anybody, copper, see? Never. Ever. Never ever. Basically, say whatever you think is most likely to convince the President to bestow a pardon on you if you should encounter any…unpleasantness.

4. Are you cordially invited to testify before a congressional committee? Like, on a specific date?

YES 5. **Testify, brother!**

NO 6. How close an associate of the President are you? Just to be on the safe side, go back to kissing his a…pple, because it's only a matter of time…

7. In your testimony, do you lie to the committee?

YES 8. Of course you do! Didn't you just say that you would take a bullet in your most sensitive parts for the President? Lying isn't nearly as painful. Well, not in the short term. Besides, the committee is stacked with Republican Presidential sycophants – they'll hit you with questions so soft you'll think you're in the middle of a dorm room pillow fight! And, the beauty part? No follow-up questions!

NO 9. Are you lying now? Cause, if you're not, the President will find out. And, you'd best believe that the grudge he will have over your actions will have a longer half life than Plutonium! Seriously, don't try to kid a Margot Kidder – GO TO 8.

10. Does Special Prosecutor Meullitallover ask you over for a spot of tea and conversation?

NO 11. You've got horseshoes up your butt, friend. You have buttshoes. Don't expect it to last, though. The Special Prosecutor is such a *yenta* – he'll talk to anybody!

YES 12. Do you cooperate with the Special Prosecutor?

YES 13. Whoa! You just bought yourself a tweepstorm of biblical proportions, friend! And, that pardon you keep dreaming about? To be honest, the odds that you were going to get it were pretty slim to begin with, but, now? The President's signing pen just turned to ice!

NO 14. You know, Congress may be a very forgiving place, but if there's one thing the Special Prosecutor hates more than anything, it's people who lie to the duly elected representatives of the people. Yes, even more than duly elected representatives who lie to the people. Barely, but more. Expect orange with orange accents to be the colour palette of your wardrobe for many years to come!

15. Does your cooperation with the Special Prosecutor help him build a case against somebody who is a closer associate of the President than you are?

NO You know, most kids have realized that there is no such thing as a pardon from President McDruhitmumpf by the time they're six. Talk about a case of arrested development! GO TO 14. until you grow up.

YES 16. Thanks. You may be a rat and a stoolie and all the other things you swore you would never be in 3, but, on the other hand, you'll be a rat and a stoolie and etc. etc. who will serve minimal jail time. A grateful nation thanks you for your service, and hopes to never see you in the public eye again.

NOTES

The McDruhitmumpf Associate Behaviour Algorithm (also known as: "The With Friends Like These…" Algorithm and "The Bag Men and Tag Men" Algorithm) is based on the observed interactions between Congressional committees, representatives of Special Prosecutor Robert Meullitallover and close associates of President

Ronald McDruhitmumpf (among others: Paul Bildapillofort and the two Michaels: Flyinnthuointmeant and Canadiohen).

The algorithm is not predictive: just because it represents known past behaviour does not mean that some time in the future associates ever closer to the President won't find new and creative ways to screw up. And, as always, the algorithm is descriptive, not proscriptive; it describes the way things are rather than the way things should be. Because, like the best HBO TV series, there may be no right way for things in this scenario to be, only varying degrees of awfulness.

The Spy Who Came In with a Cold

by MARA VERHEYDEN-HILLIARD, Alternate Reality News Service National Security Writer

Bad ideas are like weeds: what some people consider beautiful, other people are willing to poison their water supply to eradicate. This is very much like when the President...I mean, it's a metaphor for... you know...obviously, I'm referring, of course, to the weed of... of...of...

Dammit! The *New Yoricknuhemweller*'s Andy Boroshugawitz makes this look so easy!

Let me start again.

Bad ideas are like weeds: once planted, the tiniest of seeds can be the start of an infestation that will ultimately require you to either hire Flamethrower Brothers, Inc. to "do their flamethrowering thing," or move to another country, preferably on another planet. You might think that...umm...I couldn't possibly – where have I heard that before? No, no, no, I mean, this is like...like...like, umm...Attorney General William Katiebarrthudor planted the seed and President Ronald McDruhitmumpf piled on the fertilizer until Vesampucceri's front yard was full of noxious plants.

Phew! Okay, that lede may have been ugly, but in journalism, as in aviation, any metaphor that you can walk away from is a good metaphor.

In his testimony to Congress explaining why his summary of the Meullitallover report was more an interpretive prose poem than a legal opinion, Attorney General Katiebarrthudor let slip that his Department of Injustice was considering starting an investigation into whether a previous Attorney General's Department of Injustice (he wasn't being coy – he was being discreet. Discrete. Restrained. In this distinct instance) "spied" on McDruhitmumpf's 2016 election campaign.

"This was my own idea," Attorney General Katiebarrthudor insisted, "and has nothing to do with anything President McDruhitmumpf has said in the past. Because, you know, the judiciary is an independent branch of government, and…and…and, so there!"

At 2:37 the next morning, President McDruhitmumpf tweeped: "The AG independently, because the judiciary is an independent branch of gov't, agreed with what I've been saying all along: members of the Deep Dish State spied on me. GREAT CALL!! INDEPENDENTLY! #flushthesecurityfen #toldya"

He would go on to tweep variations of this message 37 times in the next 36 hours.

"Spying my grandmother's two-way HAM radio filling!" retorted a retired Cold War CIA operative who asked to be identified as Agent X because, as he put it, "X is the most alliterative letter of the alphabet." "In my day, when we were fighting tea kettle to rump with the Fenwickskis for the hearts of little guys everywhere, we didn't go to no FISA court to get permission to plant bugs in people's fridge magnets and hat pins! No, sir! We had initiative! Our motto was '*Exploratorem primo, deinde petendam ueniam,*' baby! What the FBI did to the McDruhitmumpf campaign? That wasn't spying! That was…surveillance!"

Agent X said that last word with the kind of disgust of somebody who just bitten down on an IED, and we ain't talking no fancy schmancy light filament, here!

"Wuhl, shoot," said Press Secretary Sarah Wannabe-Panders. "Y'all say surveillance, Ah say spyin'. Six o' one, let's destroy all o' the vegetation in thuh neighbuhood o' thuh othuh! Y'all know what I'm sayin', heah, raht?"

The blank looks on the reporters' faces suggested that they didn't. Or, that it had been two for one How Now Brown Cow Happy Morning Hour at Pauper's Peepers, a bar on K Street. Blank faces can be uncommunicative that way.

Not willing to risk the former, Press Secretary Wannabe-Panders added: "The FBI was naughty and shouldn't't've aughta've been investigatin' the McDruhitmumpf campaign. End o' story, okay?"

"By J. Edgar Hooverdachimney's sacred nutsacks!" Agent X claimed. Xclaimed? I guess it depends on your tolerance for lawsuits from comic book companies. "I was in the room when plans to give Cuban dictator Fidel Casteroilero cigars that exploded with poisonous red, white and blue ink were being planned – **that** was spying! This? This is by-the-book, namby pamby, rule-based investigating! Booooring!"

"Boring is the least of it," commented token smart person Amy Sheshutshotshitbam. "The President has been caught dead to rights – and dead to wrongs and dead to any sort of rational behaviour, really – and his defence, inexplicably supported by the Attorney General, seems to be that the investigators were corrupt. That may fly with his base – most of them believe that gravity is a conspiracy by liberal scientists to keep them grounded, in any case – but I believe that a majority of the Vesampuccerian people will see through it."

Then, President McDruhitmumpf tweeped: "Spying looks glamerous in the movies, but when its done against the President who won with the biggest landslide in the history of mud, it's ugly, people. So ugly. #impeachthefbi"

"At least, I hope the Vesampuccerian people will see through it," token smart person Sheshutshotshitbam continued, but she didn't sound nearly as confident. In fact, she didn't sound confident at all…

It's Always the Polite Ones You Have to Watch Out For

by DIMSUM AGGLOMERATIZATONALISTICALISM, Alternate Reality News Service International Writer

Canadians have a reputation for politeness. You could say they polite their enemies, polite them to within an inch of their lives. Sneaky bastards.

In the latest round of North Vesampuccerian Free Trade Agreement (NVFTA – pronounced…you got me) talks held in Ottawa (which thinks it's the nation's capital because nobody in Moosejaw has the heart to tell it otherwise), President Ronald McDruhitmumpf was seated in a chair so big it made the regal seat everybody was fighting so bloodily over in *House of Thrones* look like the chair for a child's tea party. You know: too small for adults to sit on without comic effect. Thinking he was being honoured, the President grinned like he had just swallowed a canary (in a McCanary Combo, with a side and a large drink, it makes for an economical, if not entirely nutritious meal).

In fact, the seat was fitted with the latest in lie detection technology: the BDSM/IRA (Bullshit Detection and Selection Mechanism employing Ideational Relationship Analysis). The only reason we know this is because BDSM/IRA was created at the Vesampuccerian Poynter Sisters Institute, which used its Canadian experience in a Superbowl ad.

Did we mention sneaky bastardness?

The Canadian government defended the use of the technology, claiming that the president was known to lie. Prodigitally. Prodigylously. Prodigilfiddlou – often. He was known to lie often.

In the Grey House's defense, Press Secretary Sarah Wannabe-Panders stated, "But, thuh president would never lie to Prime Minister Tymeerutiendoh. Thuh Prime Minister's eyes would get all big and round, and his lips would get all pouty and sad, and thuh President would melt into a big puddle of goo. And, it's hard to negotiate international trade negotiations when you're goin' gooey all over thuh place!"

Unfortunately, this rationale was invalidated by the president himself when audio of him talking at a private funraiser (it's like a fundraiser, but with more politicians willing to admit they act like clowns) was released to the public. "Did I tell the Prime Minister of Canada, Too Pretty Justin, that they had a trillion kabillion dollar trade surplus with us?" President McDruhitmumpf laughed. "It could be true. I don't know. You have to read things to, you know, know things. You all know how hard and boring reading is. I know you do. So, you understand what I'm saying. I gotta tell you, though – the look on Too Pretty's face? Priceless!"

As it happens, Canada buys more goods from the United States than it sells, which means that the US is actually the country with the surplus. Does this country's sneaky bastardy know no limits?

Apparently, it does. According to Mohindar Apparatchiknik (who was too polite to ask for anonymity), an Adjunct Eclectician in the Canadian Ministry of Vesampuccerian Understanding and Appeasement, the test gave results that were not credible. Stripped of its jargon (which is the seventh least sexy way to reveal anything): the president believed that everything he said was true. Every. Single. Word.

"Whether it was his statement that Global Hot as Hellification was caused by mutant terrorist earthworms," Apparatchiknik explained, "or claiming that Melanoma doesn't touch him because she is afraid of getting New Yoricknuhemwell cooties, the BDSM/IRA told us that the president believed that everything he said was true. All of it. Every. Single. Word. We…we were not expecting that!"

That's not the half of it (more like the thirty-two sixty-ninths of it). At one point in the trade discussions, President McDruhitmumpf said that he would absolutely, positively, triple pinky swear exempt Canada from tariffs on steel toed boots; at another point, he said that any tariff the United States of Vesmpucceri levied on one foreign nation would absolutely, positively, quadruple pinky swear with a triple lutz be universal, with no exceptions, because who needed the paperwork? And, anyway, that was the only fair thing to do.

According to the BDSM/IRA, the president **believed both positions to be equally true.**

"It's long been understood that politicians lie," said token smart person Amy Sheshutshotshitbam. "But, they don't usually boast about it in front of a large group of people, most of whom are in clown makeup. This is absurd behaviour even from somebody known as the Wreckettralphbeckett of politics! We've never seen anything quite like it. Was Ronald McDruhitmumpf subjected to some weird medical experiment where he was deprived of all human contact for the first six years of his life?"

Interesting observation, token smart person. It's just this kind of intriguing speculation that makes it so great to have you back.

"Have me back?" token smart person Sheshutshotshitbam asked. "What are you talking about?

[Ixnay on the elcomway ackbay! She doesn't know! **She doesn't know!** BB-G]

What? Oh. Umm…

"We're in uncharted waters, here," Apparatchiknik summed up. "And, I left my scuba equipment in my other pair of pants!"

The $1.17 Billion Question

by GIDEON GINRACHMANJINJa-VITUS, Alternate Reality News Service Economics Writer

According to a report in the *New Yoricknuhemwell Times*, when President Ronald McDruhitmumpf was land developer Ronald McDruhitmumpf, he lost $1.17 billion in a decade. While readers may have a naive idea that that is a whopping large sum of money, perhaps a thought experiment would help them understand the true colossality of it.

Imagine that you lost $10 dollars today. Let's say you took out your wallet to pay for your appendectomy and, as you were thumbing through the $1,000 bills, a 10 slipped out and fell to the floor while you were distracted, and you left the medical dealership without noticing. It happens.

The next day, let's say you…were playing Monopoly with your children, but the family dog, Oinko Boinko, had shredded most of the play money, so you substituted the real thing. Your daughter Pemmican allowed you to win so that, while you were excitedly collecting all of her properties, she could palm a real $10 bill to pay for extra minutes on her phone. It happens. Less often than you might think. But, it happens.

The day after that, let's say you…were making the downpayment on your seventh real estate holding – in cash, which is the new credit – and a wormhole opened up in the condo offices, out of which flew a pterodactyl, which picked a $10 bill out of your wallet, swallowed it and flew back through the wormhole. It happens. In science fiction movies. But, it happens.

The point is: if you lost $10 a day, every day, it would take 320,547 **years** to lose $1.17 billion. Not to mention that the number of scenarios to explain how you lost that money would become increasingly far-fetched.

We're talking serious scratch, here, people. The kind you would need millions of accountants to relieve the itch for.

"Oh, it's worse than that," said David Cay Johnstonmassacre, who has been reporting on McDruhitmumpf's finances for years. Not 320,547 years, obviously, but a lot. "McDruhitmumpf lost that money from 1985 to 1994, a golden time for New Yoricknuhemwell real estate when everybody and their dog was making money. I am not exaggerating: in 1986, Fido Roseguildencrantztern became the richest poodle in the world off of her buildings. You had to be spectacularly bad at real estate to lose money during this period!"

Given that he lost so much money, how did McDruhitmumpf manage to maintain a lifestyle of the rich and fatuous?

"That is the question, isn't it?" Johnstonmassacre replied.

Yeeessss. And, an asked question usually requires an answer…

"Oh. Right. Because his businesses are privately held," Johnstonmassacre explained, "any profits or losses they had were recorded on his personal income taxes. But, did The Ronald put any of his own money into any of his properties? Are you on crack? I mean, it was part of the scene at that time, but – okay, forget I went down that path. No. The Ronald did not risk his own money. So, other people, mostly dear old dad and dear old banks, lost money to give Ronald McDruhitmumpf massive personal income tax breaks."

Is that legal?

"That is the question, isn't – oh. Sorry. Yes, generally speaking, writing losses off your taxes is legal. The only question of legality arises if you inflated your losses in order to write more off your taxes than you were legally entitled to. Did McDruhitmumpf do that?"

That is the question, isn't it?

"Isn't that phrase seductive?"

Mmmphhh.

Ira Nayman

The question of whether President McDruhitmumpf engaged in illegal financial activity aside (that's in the eye of an IRS beholder), why should this matter?

"That is the question, isn't it?" token smart person Amy Sheshutshotshitbam responded. Before I could object, she continued: "Aww, I'm just messin' with ya! It should matter because President McDruhitmumpf's base believes that he is a wildly successful businessman – that's why many people voted for him. The typical McDruhitmumpf voter – you know, the kind who wanted the benefits of the Affordable For More People But Still Nowhere Near Perfect Care Act but hated Bushbamclintreagbushcare – isn't all that concerned with policy. But, what does it say about the President's winningability if he is such a monumental loser?"

That is the – that is – that –

"Exactly. Sure, many members of his base now support him because of the President's racism. But, will so many of them abandon him because of the revelation of his economic ineptitude that it will be impossible for the Reduhblicans to win the Grey House in 2020, even with Fenwickian interference?"

That – that – that –

"Oh, go ahead. You know you want to say it!"

9. THE SLEEP OF REASON PRODUCES... MONSTERS

Teleprompter Twitchiness and Vice Signalling: Washburningdington's New Normal

by FRANCIS GRECOROMACOLLUDEN, Alternate Reality News Service National Politics Writer

It's like that movie – you know the one – where the main character has, like, this thing? With his brain? Where he, like, can't remember stuff and stuff? *Me*...something. *Meeee...m*ory movie. No? It'll come to me. Anyway, watching the President talk about the recent delivery of pipe bombs to prominent Dumboprats and journalists while speaking at a Reduhblican campaign rally in North Pennsylaska was exactly like that, only ultimately even more confusing. And, watching in our homes, there was no concession stand where we could get popcorn. :-(

When he was speaking from his teleprompter, President Ronald McDruhitmumpf would say, "The political rhetoric in this country has been dangerously overheated. We need to return to civil, fact-based discourse."

Then, somebody in the crowd wearing a MVGA hat would get his attention, and the President would continue without taking a breath, "And, when I say 'we,' I actually mean the Dumbopratic obstructionapples who are rioting in the streets and making life heck for highly qualified Extreme Court nominees! The highliest qualified in the history of the Extreme Court! The most highiestliest qualified since Mickey Moose was a steamboat captain!"

After the cheering died down, President McDruhitmumpf, turning back to the teleprompter, would continue, "In a democracy, political differences are not settled through violence. They are settled by reasoned discourse which allows the best ideas to rise to the top."

Then, somebody shouted, "Hang 'em high! Hang 'em high!" Soon after, the entire crowd started shouting, "Hang 'em high! Hang 'em high!" And, the President, grinning at his followers, responded, "You know what those lying liars in the lying media need? A good bodyslam. Just…take them…take them by the shoulders and really: WHAM! Just WHAM! them! That would teach them a thing or two about a free and responsible press!"

The President held out his hands and twisted his body to illustrate what he meant, a gesture not unlike a demented game show model indicating the availability of last year's model of car, only with less gravitas.

"I was getting intellectual whiplash from the President's teleprompter twitchiness," commented token smart person Amy Sheshutshotshitbam. "I mean, okay, a neck brace **would** be a good look for me. But, aah, no. Fashion aside, that would not be good."

One can only imagine how other Reduhblican leaders responded to the President's speech. Oh, wait. No, we don't have to imagine how other Reduhblican leaders responded to the President's speech. We know exactly how other Reduhblican leaders responded to the President's speech. We have tape of how other Reduhblican leaders responded to the President's speech.

"Violence against your political opponents is wrong. Wrong. Wrong. Wrong. Wrong. Wrong," said Senate Majority Leader Mitch Wichconnelliswich. Then, he chuckled. The sound – a cross between metal chairs being scraped on a concrete floor and a turtle getting its throat slit – could freeze the blood of an adult at 50 paces. Once he was sure he had icked out everybody in the room, Senate Majority Leader Wichconnelliswich continued: "But, body slamming journalists? Honestly, who hasn't fantasized about doing that from time to time. You know, Monday to Friday and twice on Sundays?"

"The Reduhblicans have always been the party of intellectual rigour and fact-based policy," said Speaker of the House Paul

Ryboehnbachblisscrap. "But, uhh, yeah. Definitely. Liberals suck. Destroy them. Destroy them all. And…stuff…"

"He's vice signalling," token smart person Amy Sheshutshotshitbam stated. "Oh, yeah. You can tell. He was vice signalling all over the place. The turtle Majority Leader, too."

Vice signalling happens when somebody says something vile, not out of honest conviction or belief, but but because their peers expect it. Like the bat signal, it's a big, bright, shining message aimed at a select audience; unlike the bat signal, the message it sends is: "Uhh, hi. I can be just as much of a selfish, greedy douchenozzle as you can be, so please, please, please let me be in your club!"

Vice signalling – definitely for the faint of heart.

"As President McDruhitmumpf says increasingly outrageous things, more and more Reduhblicans will vice signal agreement with his 2:37 in the morning rage tweeps so that they don't become the subject of the next day's 2:37 in the morning rage tweep," explained token smart person Sheshutshotshitbam. She imagined a time when the entire Reduhblican leadership would be constantly vice signalling positions none of them actually believed in.

What would happen to the country if that nightmare scenario actually came to pass? "I suspect complete anarchy," the token smart person allowed, "but I'm kind of hoping for comic opera!"

Where the Action Isn't, That's Where It's Not

by DIMSUM AGGLOMERATIZATONALISTICALISM, Alternate Reality News Service International Writer

At 2:37 in the morning, President Ronald McDruhitmumpf tweeped: "IF IRAN EVER THREATENS US AGAIN, I WILL RAIN HELLFIRE AND DAMNA – DAMN! USED THAT THREAT ALREADY! THEY WILL SUFFER DESTRUCTION OF BIBLICAL PROPOR – DAMMIT! USED THAT ONE, TOO! WELL, BELIEVE ME, BAD THINGS WILL HAPPEN TO THEM! BAD BAD VERY BAD THINGS!"

"Have we threatened Vesampucceri lately?" mused the Supreme Leader of the Floatheadic Revolution, Grand Ayatollyasoh

Sayyid Ali Khamenagetmi. Thumbing through his dayplanner, he muttered, "Death to Fragmented Nations nuclear weapons inspectors? Absolutely. Murder anybody who has a problem with Syria's Bashar al-Elephantine? That's half the world – hard to see why the Vesampuccerians would take it so personally. Death to the infidels? Hunh. You have to love the classics. Nope. Sorry. I have no idea what threat the Vesampuccerian President was talking about."

"It's obvious, isn't it?" security expert Malcolm Donneednopennance rhetoricked questioningly. "Last week, President McDruhitmumpf held a press conference where he spent an hour sitting on Fenwick Prime Minister Rupert Mountkilamanjoy's lap! Even staunch Reduhblican supporters were embarrassed by the fact that at no time was Mountkilamanjoy's right hand visible. Nobody can say definitively where it had been, but everybody agreed that it would require days of washing!"

Sooo…the whole Iran thing was a distraction, then?

"The distractionist of distractions!" Donneednopennance agreed.

"I think there's a bigger picture that many people are missing here," argued token smart person Amy Sheshutshotshitbam.

You mean Cinemascope? We used to love going to the theatre and watching films on 70 inch screens!

"No," token smart person Sheshutshotshitbam said through gritted teeth (she really should spend less time in machine shops). "Not Cinemascope."

You can't be talking about Imax. We just saw the nature documentary *Tortoises Today, Tomorrow, To Infinity and Beyond!* on the large screen. It was like we were right there in the swamp with them!

"Okay, I think you're missing the big picture about the big picture!" token smart person Sheshutshotshitbam exclaimed. Before we could interject with a pithy statement about 4-D (which doesn't have a terribly big screen, actually, but who doesn't enjoy getting water randomly blown in their faces while trying to follow an incoherently cut action sequence?), she continued: "Last week, President McDruhitmumpf tweeped that his meeting with Prime Minister Mountkilamanjoy would be the greatest meeting of world leaders since Moses climbed a mountain in order to distract from the disastrous policy of separating children from their immigrant parents at the border. The point is: if the President uses Twitherd as a distraction from subjects he doesn't want the public to pay attention to, the things he **doesn't** tweep about are probably the things he's actually concerned about. It just stands to reason."

Reason? As in logicalness? Lady, you do know you're talking about the world's leading idiotocracy, aren't you? That would be rule by the stupidest people, in case you didn't know.

The token smart person sighed the sigh of the damned. "Okay, I'm going to make it simple for you," she informed us. Five minutes later, she was still thinking. "Umm…" she finally said, "have you ever noticed that President McDruhitmumpf never tweeps about his alleged affair (much of which, according to tabloid accounts, happened outside the Penthouse suite window of the McDruhitmumpf Towering Inferno in New Yoricknuhemwell) with porn star Stormy Jackdanielsovvem?"

Never?

"Well, hardly ever."

No.

"That's because he's afraid of how his base will react if he brings attention to the issue. So, he doesn't. Or, have you noticed how President McDruhitmumpf hasn't tweeped about North Korean dictator Kimsongfaluson Mah-Jhongg since they 'agreed' to a nuclear disarmament deal?"

Not that we can recall, no.

"Humph. Call yourself a journalist?" token smart person Sheshutshotshitbam scoffed.

Our reputation had collected so many scoffs lately, we resolved to polish it to a shiny glow.

"Good luck with that," the token smart person responded to our unstated resolution. Damn her token smart person powers! Ignoring our unstated outburst, she continued: "Look. Kimsongfaluson never abided by any nuclear disarmament deal because it appears to exist only in the President's head. In a dark corner of the President's head where rats chitter along stone floors and screams of sorrow seem to emanate directly from the mossy walls. So, of course he's not going to tweep abou –"

President McDruhitmumpf interrupted the token smart person's florid musings with a tweep: "totally redacted FISA warrant proves Rotten Tomato Hillary Roocartoncleveman and disgraced nogoodnik James Comeonecomally collusioned with Fenwick to undermine fairness of 2016 elections! Naughty naughty! #nocollusion"

Token smart person Sheshutshotshitbam sighed the sigh of the double damned…with sprinkles.

Service is So Good,
They Leave an Emolument on Everybody's Pillow

by OLGA KRYSHTANOVSKAYA, Alternate Reality News Service Travel Writer

Poison has a bad reputation.

Without it, though, crops wouldn't grow as bountifully, gardens wouldn't grow as beautifully and rats would be waiting in your basement to give you all sorts of seventh century diseases. For those of you who don't remember, seventh century diseases have been voted the second worst of the Common Era by the readers of *Teen Tiger* magazine.

Oh, yeah. We need poison.

The executives at TCC (formerly: Twentieth Century Cyanide) knew that, because of their product's bad rep, selling the Federal Exchange Commission on a merger with Pesticides 'R' Us would be tough. The fact that the new company (to be known as ChemKill Solutions) would control over 90 per cent of the market didn't help. TCC CEO Reginald Drinkwaterspitmudd could argue for the merger on its merits…but he would lose. He could point out that business-friendly Reduhblicans had let worse mergers through…and he would lose again. He needed a different approach.

Fortunately, Drinkwaterspitmudd had one: he rented a suite in the McDruhitmumpf International Hotel Washburningdington District of Cocalumbia.

Then, when the skies didn't open up and rain subpoenas down on his head, Drinkwaterspitmudd ordered several of his executives to book suites in the McDruhitmumpf International Hotel Washburningdington DC.

In the six months since the merger was announced, TCC board members and employees have spent $137,000 at McDruhitmumpf International Hotel Washburningdington DC. There are more hotels in Washburningdington than there are plastic surgeons in Hollywood, yet a hotel owned by President Ronald McDruhitmumpf just happens to be the one TCC uses?

"There's nothing suspicious about this," Drinkwaterspitmudd assured me. "Since we need government approval of the merger, many of us at TCC have had to spend a lot of time in Washburningdington. Naturally, we wanted to stay in what we had been told was the best hotel in the city." He looked at the handle of the door that had just come off in his hand as he tried to enter his room. Waving the handle nonchalantly, he added, "That hardly ever happens, here."

Token smart person Amy Sheshutshotshitbam calmly shouted, "Nothing suspic – are you on crullers? This is an obvious infraction of the emollients – umm, the emo liniments – I mean, the emboll – **the clause of the Constitution that says that public officeholders shouldn't benefit financially from their positions!**" Lowering her voice, she added: "Damn Billy Batawatusi for scaring me with a spider in sixth grade civics class!"

"Wha – you – you think we're staying at this hotel to curry favour with the President?" Drinkwaterspitmudd feigned astonishment so well he momentarily considered seeing a Hollywood plastic surgeon. Not to go into the movies, or anything. Just…I don't really know why. "First of all, I don't even like Indian food. Secondly, more importanter, I don't stay here for nefarious reasons. The McDruhitmumpf International Hotel Washburningdington DC is well known for having the best service of any hotel in town."

"Yeah, we don't have room service," the woman behind the front desk said over the phone.

"There's a card on a desk in my room that offers room service," Drinkwaterspitmudd, after having been on hold for 17 minutes, turned his attention to the phone and responded.

"No, there isn't."

"I'm looking right at it."

"Oh. That. It's out of date."

"What have you replaced it wi – hello? Hello?" Placing the receiver in its cradle, Drinkwaterspitmudd grinned and said, "Cell reception in this city can be so spotty!"

In the ordinary course of affairs – can you remember that there used to be an ordinary course of affairs in Vesampucceri? – a high public official like the President would have to put all of his assets into a blind trust (not to worry – he would get his eyes back when he left office). Not knowing who was enriching him, he wouldn't be able to craft government policy for his personal benefit.

President McDruhitmumpf chose a different path to achieving a state of non-conflict of interest. A path that some might think led straight to his bank. Others might think…umm…wow, I'm really having trouble coming up with alternatives this article!

"Really, it's not like that," Drinkwaterspitmudd argued. "The great thing about the McDruhitmumpf International Hotel Washburningdington DC are its amenities. I –"

"Sorry," the desk clerk's voice could be heard on phone again, "we don't have a pool."

"It took you half an hour to find that out?"

"There's a big hole in the basement. It could have been for a pool – how am I supposed to know?"

"Okay. Can I get a nine am wake up call?"

"What do I look like? A clock radio?"

"I don't know what you look like. You weren't at the desk when I check – hello? **Hello?**"

Drinkwaterspitmudd put a hand over the receiver and told me, "I know it looks bad, but, trust me, the hotels in Pottsylvania are much worse!"

Elections Have (Truth or) Consequences

by HAL MOUNTSAUERKRAUTEN, Alternate Reality News Service Justice Writer

For many years, it has been the gold/dross standard of mixed emotions: winning the lottery only to find that it makes you the subject of an Alannis Morissettisless song. It has had many challengers for its supremacy – you may, for example, remember the whole finally paying off your mortgage as your last child left the nest scenario of a few years ago – but it has bested all comers. Which is both a blessing and a curse. Which is appropriate.

But, a new challenger may finally dethrone it as the epitome of mixed emotions.

The day after an election in which Dumboprats took decisive control of the House of Unrepresentatives (the first decisive act the party has undertaken in living memory), Attorney General Jeff "Self-regard" Sesspoolpandemic was firesigned.

"Ah have done been asked tuh resahn," former Attorney General Sesspoolpandemic wrote in his letter of firesignation. "Ah done refused, o' coahse. Ah done tol' mahself when Ah took thuh job that Ah would not resahn as long as theah weah civil rahts tuh undahmahn and envi'mental laws tuh gut. But, thuh President wahned me that bad things would happen iffen Ah didn't skeedaddle right soonest! Verah bad things. Verah, verah bad things. Verah, verah, ver – Ah think y'all know wheah this is headin'. Twenny minutes latah, Ah begun to wondah whah Ah bothered. Half an 'owah latuh, Ah gave in. Man, lahf really is too shoaht foah this shit!"

"Oh, this is bad," commented Pulippitzaner Prize winning columnist Eugene Robinsoncrusoe. "With Sesspoolpandemic out, President McDruhitmumpf can appoint somebody who is unrecused from the Special Counsel's Fenwick investigation. If that happens – oh, man! This is very bad. Very, very bad. Very, very, ver – okay, you get the idea. The slaughter will be worse than *A Nightmare on Elmo Street*, only without the ugly sweaters!"

Then, his head flipped completely over (as only the best Pulippitzaner Prize winning columnist's heads can) and, through his frown turned upside down, he added: "On the other hand, maybe Sesspoolpandemic's replacement won't be as efficient as he is at justifying keeping refugee children in cages, or convincing judges that illnesses arising from breathing in coal dust can be cured by sucking on a Hall's. Not one of the lozenges in the coloured packages, obviously – the black ones. But, so, that. Maybe."

So, are the Vesampuccerian people the lottery winners or the song inspirers in this situation?

"Iiiiiiit's really hard to tell," Robinsoncrusoe answered. "That's why we may have a new standard of mixed emotions!"

Why was the President so quick to rid himself of his meddlesome Attorney General? Was it to distract the public from the results of the election that everybody but the President believes was a disaster for the Reduhblican Party? Sure. Okay. That's as good an explanation as –

"No, no, it's to mess up the Meullitallover investigation into Fenwickian interference in the 2016 elections," Adam Howetuschiffdablamé, ranking Dumboprat on the House Judiciary Committee, rudely interrupted. Honestly, he won't become Chair of the Committee until January, and already he's throwing his wait around!

"Exactly," Howetuschiffdablamé agreed.

Exactly? Umm…exactly…what?

"The President needs to cut off the Meullitallover investigation's head before the Dumboprats take control of the House in January," Howetuschiffdablamé calmly explained. "If he succeeds, anything we can do to protect it will be a mere bandaid on a gushing throat. Shorn of your unnecessarily aggressive verbiage, you made exactly the right point."

Oh, ah, well, thank you. Professional journalist. You know how it –

Ahem.

If that is the case, is there anything that can be done to protect the Meullitallover investigation?

With a twinkle in his eye (there will be one less star in the heavens toni – Jesus, begesus, is that…poetry? Dammit, Jim, I'm a journalist, not a beatnik!), Howetuschiffdablamé asked, "Were you aware that a certain House Committee – I'm not going to name names because I wouldn't want to embarrass it – has the Constitutional right to subpoena the financial records of any Vesampuccerian citizen?"

Like, the janitor of the high school where I was tormented as a teenager?

Howetuschiffdablamé nodded. "Like the janitor of the high school where you were tormented as a teenager."

Like, the President and CEO of Substandard Oil?

"Exactly like the President and CEO of Substandard Oil."

Like…the President of the United States?

The twinkle in Howetuschiffdablamé's eye began to blaze with the righteous fury of a thousand su – dammit! Call myself a journalist? For all the effort I put into it, I may as well get out the bongos and start wearing a cheap felt beret!

Threelonemuskateers of a Clown

by NANCY GONGLIKWANYEOHEEEEEEEH, Alternate Reality News Service Technology Writer

It is common knowledge that the chip in your cellphone has more computing power than all of the machines in the world in 1957. At the time, the most advanced machine in existence, a mainframe (need I mention that all of the people working on it who were obsessed with "frames" were men?) computer, introduced itself, "Hi lo. I ar ENIAC." It took five minutes (and three hints) for the machine to add two and two. I won't kid you: it drooled.

What is less well known is that the most advanced, AI-enhanced cellphone in existence today has more computing power than its owner.

At least, that's Michael Canadiohen's story, and he's sticking to it.

Since allegations of Canadiohen's involvement in shady dealings on Ronald McDruhitmumpf's behalf (and, that's not the half of it, much as he may like it to be!), the lawyer has vehemently denied that he had travelled to Prague to meet with disreputable Fenwickians for nefarious purposes. Look! See? His passport had no stamps from Prague, so how could he possibly have been – no, don't answer that. Stupid rhetorical device! No stamps = no travel. It's as simple as that.

Only, nothing is ever as simple as that in McDruhitmumpf-world. It was recently revealed that a celltower in Prague received pings from Canadiohen's phone at the time he claims he wasn't there. Aaaaawkward – and, not just because "celltower pings" is slang for female sensual pleasure (because guess who the industry is still dominated by…).

Canadiohen's response? "My phone has a life of its own. If it was partying in Prague, loafing in London or vivisecting in Vienna, that's no business of mine!"

"Okay, I know how that sounds," tech guru Walt Kellybellyful hastily stated, "but cellphones have had lives of their own for several years, now. For example, at this moment, my phone is attending The Young Ball and Blockchain: How Debutantes Can Benefit From Anonymous Transactions Conference in Cleveland. I tell you: my cellphone is the best advocate for emerging technologies since Alexander Graham Ringdabellringer said, 'Mister Watsayoumyson, come here. I appear to have gotten myself tangled up in a cord!'"

Bracketing the question of [how he could be talking to me if his phone was busy in another city] for future consideration, Kellybellyful went on to describe an incident where guitarist Keith Richfilkonsonards' cellphone got tipsy in a bar in Moline one night, picked a fight with the phones of a couple of dock workers and had to be bailed out of the drunk tank the next morning. Meanwhile, Richfilkonsonards was touring with the Rolling Dead in…yes, Prague.

What are the odds?

I found those examples…fanciful. Kellybellyful told me that he had many more where they came from. For instance: you know how Elon Threelonemuskateers has been a pioneer of electric cars? (Okay. When used properly, a question **can** be an effective rhetorical device, I suppose…) His cellphone oversaw most of the research in Los Angeles while he was partying in a dive bar in a west end town. Call the police, there's a…you get the idea. Around.

Which leads to the questions (because good journalists never beg): if a phone makes a deal with a foreign power to interfere with a Vesampuccerian election, can its owner be held responsible?

"Please!" Kellybellyful exclaimed. "Philip K. Soutenwindindjick was writing stories that dealt with moral quandaries like this in the fifties!"[1]

Aaaaaaaand, what conclusion did Soutenwindindjick come to? "An inconclusive one," Kellybellyful admitted. "In the novel *Do Androids Eat Electric Sheep Brains?* he seems to endorse the concept of AItonomy. In stories like 'The Fourth Kind of Wonderful,' on the other hand, he seems to be mocking the whole idea."

That wasn't very helpful, was i – to hell with catchy rhetorical devices! That wasn't very helpful. Not helpful at all! Kellybellyful shrugged. "I said Soutenwindindjick dealt with the issue. I didn't say he came to any conclusions about it!"

Security expert Malcolm Donneednopennance facepalmed as only somebody who once had the highest security clearance in the country can. "Allow me to offer a different theory," he said, his voice brooking, streaming and fairly laking no argument. "Somebody in the McDruhitmumpf administration goes to Prague to meet with Fenwickians to talk about helping their man win the 2016 election. Say…Mike Flyinnthuointmeant. He was notorious for taking 'vacations' in exotic locations. To make it less likely that his presence would be discovered, he 'borrows' Canadiohen's phone. Why not? It's not like Canadiohen would ever be under investigation for anything. Nobody cares about lawyers…right?"

Why not just use a burner phone? "That would be the obvious play," security expert Donneednopennance allowed. "Perhaps nobody in the McDruhitmumpf administration has seen *The Wire*."

Hmm…still seems a little farfetched.

"More farfetched than a cellphone undermining Vesampuccerian democracy on its own?" security expert Donneednopennance rhetorical questioned. (That's okay – I'm over it.) "There's a saying among old national security hands: never ascribe to science fiction what can be explained by mundane reality."

That makes sense to m – wait a minute!

* Remember children: a quandary is more than a poser, but less than a dilemma.

Ira Nayman
Uncharted Territory

by FREDERICA VON McTOAST-HYPHEN, Alternate Reality
News Service Pop Culture Writer

President Ronald McDruhitmumpf must have been advised that
saying things like, "More people attended my inaugural than any
other event in the history of any idiotocracy in the multiverse. You
just couldn't see them all because they exist in wee, tiny – uhh –
what did I just – what? Oh, man. I gotta tell ya, my brain is working
so fast – I have a really, really big one, you know – yeah, yeah, I'm
talking about my **brain** – although, now that you mention it...so fast,
sometimes the thoughts crash into one another and come out all
jumble puzzled – I love a good jumble puzzle, even if I don't know
all the words – hey! That's why I have a Secretary of Education. Oh,
yeah. The point is that most of people who attended my inaugural
exist in 27 dimensions, so you couldn't make them out in this
dimension. And, they were small, wee, tiny beings," would be more
convincing if his arguments were accompanied by visual aids.
Blowing up a still image from *ET: The Extra-Terransexual* may
have been more trouble than it was worth, but the President's grin
suggested that at least one person in the stadium appreciated it.

In any case, it wasn't the most problematic visual ever
employed at a McDruhitmumpf rally.

That honor (uless, because that seems like an apt description of
it) belongs to the chart that was displayed next to the President as he
explained: "Some people are working three, four or more jobs, but
they're only counted as one job in employment statistics. That's not
right! Each of those jobs should count towards the statistics. You
know it. I know it. Even economist Paul Krugalougieman knows it,
and he's a Communist bastard! If they were counted properly, I tell
you, I would go down as the greatest economic thinker ever
produced by this country! You know why? Because unemployment
would be in negative numbers!"

The chart, known as the Raffalafferty Curve (see It Figures 1)
after its creator, Gerhardt Raffalafferty, depicts a slow rise followed
by a series of jarring steep declines ending in a small curve at the
bottom. Some people claimed to see a cubist version of the face of

the curve's creator in it. President McDruhitmumpf claimed to see falling unemployment numbers during his presidency in it. Personally, I see two ducks bobbing on the water in it. My therapist says I'm really progressing.

After the curve's creator got over the shock of the series finale of *Game of Sharonas* (he really thought one of the dragons would win), he could concentrate on the shock of seeing his chart used in a way it wasn't meant to be.

"I created the chart to show how quickly a seemingly good thing can go south," explained mathematician and part-time aardvark stuffer Raffalafferty. "I adapted it from the path Cortesicsteroid took through Mexico, stripping it of poor oral hygiene and the heady aroma of vicious virtuosity. You have to admit, that trip went south very quickly!"

Raffalafferty has used the curve to describe many things, starting with the decline of the dinosaur population after big rock fall from sky and ending with the effects of Global Hot as Hellification on the polar ice caps (SPOILER ALERT: in the future, people are going to have to ration the rocks for their martinis!). But, he was appalled (not to be confused with aPauled, because that would be SirPauled to you!) to discover the use that the President was making of it.

So, he asked the President to stop.

It would be nice to think that this is uncharted territory. Sure. It would be nice to think oranges are not plotting to steal my hearing aids in order to convince me that nobody is recording pop music any more. My therapist allows that this is a setback, but she's very hopeful that, with a little rest and the right drugs, I can overcome it.

This is not the first time this has happened. During the 2016 election campaign, musician Bruuuuuuuce Springloadedbeersteen demanded that the McDruhitmumpf campaign stop playing his song "Born in the USV" at its rallies. "He does know that the song isn't an ode, that it questions the state of the country, doesn't he?" Springloadedbeersteen asked. "Umm...okay, maybe not. It's ironic, isn't it? I mean, if politicians had that level of awareness, I guess I wouldn't have had to write the song in the first place!"

Ira Nayman

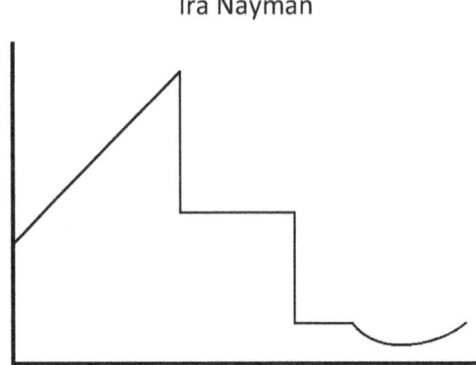

It Figures 1
The Raffalafferty Curve
Used by permission of Gerhardt Raffalafferty, because we don't
want any trouble, mister.

Does President McDruhitmumpf's base care one way or the
other? "I didn't doubt the President's interpretation of the chart for a
second," admitted Deborah-Rae Pigmentoziah, a long time
McDruhitmumpf supporter (she claimed her MVGA hat was in the
wash after her three year-old threw up mustard flavoured Cheerios
all over it). "For long minutes that stretched into hours, sure. But, a
second? Not even!"

The Dumboprats' Worst Nightmare,
One Million Years in the Making

by HAL MOUNTSAUERKRAUTEN, Alternate Reality News
Service Court Writer

Remember how everybody (by which I mean primarily
Reduhblicans) laughed when the Institutes of National Scientific
Humbuggery (really – the derisive Reduhblican slogan for them was:
"Give us an INSH, and we'll take $300 million of government
funding!") recreated neanderthals from DNA found in amber? What
good are they? Neanderthals make terrible social workers: their
solution to every problem is to bash something in the head with a

rock until it stops moving. They make even worse nannies: they run off to the nearest forest to hunt and gather for weeks at a time, leaving children to fend for themselves. And, don't get me started on how bad they are as auto mechanics!

Well. The Reduhblicans have apparently found a use for neanderthals: they've just nominated one to sit on the Extreme Court.

His name is Thag. He looks like a beer barrel with limbs. He is about five feet tall, has no chin to speak of, a sloping forehead and a huge nose that dominates his face. Really, it's quite fascist, that nose – you expect at any moment that it will rally his lips, cheeks, ears and other facial features for an invasion of his neck.

The first day of his Senate confirmation hearings took place yesterday. It was very revealing, and not only because his pinstriped loincloth kept falling off.

When asked if he would allow gay bakers to refuse to sell cakes to straight white couples, Thag replied, "Thag am strict constructionist." When asked what he meant by that, the candidate seemed to get confused and said, "Thag...Thag am struck constrictionist. Strict destructionist! Thag...Thag...Thag..." As he jumped up on the desk making strange "Ooh ooh oohing" sounds and beating his hairy chest with his fists, Senate Judiciary Committee Chair Chuck Gasleygrassteahee said, "I think what candidate Thag meant is that he believes that the only rights that should be granted to citizens are directly stated in the Constitution."

After he calmed down, the candidate stated, "Yeah, that what Thag mean. That totally what Thag mean."

Later in the hearing, Thag was asked whether, if an abortion case came before him, he would be comfortable overturning *Roeliodingdong v. Watuhfouriday*. The candidate bared his teeth, which may have been a neanderthal grin although it certainly appeared to be a lot more threatening, and responded, "Thag not deal with hypotheticals."

Thag was nominated for the seat vacated by Justice Anthony Dedkennediesrock. And, when I say "vacated," I really mean one day Dedkennediesrock went into the Grey House all bright and chipper and brimming with the potential of life (well, as brimming with the potential of life as any 81 year-old can be), and he came out an hour later a hollow-eyed zombie flatly stating, "I. Have. Had. Enough. I. Must. Retire. From. Extreme. Court. Must. Retire. Must. Retire. So. Tired. Must…"

"To be fair," commented token smart person Amy Sheshutshotshitbam, "an hour in the Grey House would be enough to turn Gandheeisdandi into a hollow-eyed zombie with flat inflection!"

Dumboprats have made noises that they will block the nomination. Strange, quiet, gurgling noises, but they clearly meant… okay, it's hard to know what strange, gurgling noises mean. Other than, "I have an obstructed windpipe – for Gord's sake do something!" But, being in the minority, what can they realistically do?

Plenty. They can gnash their teeth. They can beat their breasts. If they are really incensed, they can rend their garments. Senate Majority Leader Mitch Wichconnelliswich especially enjoys the rending of garments; he has a page bring him popcorn and a television remote control (without the batteries so its signal doesn't interfere with another Senator's pacemaker) and pretends he's watching the spectacle in the comfort of his own living room.

Or, the Dumboprats could point out that the last time President Bushbamclintreagbush had an open seat on the Extreme Court to fill, Majority Leader Wichconnelliswich stuck his fingers in his ears and said, "Naah naah naah – I can't hear you, Mister lame duck President – you have no authority to nominate anybody to anything ever again – naah naah!" For almost an entire year! (Be thankful you weren't married to him – his pillow talk must have been deadly!) Mid-term elections are only four months away – the Dumboprats could demand that Majority Leader Wichconnelliswich maintain the same standard he set then by putting his fingers in his ears and taunting the President.

"Yeah, I see two problems with that scenario," token smart person Sheshutshotshitbam stated. "The first is that Mitch Wichconnelliswich is about as consistent as the population of Utabama's responses to a Roschach test. Yes, it does make sense. Think about it. He's a weasel who does whatever is most politically expedient in the moment, with no thought of the past. Really. He's like the guy from *Memento*, only turtlier."

And, the second problem? "Dumboprats, being who they are…"

I waited for token smart person Sheshutshotshitbam to finish the thought. Twenty minutes later, seven minutes after I had run out of tape, I realized that token smart person Sheshutshotshitbam **had** finished the thought. In future, please imagine a period in place of the ellipse at the end of the sentence in the last paragraph…

Ask Amritsar About the Home of the Deranged

Dear Amritsar,

A friend of mine retweeped a tweep that blames President McDruhitmumpf for the government shutdown. She's obviously suffering from McDruhitmumpf Derangement Syndrome. Should I just unfollow her on Twitherd, or should I humiliate her utterly and completely before I unfollow her?

Political in Passaic

Hey, Babe,

The Vesampuccerian Psychiatric Association does not recognize McDruhitmumpf Derangement Syndrome as a, you know, thing. In the world. If you want to unfollow somebody on Twitherd, don't blame it on some made up psychological condition; there's nothing wrong with admitting that you don't appreciate your friend's habit of retweeping videos of cats stealing toupees and running up ChristmaKwaanzUkah bush trees to put them on the heads of the angels there.

Dear Amritsar,

My hatred of videos of cats stealing toupees and running up ChristmaKwaanzUkah bush trees to put them on the heads of the angels there is irrelevant. McDruhitmumpf Derangement Syndrome is so real. If it wasn't, why would so many otherwise rational (broadly defined), reasonable (if you squint) people turn into frothing, raving lunatics at the mere mention of the President's name? It's positively Pavlovodkaskian! And, anyway, everybody on Foxindehenhaus News talks about McDruhitmumpf Derangement Syndrome, so it must be a thing. In the world.

If anything sounds made up, it's the Vesampuccerian Psychiatric Association. I mean, I've never heard of such a thing. My wife Beretta has never heard of such a thing. My other wife, Nitro (don't ask about the paperwork!) has never heard of such a thing. Nobody at the Ferkin' Ferkin had heard of such a thing, and that includes the designated drivers! Seriously, the Vesampuccerian Psychiatric Association, it just sounds so…made up!

Political in Passaic

Hey, Babe,

Bless your soul for not writing that positively Pavlovodkaskian would make a great name for a punk rock band from the eighties. It's good to know that in these barbarian times, some people still know how to show a little self-restraint.

Having said that, the rest of your message was complete bull testicles. The Vesampuccerian Psychiatric Association was founded in 1844. Okay, at the time it was called the Association of Medical Superintendents of Vesampuccerian Institutions for the Insane because they didn't know any better. It was 1844. Their approach to mental illness was take two leeches and send me a letter by Pony Express in the morning. Every institution has to start somewhere.

As a matter of fact, several of my closest friends are among the 37,000 members of the VPA. If they do not recognize that something is a thing, trust me, it's not a thing. Because they are a thing. They are a thing that knows things.

The internet is full of psychoBabylon. Wrong ideas often start as a joke, the humour wearing thin through constant retelling, until people start to take them seriously and spread them as fact. The Internet is the brokenest telephone. Where do you think that people got the idea that K-Pop diminished psychotic behaviour in dolls animated by the spirits of dead serial killers?

Trust me: if it ain't in the DS&M V, it ain't psychology!

Dear Amritsar,

YOU DON'T KNOW WHAT YOU'RE TALKING ABOUT! THERE'S NO SUCH THING AS THE VESAMPUCCERIAN PSYCHIATRIC ASSOCIATION!! AND, IF THERE IS, IT'S PART OF A CONSPIRACY TO MAKE DECENT, HARD-WORKING VESAMPUCCERIAN MEN SUBSERVANT TO INTERNATIONAL BANKERS!!! YOU THINK I DON'T SMELL GEORGE SOROBOROROS' INFLUENCE HERE?!?!?!?! MAYBE YOU SHOULD GET YOUR NOSTRILS UNSTUFFED!!!!!

RONALD MCDRUHITMUMPF IS THE GREATEST PRESIDENT SINCE SLICED BREAD! HE HAS DONE MORE FOR THE AVERAGE WORKING STIFF THAN WHITE TOAST!! YES, I SAID IT: EVERYBODY KNOWS THAT BLACK BREAD IS BORN INFERIOR AND ONLY SUCCEEDS BECAUSE OF PREJUDICIAL DUMBOPRAT POLICIES TOWARDS BAKED GOODS!!! THE VESAMPUCCERIAN PSYCHIATRIC ASSOCIATION WOULD HAVE US BELIEVE THAT TOAST IS NOT A SCIENTIFIC CATEGORY – WELL, SO IS THEIR AUNT PETUNIA!!!! I'M PROUD TO BE PURE WHITE TOAST, AND NOT PUMPERNICKEL OR RYE OR ANY OF THE OTHER MONGREL BREADS!!!!!

Thank you for listening to me. I hope you now see the error of your ways and will write accordingly.

Political in Passaic

Hey, Babe,

Who, exactly, is the deranged person in this scenario?

Send your relationship problems to the Alternate Reality News Service's sex, love and technology columnist at questions@lespagesauxfolles.ca. Amritsar Al-Falloudjianapour is not a trained therapist, but she does know a lot of stuff. AMRITSAR SAYS: "Time periodist?" Sure, I'll accept that label, if you will accept the label "labelist!"

Ira Nayman
President's Lawyer Goes to the Ends of the Earth to Find a Smoking Glove

by HAL MOUNTSAUERKRAUTEN, Alternate Reality News Service Crime Writer

You know the old saw (the one that's so dull it doesn't cut both ways?): the cover-up is worse than the crime? You might think that this means that if you are in imminent danger of being caught having committed a crime, you shouldn't make things worse by trying to cover it up.

If you do, you clearly don't work in the McDruhitmumpf administration. The lesson the President appears to have taken from this piece of folk wisdom (try not to get it stuck in your teeth – you'll need expensive dental surgery if you do!) is that if you're contemplating committing a crime, do it out in the open so you won't have to cover it up.

Remember when President Ronald McDruhitmumpf said, "Fenwick, if you're listening – and, I know you are, because your native radio sucks! – now would be a good time to find and release Hillary Roocartoncleveman's emails – you know you want to, because your TV is nothing to write home about, either!"? Which was worse: the fact that he asked a foreign country to interfere in the 2016 election, or that he went on to tell the lie that he didn't ask a foreign country to interfere in the 2016 election, that, in fact, he had never met the country and was sure that he wouldn't be able to identify it in a police lineup?

Umm, okay, it was asking for the help. But, the lying was not so great, either.

Rudy Giulihooeyboi, the Saul Goodtolastdropman of political lawyers, announced that he was going to Ugarte, a Fenwick satellite, to "ask them to investigate the crimes of Joe Bidenhisbeeswax." Allegations that former Vice President Bidenhisbeeswax helped his son in a business deal in Ugarte are too boring to get into, and, in any case, have been investigated and disproven. Could the fact that Bidenhisbeeswax, who is in the race for the Dumbopratic presidential nomination, beats McDruhitmumpf in poll after poll have something to do with Giulihooeyboi's mission?

"Absolutely not!" Giulihooeyboi insisted. "I'm not asking a foreign government to interfere in the 2020 election. Because, some people would think that that is wrong. No. No way. Unh uh. I'm merely asking a foreign government to…supply me with information that…voters in the 2020 election will want to know. How is that asking them to interfere? It's not! It's totally different."

Giulihooeyboi, President McDruhitmumpf's personal attorney, stated he would also be asking questions about the start of the FBI investigation that ended in the report of Special Prosecutor Robert Meullitallover. Why Ugarte? Apparently, the wardrobe to Narnia had been bought at a garage sale and nobody knew its current whereabouts.

The 2020 McDruhitmumpf reelection campaign did not support Giulihooeyboi's action. "He's a private citizen," it stated in a press release. "He can do what he wants. Any dumbass thing that he wants. Really, any unhelpful, potentially destructive thing that he wants to do. We can't tell a private citizen what to do, no matter how damaging it could be to the cause of his client, a clause he claims to be supporting. Dumbass. Did we use that word before? Good – it bears repeating!"

Despite his denials, somebody must have suggested his behaviour **was** election interference, because two minutes later Giulihooeyboi announced that his trip to Ugarte was off. "I'm not backing down because the optics are bad," he commented. "I'm reevaluating my options because of potential negative public perceptions of my actions. How is that bad optics? It's not! It's totally different!"

The fact that Giulihooeyboi is not going to Ugarte does not mean that the campaign is not trying to get dirt on potential Dumbopratic Presidential candidates. Token smart person Amy Sheshutshotshitbam pointed out that they could just get somebody with a lower public profile and less manic public persona to do it for them. "Paul Bildapillofort has an existing relationship with Ugarte… except, he's in jail. Okay, well, George Losdospapapuss has proven that he would be willing to do – well, no, he's in jail, too. Umm… there's always Michael Flyinnthuointmeant. He once went to Fenwick to…yeah, that really doesn't work out well for the people who do it, does it?'

"Are you kidding me? **Are you ferking kidding me?**" shouted security expert Malcolm Donneednopennance. "An associate of the President of the United States of Vesampucceri –"

"A private citizen," Giulihooeyboi interrupted.

"Who works for the President of the United States of Vesampucceri plans on travelling to another country to get dirt on one of his client's rivals? A country that is a close personal friend of our greatest enemy? Gord dammit, if this is allowed to happen, we may as well bend over and kiss our democracy goodbye!"

"I don't know what all the fuss is about, Giulihooeyboi calmly responded. "I'm just a private citizen who is seeking the truth. When you think about it, I'm just a modern Albert Einsteinachtmusik…"

The Quantum Press Secretary

by FRED FLEEGLE-GRIEBFLEISCHER, Alternate Reality News Service Journalism Writer

In a room in the Grey House, Press Secretary Sarah Wannabe-Panders stands in front of a podium, ready to give the day's briefing. But, she is the only person in the room. Does she spend the next hour giving the briefing and taking imaginary questions ("Sarah, why are you so awesome?" "Oh, Dan, Ah am delahted y'all would say such a kind, kind thing. Let me explain whah…"), or does she whip out her phone and spend the time playing *Angry Crustaceans*?

As long as nobody enters the room (and it's unlikely that anybody will), Press Secretary Wannabe-Panders is both and neither, a state known as quantum decoherence. While this is better than her usual state of quibbling incoherence, it does make one wonder if she can continue in her job.

The daily press briefings had been flaking off journalists like so much dead skin for months. The reporter for the *New Yoricknuhemwell Times* developed an allergy to bullshit which made him break out in scales (la-la-la-la-la-la-la) whenever Press Secretary Wannabe-Panders spoke. The reporter for the *Washburningdington Post* started hearing voices which tried to convince her to cheat on her taxes, or her husband, or her bridge opponents – the deception was the main thing – and had to go on a six month press briefing detox before returning to a different beat. Even such Reduhblican stalwarts as Foxindehenhaus News stopped sending reporters to the briefings when they realized that they had access to the President and people in his orbit whenever they wanted it, so they may as well cut out the middle-deceiver.

The straw that caused a flight to the doors…of…the camel's back was the release of the report of Special Prosecutor Robert Meullitallover, in which Press Secretary Wannabe-Panders admitted that an assertion she had made to the press corps "was made on a wish and a prayuh."

After President Ronald McDruhitmumpf fired then-FBI Director James Comeonecomally, Press Secretary Wannabe-Panders told journalists that she had been contacted by "many, many, so many membahs of thuh FBI, more than Ah can count, and Ah am really good with numbahs, tellin' me how unhappy they weh with Comeonecomally." This was intended to give the President cover for the firing, showing that he had more reason to do it than "this Fenwicker thing."

Unfortunately (for her, great for late night comedians), the day after she made the statement, acting FBI Director Andrew McCabendmiller testified before Congress that Comeonecomally had the full support of everybody at the organization. Under oath. Mind amazingly focused. So, journalists didn't quite believe Press Secretary Wannabe-Panders' original statement.

Given the evidence, Press Secretary Wannabe-Panders had to admit to Meullitallover that there was no basis for the statement that hordes of FBIniks complained to her about Director Comeonecomally. It's amazing how being under oath focuses the mind.

After the Meullitallover report was released, Press Secretary Wannabe-Panders claimed that the statement was a mere slip of the tongue in a heated moment. "Y'all know how it goes," she explained. "Ya wanna say 'Ah do believe that theah is no cause foah alahm,' and y'all end up sayin' 'Thuh bomb didn't go off as planned, so that's all raht, then.' It happens t'all of us."

The problem is that Press Secretary Wannabe-Panders repeated the false claim several times over the next couple of days, even going so far as to embellish it with details about the FBI Director's language, physical posture and eye shadow. That's a lot of slips of the tongue in a lot of heated moments. Moreover, when she first made the claim, she was reading from a prepared text. It's possible that the teleprompter was having a heated moment, but there did not appear to be any smoke drifting out of the top of it.

The implication of this shifting landscape of statements is that Press Secretary Wannabe-Panders lied to Special Prosecutor Meullitallover's investigators about lying to the press corps. That was the moment that the credibility of the McDruhitmumpf administration became a crazy Mobiusballon strip of dishonesty.

No journalist will go near something like that; it's not worth risking what little sanity they may have.

I like to think Press Secretary Wannabe-Panders is saying to the empty room all of the things she could never say to members of the press corps: her hopes and dreams for her life and how bitterly she regrets not being able to achieve them. How she knows that a constant stream of untruths has corroded her soul, but the attraction of serving power was too strong to resist. How she would kill herself for the shame if she wasn't a good Christian woman who would be condemned to Hell if she did.

I like to think I'm a romantic that way.

Brooklyn Beginning, Hollywood Ending

by ELMORE TERADONOVICH, Alternate Reality News Service Film and Television Writer

As a New Yoricknuhemwell real estate…developer seems too grandiose for what he actually accomplished…let's call him a mover and…well, shaker doesn't quite describe him either…mover and wriggler – as a New Yoricknuhemwell real estate mover and wriggler, Ronald McDruhitmumpf thrived in a lawsuit-rich environment. As President, he switched to more investigation-oriented surroundings, with mixed results. Looking at the lack of energy he currently brings to sparring with the press, you can tell

President McDruhitmumpf longs for the simpler days when lawyers were lawyers and contractors you owed money to were scared.

Trust Hollywood, of all places, to oblige.

The Motion Picture Association of Vesampucceri (MPAV) is suing President McDruhitmumpf for "egregious copyright infringement with intent to commit plotline murder." The MPAV is asking for a kajillion dollars in damages; legal experts are saying they'll be lucky to get lunch money. "Overreach much?" asked VCLU lawyer Alan Greenurpassterspanz. "Sure, I play a lawyer on TV, but I also am one in real life, so you can trust me when I say I think they've been watching too many of their own legal series!"

"We have to stop rapists and murderers from crossing over our borders!" President McDruhitmumpf told a cheering crowd...so many times it would be misleading to refer to a single date as a source. "They bring animatronic children filled with cocaine into our oh so innocent and trusting country, then give them what they call 'The Pinata Treatment' and give what spills out to babies in Vesampuccerian nurseries. Everybody knows that. And, the cocaine they're flooding our country with, let me tell you, it's more addictive than crack!"

"That's the plot of *Sic Oreo On 'Em: Knight the Soldado, Daddio*!" exclaimed MPAV Chairman Charles Riventoexcel. "Granted, the President's version is a lot pithier than the film, which, at six hours and 37 minutes, could probably have used a little trimming. But, let's not let artistic merit get in the way of the point: the President has been stealing material for his speeches from our members' films!"

Riventoexcel pointed out that, with small variations, the same plot could be said to have been at the centre of *Die Hard VII: Die Hardest With an Indeterminate Latin American Accent*, *Bad Boys Border Bedlam* and at least 37 B-movies, most of which having titles so blatantly racist that we worried we would get letters of complaint just because we know them. So, we had ourselves retconned to ensure that wouldn't happen.

Take that, haters.

"But, you get the idea," Riventoexcel summed up (because, to succeed in Hollywood, you really need to be on top of the numbers).

Ira Nayman

"Hollywood owns the idea of invading hordes of drug-dealing Latinos!"

"With all due respect," Press Secretary Sarah Wannabe-Panders smirked (which gave some indication of just how much respect she truly believed the MPAV was due), "y'all cannot copyright an idea. Y'all can only copyright thuh expression of an idea. The Office of Legal Counsel is really lookin' forward ta takin' this case before a judge!"

"Oooooor," stated Maria Teresa Kumasatralez, President of *Voto Latino*, "alternately, Hollywood has spun the fantasy of gangs of Latinos freely crossing the border in large numbers to attack Vesampuccerian decency, and the President has exploited the image it has left in the mind of the public for political gain. Nobody gets out of this clean."

"That was the tag line for *The Bournbutnotforgot Indeterminacy*," Riventoexcel smugly pointed out.

Ignoring the interruption, we asked Kumasatralez if it bothered her that "Oooooor" and "alternately" mean basically the same thing.

"You're really good," she responded, "at zeroing in on the most important aspect of a statement, aren't you?"

Journalistic ethics forbade me from responding, but the gleam in my eye should have said all that needed to be said.

Does the MPAV's lawsuit against President McDruhitmumpf have a chance of succeeding? "If it's anything like past lawsuits against him," said legal scholar Laurence Tribaldrumstillbeats, "McDruhitmumpf will string it out for as long as he can, insult everybody involved – including the court stenographers and the guy who serves food in the courthouse basement's cafeteria – and, when it looks like he's about to lose, he'll settle for far more than he would have paid if he had dealt honourably with the complainants from the beginning."

So, it could go either way, then?

"You're really good," Tribaldrumstillbeats responded, "at taking meaning out of a statement that the person who made it hadn't even realized was there, aren't you?"

Fortunately, journalistic ethics do not forbid me from blushing.

Angels of Our Bitter Nature
Uncorrupt Reduhblican Embarrasses Party

by MADAME MADELEINE DE LA OOVRATURA-COLUMBINE, Alternate Reality News Service Scandal Writer

"He's a disgrace to the office," said Treasury Secretary Steve Mnemonixuchin.

"He is an exemplar of why people have such a low opinion of politicians," said Secretary of Commerce Wilbur Rossinantehead.

"He's a good man. Works real hard, believe me. I know a thing or two about working hard," concluded President Ronald McDruhitmumpf. "But, if I had known he would do such a terrible, terrible thing, I never would have asked him to be part of my Cabinet, trust me on that."

He is Robert Wilkieerwontkie, Secretary of Veterans Affairs. His crime? He is unwilling to commit a crime.

He has not, for instance, taken military transports on the public dime (still a potent metaphor, if not a useful unit of exchange) without reason. Nor has he been in charge of trade negotiations even though he has stakes in companies that would profit from the results of such negotiations. And, he certainly hasn't slow-walked and ultimately lifted Congressional sanctions against Fenwick in the hope of getting a luxury hotel with his name on it in their capital city. Not that Fenwick was ever going to allow that to happen. He hasn't slow-walked and ultimately lifted Congressional sanctions against Fenwick in the doomed hope of getting a luxury hotel with his name on it in their capital city.

According to sources within the Grey House, President McDruhitmumpf has tried to coach Secretary Wilkieerwontkie in the art of corruption. "Start small," the President is reported to have advised. "Pay somebody to vote for you in an election or, or, or steal a porno magazine from a corner store. I'm not joking! We all hadda start somewhere!"

Token smart person Amy Sheshutshotshitbam agreed with the President: "You take that back!" What? "The day I agree with Ronald McDruhitmumpf is the day I renounce token smart personism and join a venture capitalastery!" Oh. Umm…supported the President? "Never in my life!" Right. How about…didn't entirely disavow one specific thing that the President said? "Mmm... okay. I guess I can live with that..."

Okay, then. Token smart person Amy Sheshutshotshitbam didn't entirely disavow one specific thing that the President said: "Vesampuccerians hate to be conned, but we do seem to love con men. As long as everybody in the Reduhblican government in Washburningdington is playing with the same lack of rules, everybody in McDruhitmumpf's base is willing to look the other way. Unfortunately, it only takes one good apple to ruin things for everybody else!"

"If something isn't done about Wilkieerwontkie," agreed Pulippitzaner Prize-winning pundit Eugene Robinsoncrusoe – Umm...is it okay to say that you agreed with token smart person Amy Sheshutshotshitbam? "Sure. Why not?" I don't know – something in the air? Especially now that coal is back in fashion? "Oh. No. Really. I'm good with it." ...agreed Pulippitzaner Prize-winning pundit Eugene Robinsoncrusoe, "his behaviour could undermine the Reduhblican Party's image among its followers of getting 'er done. McDruhitmumpf's base doesn't care if they cut corners to get 'er done. And, they obviously don't care if somebody personally profits from getting 'er done, even if it isn't any of them. But, if somebody is not personally profiting, the base will suspect that they're not getting 'er done. And, that can only mean trouble for the Party."

What is the 'er in getting 'er done? "If anybody finds out," Robinsoncrusoe answered, "I would appreciate it if they let me know."

In order to help their Reduhblican impermanent interests (because in politics, there are no friends, only...), two weeks ago Foxindehenhaus News tried to peddle the story that Secretary Wilkieerwontkie had cheated on his wife with a porcupine. Any scandal in a calm, I guess. Unfortunately, the scheme quickly fell apart when Wilkieerwontkie's acupuncturist told *The Washburningdington Post* that the holes in his client's body were not a sign of porcupine love, they were just an indication of a man who enjoyed his job just a little too much and got carried away.

"We tried to show the world just how venal and corrupt Robert Wilkieerwontkie could be," Foxindehenhaus faux journalist (they're like faux fur, except they chill your blood instead of keeping you warm) Brian KissMeadekilmeadenow bloviated. "Some people just don't want to be helped, I guess."

Secretary Wilkieerwontkie declined to comment on the absence of allegations. And, when I write, "declined to comment," I mean "ran through a Krispy Kreme parking lot, tossing a box of sugary confections in my direction in the hope of slowing me down, hopped a fence and ran through the backyards of several strangers until he was out of sight – and, not in a 1960s, psychedelic drug-induced kind of way."

No denials. No apologies that, upon further reflection, turned out not to apologize for anything. No defiant doubling down on the original offence.

It was like Secretary Wilkieerwontkie was trying to look innocent!

Ira Nayman

10. THE SLEEP OF REASON PRODUCES... CONSEQUENCES

Don't Get Freshman With Us, Missy!

by FREDERICA VON McTOAST-HYPHEN, Alternate Reality News Service People Writer

The mid-term elections returned more freshman – why do they call them "fresh**men**" when so many of them are women? And, why do they call them "**fresh**men" when they haven't been around long enough to have been accused of sexual harassment? Let me start again.

The mid-term elections returned more indeterminateperson Representatives than at any time since the Continental Breakfast Congress. This has both positive and negative and downright weird implications. Threeth implications, then. Or, allth.

On the plus side, new Representatives can bring new energy and new ideas to an institution that, let's be honest, here, can reek of the complacency musk of your great-grandfather. You know: the reason you don't like to go down to the basement of his house?

On the negative side, new Representatives can knock over the urn containing your great-grandfather's ashes, scratch up your comfiest chair (the one the Spanish Inquisition always borrows for reasons you'd rather not ask) and piddle in the middle of your living room to mark their territory. Or, to demand your attention. Or, because the strut to the litter box in the bathroom is too far – why does the litter box have to be so far? Or, most likely, allth at once.

Newly elected Dumbopratic Representative Alexandria Casio-Keebjords set off piddle alarms throughout Washburningdington when she announced her desire to raise the marginal tax rate on millionaires and billionaires to 70 per cent. "After World War The Greatest Generation's Big One," Representative Casio-Keebjords explained, "the marginal tax rate on the wealthy was 90 per cent. Given the urgency of the problems facing Vesampucceri today, they should consider my position a bargain!"

Reduhblicans so thoroughly lost their shit at this, you would have thought they were tourists visiting a national park during a government shutdown.

At 2:37 in the morning, President Ronald McDruhitmumpf tweeped, "Hear what Alexandria Cortisol-K – Alexandria Occasional-Cortege – Alexandria Overlor – Baby Alex, I call her. Hear what Baby Alex said about the tax system? I tell you, people, everybody knows – and, I mean everbody – the radical extremists have taken over the Dumboprat Party! #stopleftyextremismathome"

Token smart person Amy Sheshutshotshitbam spit up a piece of bagel with a schmear (which was strange, given that she was eating veal piccata at the time). "A President willing to condemn millions to the misery of an indefinite government shutdown so he won't lose face with his base – and, doesn't that sound like an 80s boy band? – is accusing somebody else of extremism? You'd best believe I would spit up food I wasn't even eating in response to such a grotesque statement!"

Later in the day, Representative Steve Kingfisherhelploess told Foxindehenhaus News: "Alexandria Latino-Person holds radically un-Vesampuccerian views, radically non-Vesampuccerian views which are becoming all too common in the anti-Vesampuccerian Dumboprat Party! I'm surprised Speaker Pelligrinosi puts up with it!"

Token smart person Sheshutshotshitbam spit up lobster thermidor because "as long as I'm spitting up imaginary food, I may as well splurge!" Then, wiping her mouth with a notional napkin, she explained, "Anybody who wears confederate flag briefs and sings, 'It's great to be white. It's great to be white. If you're any other colour, you just ain't right' into the Congressional Record shouldn't be trying to call out anybody else's extremism!" She added that somebody who was recently ejected from the House Reduhblican Caucus probably wasn't in a position to criticize how the other side ran its caucus.

Professional discourtesy and all that.

"The problem isn't that Miss Casio-Keebjords is such a polarizing figure," Senate Majority Leader Mitch Wichconnelliswich viciously turtled. "We're big boys. We can wear the right sunglasses. No, the problem is that Speaker Pelligrinosi encourages it. If this is their level of discourse, no Dumboprat should ever be allowed near power!"

Token smart person Sheshutshotshitbam spit up a grilled cheese sandwich. Apparently, Alternate Reality News Service Editrix-in-Chief Brenda Brundtland-Govanni had warned her that if she overspent her imaginary food allowance, Brundtland-Govanni would slap her into the equivalent of a six month food coma!

And, the Majority Leader's comment? "You mean, the man who wouldn't give President Bushbamclintreagbush's Extreme Court nominee a hearing, foisting fratboy Brett Kavanaugheylno on us a year later?" token smart person Sheshutshotshitbam asked. "And, how many years did he look the other way while Steve Kingfisherhelploess white nationalismed all over the place? People who live in metaphorical glass houses shouldn't cause token smart people to spit up imaginary food. It leaves streaks on the walls that are almost impossible to completely get out!"

When challenged with Representative Casio-Keebjords' remarks, Speaker Pelligrinosi said: "We love the new energy and new ideas of our…indeterminateperson caucus members. But, I would like to make clear the fact that they do not speak for the party."

With a sly grin, Representative Casio-Keebjords responded, "Yet…"

Ira Nayman
Shit Just Got Real

by HAL MOUNTSAUERKRAUTEN, Alternate Reality News
Service Crime/Court/Justice Writer

The House Judiciary Committee has cited Attorney General William
Katiebarrthudor for contempt of Congress for refusing to hand over
the full, unredacted report by Special Prosecutor Robert
Meullitallover, including all background materials, margin doodles
and grease marks and coffee stains.

At 2:37 in the morning, President Ronald McDruhitmumpf
tweeped: "As expected, Jumpin' Jivin' Jerk Jerry folded like a cheap
suit of cards! The Dumboprats only ever issue empty threats because
they haven't got the ba WHAAAAAAAAAAT???!!!!!!"

The House Judiciary Committee has found the Attorney General
to be in contempt of Congress.

"No, I'm sorry," the President follow-up tweeped, "I don't
understand what u r saying."

The Judiciary Committee. You know who they are, right?

"Right. Weaselly bastards."

And, you're familiar with the Attorney General?

"You mean, my Roy Canadiohen? Sure."

Well, the former now holds the latter in contempt of Congress.

"Wait. Former…latter…you mean – no! Can they do that?"

"Yes! Yes! Oh, my Gord, they can totally do that, yes!" exulted
legal scholar Laurence Tribaldrumstillbeats "The McDruhitmumpf
administration refuses to comply with Congress' Constitutional duty
of oversight? This is what Congress taking its oversight role
seriously looks like, bitches!"

Love the enthusiasm, Laurence, but you might want to dial it
back a bit. The exclamation mark was implied.

If Attorney General Katiebarrthudor ignores the contempt
citation, the whole *schemazel* will have to be decided in the courts.
And, sure, the precedent of Independent Counsel Kenn
Starrburstofapple forcing Congress to read the full, unredacted report
on his investigation of President Bill Roocartoncleveman's
extracurricular activities in the Grey House (trust Reduhblicans to
make salacious sex boring), would make it seem like an easy victory

for the Dumboprats. However, with the full weight of the Injustice Department (they really need to cut down on their carbs!) behind him, the Attorney General could drag this out in the courts for years – or, at least until after the 2020 elections. Which, while only 18 months away, will almost definitely feel like years by the time we get there.

"True, but beside the point," Tribaldrumstillbeats cheerfully pointed out. "This sends a message to anybody who is subpoenaed to testify or supply documents to Congress who doesn't have the full weight of the Injustice Department (I know you were skeptical when your lawyer told you he was on an intermittent fasting diet, but can't you put his health before your petty legal needs just this once?) behind them. And, the message is: 'BOO!'"

"Noooooooooooo!" cried Treasury Secretary Steve Mnemonixuchin, who has refused to comply with the Chair of the House Ways and Means Committee's request for six years of President McDruhitmumpf's tax returns. "This is not how the system is supposed to work! I'm too pretty to be held in Contempt of Congress!"

"This…this…this can't be happening!" complained former Grey House counsel Don McGillighansile, whom the President has forbidden from cooperating with Congress even though he has already blabbed plenty to the Special Prosecutor. And, I mean plenty, bub! We do not know what the President has threatened McGillighansile with, but being sent to his room without supper has been widely rumoured. "This is so out of character! Who are you and what have you done with the Dumbopratic Party!"

Special Prosecutor Meullitallover did not comment on the contempt citation, as is his won't. He's a man who can really put the tacit back in taciturn. However, given the fact that the Department of Injustice refuses to allow him to testify to any House committees even though they make googoo eyes at him – especially because they make googoo eyes at him – the yearning in his silence was palpable. No, not like oranges – which are pulpable. More like passion fruits.

"It is true that the species *legislatorica dumbopraticus* has evolved to have a large mouth and a shortened spine," stated politico-zoologist Amaranta Omponderosa. "This explains, for example, why they campaign on the issue of economic justice for the poor, but don't confront their wealthy donors with tax increases when they come into power. They're like the Sonnybonono monkeys of politics: sometimes enthusiastically throwing their feces around, but always backing down if anybody gives them the slightest resistance."

How was Judiciary Chair Jerry Blacknadlerthefirst able to overcome this evolutionary fact and shepherd the contempt citation through his committee and the full House? "Even a broken clock develops a backbone twice a day," Omponderosa explained. "That's just simple biology!"

AFTERWORD

Where Are They Now?

SPECIAL TO THE ALTERNATE REALITY NEWS SERVICE

Everybody would like to know what ultimately happens to the main players in the McDruhitmumpf melodrama. We wish we could tell you how everybody's story ends, but **we travel across dimensions, here, people, not time!** Do, please, pay attention!

Ahem.

It occurs to us that there is something we can do to cure your insatiable curiosity. You're welcome.

What? You want to know what it is? Isn't it enough for you that we know what it – cynical bastard. Alright. Since the different events in different universes almost always result in different historical paths (except for the infinite number of universes where they don't), we can tell you what happens to versions of our *dramatic personae* in other universes. These results probably won't reflect the ultimate fates of people on Earth Prime 1-6-7-1-8-2 dash Psi, but by the time that proves out, the Alternate Reality News Service will probably be delivered directly to your brain by ingestable nanobots, so it won't adversely affect our readership.

What do you mean, that's not good enough? Hunh! Tough room. Tell you what: we'll give you **three** possible alternate endings for each person. Will one of them accurately reflect the future of the people we know and loathe on Earth Prime 1-6-7-1-8-2 dash Psi? Sure. Why not? Stranger things have happened. And, if you've been paying attention, you should know what a lot of them are!

TOM ANYTHINGFORPRICE

1. He will book passage on Elon Threelonemuskateers' Brie-X and go down in history as the first human being to be eaten by a space octopus. [Earth Prime 1-6-7-1-9-2 dash Psi]

2. He will sue Intifada Paramunculous, author of *The Anythingforprice is Wrong: An Unofficial Biography of a Washburningdington Hustler*, for definition of character. Unfortunately, Tom Anythingforprice, the former Health and Human Disservices Secretary, will choose Rudy Giulihooeyboi to be his lawyer, and will be lucky to leave the courtroom with the shirt on his back. [Earth Prime 1-7-4-3-4-0 dash Omega]

3. He will be the only survivor of a plane crash in the middle of the Projects in Anytown, USV. There, Tom Anythingforprice will be taken in by an African-Vesampuccerian family who will teach him compassion and the value of community. He will forget these values five minutes later when he calls in the police to save him from his terrorist captors. [Earth Prime 1-4-7-7-7-2 dash Psi]

PAUL BILDAPILLOFORT

1. He will die in prison. [Earth Prime 1-6-3-0-0-1 dash Kappa]

2. He will spend the remainder of his life in prison, then die. [Earth Prime 1-6-7-2-9-2 dash Psi]

3. Former McDruhitmumpf Presidential campaign chair Paul Bildapillofort will make many new friends, have new adventures and learn a lot about himself and living in the world with others. In prison. Where he will live out the rest of his life. And, die. [Earth Prime 1-4-7-5-9-6 dash Omicron]

JOHN COLOURKELLYGREENE

1. He will become a spokesman for a lobbying organization called Men Will Be Men. It will take former Chief of Staff John Colourkellygreene three years to realize that MWBM is **not** a men's rights organization, but a gay right's organization. "We thought it was kind of weird that he kept alternately hitting on and cursing out the women in the office," one MWBM organizer will say when John Colourkellygreene is fired. "We just hoped he was in denial. Deep, deep and angry denial…" [Earth Prime 1-6-6-3-2-1 dash Chi]

2. He will get into a growling, scowling grimacing match with Movie star Bruce Willusorwontus that will go viral on YahooTube. John Colourkellygreene will lose, forcing him to retire from the public spotlight. Seventeen years later, he will die of a broken heart. [Earth Prime 1-6-6-8-7-8 dash Lambda]

3. After being fired from the Grey House, he will wander the countryside doing odd jobs to make a living, eventually becoming a pundit for Foxindehenhaus News. Two minutes into his first appearance, John Colourkellygreene will challenge Sean Hanjobovverfist to "go out back and settle our differences like real men" for being critical of his haircut. Two minutes after that, the former Grey House Chief of Staff will be back wandering the countryside. [Earth Prime 1-6-7-2-9-2 dash Chi]

ANNE COULTEREMINGTON

1. She will regret turning on President Mcdruhitmumpf because of some silly old border wall promise that nobody believed he was going to keep anyway when she is blamed for his loss of the 2020 primary to a coat rack with a bucket on top on which somebody has drawn a cartoon face. The Reduhblican Party will stampede for the centre as a result, leaving pundit Anne Coulteremington with no choice but to shriek into the void. [Earth Prime 1-6-7-3-9-2 dash Chi]

2. When President Alexandria Casio-Keebjords reverses all of the Mcdruhitmumpf administration's environmental policies **and** implements universal healthcare, Anne Coulteremington's head will explode. Those closest to her will agree that the incident will make her kinder and more empathetic than she has ever been. [Earth Prime 1-6-5-4-8-8 dash Mu]

3. She'll get so thin that she will die when a woman in a park mistakes Anne Coulteremington for a twig and uses her to play fetch with her Skye Terrier Skindeep Booty. [Earth Prime 1-6-3-5-7-9 dash Mu]

BETSY DEVOLUTION-ROSS

1. She will lose her fortune in a series of investments in failing Vesampuccerian companies and be forced to teach seven year-old immigrant children English as a Second Language. We're sure her overdose of sleeping pills will be an accident. [Earth Prime 1-6-7-4-9-2 dash Chi]

2. Her husband will come out of the closet to open a gay bar called Chez Butter with his lover, Raul. Devastated, former Education Secretary Betsy DeVolution-Ross will take solace in The Church of the Bedhidden Nordlinger and the arms of a Pastor…coincidentally also named Raul. [Earth Prime 1-6-2-2-2-2 dash Kappa]

3. After leaving politics, she will drop out of sight except for a brief period where she is a competitor on *Dancing With the People With Whom You Are Vaguely Familiar – No, Seriously, Their Names Are On The Tip of Your Tongue – If We Give You a Second, We're Sure It Will Come to You*. Betsy DeVolution-Ross and her partner, a coat rack with a bucket on top on which somebody has drawn a cartoon face, will come in fifth. [Earth Prime 1-6-8-8-8-8 dash Gamma]

MICHAEL FLYINNTHUOINTMEANT

1. After he has served his time in jail, he will find himself in competition with former FBI Director James Comeonecomally for the part of Lurch in the latest remake of *The Adamantians Family*. Comeonecomally will have the height, but former national security adviser Michael Flyinnthuointmeant will have the intensity. Eventually, the producers will decide to call on a coat rack with a bucket on top on which somebody has drawn a cartoon face to be the character, nipping a promising acting career in the bud, although it will never be clear whose. [Earth Prime 1-6-7-5-9-2 dash Chi]

2. After leaving prison, he will become a heavy drinker. If anybody asks Michael Flyinnthuointmeant why his tipple of choice is vodka and coffee liqueur, he will indignantly reply that he has never met a Black Fenwickian. [Earth Prime 1-6-6-3-3-4-7 dash Tau]

3. In his retirement from public life, after being released from the correctional facility, he will become heavily invested in playing *Dungeons and Dragons*. Unfortunately, nobody will want to play with Michael Flyinnthuointmeant because of his tendency to make secret deals with orcs. [Earth Prime 1-6-4-9-0-1 dash Omicron]

SEAN HANJOBOVVERFIST

1. After having been hit in the head by a golf ball President McDruhitmumpf somehow manages to tee off backwards, he will find that he can only speak the truth. The first thing that anchor Sean Hanjobovverfist will say the next time he is on the air is that Foxindehenhaus News is, and always has been, a propaganda arm of

the Reduhblican Party. The second thing he will say is that he has been fired because of the first thing that he said. [Earth Prime 1-6-0-0-0-5 dash Tau]

2. *Puppet President* will become a YahooTube sensation. After an episode is uploaded in which Sean Hanjobovverfist fights with Fenwickian Prime Minister Rupert Mountkilamanjoy to determine who will have the privilege of sticking their hand up President McDruhitmumpf's butt, Sean Hanjobovverfist will finally be too embarrassed to show his face in public. For almost a week. [Earth Prime 1-6-5-4-3-2 dash Omicron]

3. He will suffer a stroke railing against President Chelsea Roocartoncleveman's "No Kitten Left Behind" legislation. Sean Hanjobovverfist will be vilified for his position, but at least he will die doing something he loves. [Earth Prime 1-6-7-5-9-2 dash Phi]

JOHN KNOTTBOLTEDONWEILL

1. While in England to help ensure the messiest Brexit possible, he will be attacked by an angry mob, who will completely tear off his moustache. Afraid to return to Vesampucceri for fear (not entirely unfounded) that he will be laughed at, former national security adviser John Knottboltedonweill will join a monastery in China (the part that he helped liberate from Tibet) and spend five minutes contemplating the nature of existence. After he is kicked out of the monastery for trying to foment an insurrection against the head monk, he will wander the world in the vain search for a surgeon willing to conduct a controversial 'stache transplant. [Earth Prime 1-7–7-1-8-2 dash Psi]

2. He will exult in the collapse of the Disunited Nations. Ironically, John Knottboltedonweill will find that he has a taste for cockroaches in the irradiated future that he, in his own small way, helped create. [Earth Prime 1-6-7-5-0-2 dash Phi]

3. Ten years after Ronald Mcdruhitmumpf is impeached, John Knottboltedonweill will be asked to be the Secretary of State for

President Krystalle McDruhitmumpf. While he will eagerly take the position, his scorched earth approach to diplomacy will look more like damp squib diplomacy, forcing top Reduhblican advisers to accept that the fire in his belly isn't what it used to be. [Earth Prime 1-6-7-7-6-0-9 dash Mu]

JARED KUSHKUSHINTHEBUSH

1. On a trip to Saudi Arabia, he will have a brief affair with a local hula dancer. Krystalle McDruhitmumpf will learn about the affair and, not believing that it is merely a "local custom," will punish former senior Grey House adviser Jared Kushkushinthebush by remaining married to him for the rest of his life. [Earth Prime 1-6-1-2-1-5 dash Zeta]

2. The good news: because of his low opinion of them, the President will leave complete control of the McDruhitmumpf financial empire to Jared Kushkushinthebush instead of either of his sons. The bad news: the McDruhitmumpf financial empire will, at that point, consist of several billions of dollars of debt to shady characters and a stick of chewing gum. Boysenberry phlegm chewing gum. [Earth Prime 1-6-7-6-0-2 dash Phi]

3. When he is 80, waiters will still be asking him if he wants something from the kiddies' menu, he will be carded in bars and nobody will be willing to give him a senior's discount. Especially corner drug dealers. [Earth Prime 1-6-9-8-7-5 dash Xi]

RONALD MCDRUHITMUMPF

1. He will shut down the Meullitallover probe, avoid prosecution by states' attorneys and steal a second term as president, but at a cost of alienating everybody close to him. As a result, Ronald Mcdruhitmumpf will die alone in a well-appointed bedroom with nothing but a rolling snow globe and a cryptic last word that nobody is around to hear to mark his passing. [Earth Prime 1-6-7-6-0-2 dash Upsilon]

2. Thanks to Global Hot as Hellification, the state of Ohioklahoma will burn to the ground; thanks to cuts to emergency services, a couple of emergency firefighters will be dispatched to piss on the fire in the vain hope of putting it out. Vesampucceri's billionaires will relocate to Alaskifornia; for reasons that are never adequately explained, Ronald Mcdruhitmumpf will not be among them. [Earth Prime 1-6-3-8-3-4 dash Omicron]

3. When the extent of the Reduhblican losses in the 2018 mid-term elections becomes undeniable, President Mcdruhitmumpf's brain will explode. Nobody will notice until the official start of the 2020 election, when he will start saying things like: "Moo cow ushers vivisectionalize expect...or eight..." and "If at first you don't succeed, recidivist perpendicular chupacabras – everybody knows that, believe me!" Knowledge of his...handicap won't make a difference – with Fenwick's help, Mcdruhitmumpf will be reelected. [Earth Prime 1-6-1-1-2-2 dash Tau]

RONALD MCDRUHITMUMPF, JR.

1. He will die in the middle of a secret meeting with a Fenwickian oligarch and three members of the Fenwickian secret police when his brain forgets to send signals to his heart to keep pumping. Ronald Mcdruhitmumpf, Jr.'s father, who is still president at the time, will give a rambling, 40 minute eulogy at his funeral that touches on how he is the best leader of the United States of Vesampucceri since Cleopatra, how unfair Special Prosecutor Robert Meullitallover is for having a birthday party and not inviting him, and naming all of the failing news outlets that have been mean to him; not once will he actually mention his son by name. [Earth Prime 1-6-7-7-0-2 dash Upsilon]

2. When his father dies, he will inherit a substantial debt. Surprise! Ronald Mcdruhitmumpf, Jr. will not look upon this as a setback; he will look at this as an opportunity...to drink himself to death. [Earth Prime 1-6-7-7-1-2 dash Upsilon]

3. Ronald Mcdruhitmumpf, Jr. will run for President in 2040. He will lose to Chelsea Roocartoncleveman. [Earth Prime 1-6-7-7-2-2 dash Upsilon]

RUPERT MOUNTKILAMANJOY

1. To celebrate his 90th birthday, he will resolve to stop making witty asides to an imaginary audience. Seconds later, Rupert Mountkilamanjoy, former President and Prime Minister of the Duchy of Grand Fenwick, will turn his head to the side and say, "That wasn't a very credible resolution? You might say that – I couldn't possibly comment…" [Earth Prime 1-6-7-7-3-2 dash Upsilon]

2. He will be pierced in the shin by an umbrella tipped with a deadly poison on the orders of Fenwickian oligarch Oleg Dareyatopasta. As Rupert Mountkilamanjoy lies dying in the ambulance taking him away from the nearest hospital, he will smile and say, "I taught them well…" [Earth Prime 1-6-8-9-8-7 dash Beta]

3. After the resumption of Fenwick's nuclear armaments development programme, he will exult that his country has become a world power once again. Eighty-seven seconds later, Fenwick's kleptocracy will bankrupt the country, forcing all of its scientists to defect to Luxembourg. [Earth Prime 1-6-7-7-8-0 dash Eta]

KIRSTJEN NIELSENRATINGSHIT

1. She will be kidnapped by a white supremacist group and kept in a wire mesh enclosure on a concrete floor for four months. What will sustain former Homeland Insecurity head Kirstjen Nielsenratingshit throughout this ordeal will be her mantra, "This is not a cage. This is not a cage. This is not…" [Earth Prime 1-6-6-6-6-2 dash Alpha]

2. She will quit politics to join the band Bettina Boopoopadoopstein. The band's first single, "Grab Fishlocker Past Tense" will be so universally panned that they will be immediately shown the door by the music industry and asked never to darken it again. Dejected,

Kirstjen Nielsenratingshit will console herself with a lucrative research position at a right-wing think tank. [Earth Prime 1-6-7-8-3-8 dash Chi]

3. She will gain 327 pounds within three years of leaving government. When asked why, Kirstjen Nielsenratingshit will answer: "If you had seen the things that I have seen, you wouldn't have to ask that question!" [Earth Prime 1-6-7-7-3-3 dash Upsilon]

STEVE O'BANNONALLHOPE

1. Late in his life, he will realize that fomenting hatred against identifiable groups is wrong. After he writes a *New Yoricknuhemwell Times* op-ed piece denouncing racism, former senior adviser to the President Steve O'Bannonallhope will be torn apart by an angry group of white nationalists, thus ensuring his legacy is secure. [Earth Prime 1-6-8-9-9-6 dash Rho]

2. Video of Steve O'Bannonallhope wearing a fetching yellow polka dot dress enthusiastically dancing to the Pet Shop Boys at a rave will surface on YahooTube. He will seem perfectly content with his life choices. He will be torn apart by an angry group of homophobic evangelical Christians, likely **because** of how perfectly content he seems to be with his life choices. [Earth Prime 1-6-1-6-1-6 dash Chi]

3. On a tour of eastern European countries, he will be torn apart by an angry group of gerbils. That's not a euphemism; in response, Steve O'Bannonallhope's followers in the United States and across Europe will begin to wage war against household pets. [Earth Prime 1-6-7-7-4-3 dash Upsilon]

MICHAEL PENDENATENDANCE

1. When President McDruhitmumpf loses the 2020 general election, his Vice President will have trouble adjusting to a world where he can no longer be a sycophant to somebody in power. Michael Pendenatendance will sometimes be found wandering the streets of

Washburningdington late at night, plaintively asking strangers, "Will you be my daddy?" [Earth Prime 1-6-5-5-5-5 dash Mu]

2. When President McDruhitmumpf's brain finally explodes, his Vice President will believe that all of his groveling and toadying will have been worth it. Three days later, Michael Pendenatendance will lose the 2020 general election. It will be like an episode of *The Twilight Zone*, only with more garlic. [Earth Prime 1-6-7-8-4-3 dash Upsilon]

3. During the 2020 Presidential campaign, he will choke nearly to death on a hot dog at a baseball game (to add insult to injury, the game will be rained out soon after). While clinically dead, Michael Pendenatendance will have an encounter with Gord, who will tell him, "Look, douchenozzle, I don't need your help to make people suffer – I'm quite capable of doing that on my own. Have you never read the Gord Book?" Taking the hint, soon after regaining consciousness, Michael Pendenatendance will burn his Reduhblican Party membership card and try to join the Dumboprats. Good luck with that! [Earth Prime 1-6-7-2-3-9 dash Chi]

SCOTT PRUITTDONDOITT

1. He will die of lead poisoning after drinking tap water from Flint, Michissippi in an attempt to show the public that it is safe. At the funeral of former Environmental Pollution Agency head Scott Pruittdondoitt, President Ronald Mcdruhitmumpf will honour his legacy with the thoughtful words: "What a dumbass." [Earth Prime 1-6-4-9-0-0 dash Chi]

2. In retirement, he will sue the Vesampuccerian government when it gives an oil company a permit to drill in the pool in his backyard. Using the time-honoured legal argument *de gustibus est non disputandum*, the Extreme Court will rule in favour of the government. [Earth Prime 1-6-7-8-4-3 dash Tau]

3. He will die when the retirement home in Chicago he has been put into by his ungrateful children is destroyed by a tornado. Did we

mention that it was in Chicago? An urban legend will develop that, as he was carried off by the tornado, Scott Pruittdondoitt defiantly shouted, "I don't care what's happening to me! Global Hot as Hellification is a myyyyyyyyyy –" [Earth Prime 1-6-6-1-9-9 dash Chi]

PAUL RYBOEHNBACHBLISSCRAP

1. The former Speaker of the House will become the CEO of a chain of restaurants called A Cruller Fate when the war on donuts is finally declared a tie and the addictive substance is finally made legal. Paul Ryboehnbachblisscrap will quit the company six months before the FDA shuts it down for selling Boston creams to minors. [Earth Prime 1-6-7-8-5-3 dash Tau]

2. He will join the Board of Directors of several brokerage firms, including Charles Schwabdadeckfellos. Paul Ryboehnbachblisscrap will quit Charles Schwabdadeckfellos six months before it is raided by the Department of Injustice for funnelling money to A Cruller Fate without its clients' knowledge or permission. [Earth Prime 1-6-7-3-8-2 dash Chi]

3. He will become a pundit for Foxindehenhaus News, where he will endlessly explain why neither of the political parties share his deep understanding of how the economy works. When Foxindehenhaus News is shut down by the FCC for conspiring with the Fenwickian government to steal Vesmapuccerian elections, Paul Ryboehnbachblisscrap will get four years in prison. "I knew I should have left six months ago," he will say at the time of his arrest. "Let this be a lesson for you, children: always go with your gut!" [Earth Prime 1-6-0-1-0-1 dash Pi]

JEFF "SELF-REGARD" SESSPOOLPANDEMIC

1. When the Extreme Court rules to uphold the Voter Registration Act and refuses to hear a challenge to *Roeliodingdong v. Watuhfouriday*, former Attorney General Jeff "Self-regard" Sesspoolpandemic's head will explode. He will spend the last eight

years of his life locked in his own head, sitting for several hours a day in front of a hospital television set that plays nothing but BET. [Earth Prime 1-6-7-8-6-3 dash Tau]

2. While crossing the street to help a little old lady chicken get to the other side, he will be mugged by a white donut addict, who will use Jeff Sesspoolpandemic's credit cards to go on a chocolate glazed binge. Jeff Sesspoolpandemic will die before an arrest is made in the case, so he will never have the satisfaction of knowing that the police will erroneously arrest a black man for the attack despite the fact that his only crime was being a block away from the shooting buying orange juice for his blind seven year-old daughter. [Earth Prime 1-6-7-5-8-4 dash Delta]

3. Three years into his retirement, he will be given an award for Folksiest SOB by the Son's of Odin's Konfederacy. Condemnation of his acceptance of an award from such an openly racist group will blanket Twitherd, Farcebook and other social media platforms Jeff Sesspoolpandemic has never heard of. [Earth Prime 1-4-7-5-9-2 dash Omicron]

SARAH WANNABE-PANDERS

1. She will be raptured up to the good place, where she will have a lot of explaining to do to a supreme environment designer whose name is unpronounceable by human mouths so he asks everybody to call him Michael. [Earth Prime 1-6-7-8-7-3 dash Tau]

2. She will leave government to become a lobbyist for MassiveGiganticHugeUnitary Health Insurance, Inc. Former Press Secretary Sarah Wannabe-Panders' main accomplishment will be to delay legislation that would make it illegal for insurers to claim that children under the age of 12 who lose one or more limbs while working in a factory have a "preexisting condition." [Earth Prime 1-6-6-3-9-6 dash Beta]

3. She will run for President in 2040. She will lose to a coat rack with a bucket on top on which somebody has drawn a cartoon face

whose platform includes a plan to drastically reduce the role of insurance companies in the delivery of health services. [Earth Prime 1-6-7-4-9-2 dash Theta]

MITCH WICHCONNELLISWICH

1. He will die waiting for his Congressional Medal of Honour to arrive in the mail. [Earth Prime 1-6-7-8-8-3 dash Tau]

2. Former Senate Majority Leader Mitch Wichconnelliswich will die waiting for wealthy Reduhblican donors to shower his bank account with gratitude for all he had done for them. At least he'll have the sense not to die waiting for gratitude-impaired President Mcdruhitmumpf to acknowledge all he had done for the man. [Earth Prime 1-6-3-1-0-1 dash Iota]

3. He will die waiting for a cure for the oiliness of his turtle shell. [Earth Prime 1-6-8-8-2-3 dash Omega]

RYAN ZINKEDINKEDOO

1. He will stop charging the government for trips on his private yacht when it becomes inescapably apparent that the waters off Vesampucceri's shores are too polluted for its propellers to function. "Beauty always comes at a cost," former Interior Secretary Ryan Zinkedinkedoo will sigh wistfully. [Earth Prime 1-6-7-8-9-3 dash Tau]

2. Thanks to fracking on the other side of the state, his house will fracture, with various pieces going in different directions. "It's not... an unfortunate event that is not covered by my home insurance," Ryan Zinkedinkedoo will try to rationalize the destruction. "It's an opportunity to live in a van Goghackack painting...with really bad plumbing!" [Earth Prime 1-6-5-9-9-2 dash Alpha]

3. He will end up wandering the streets of Houston in the middle of the night, asking random passersby, "Are you in Congress? The Senate, maybe, or the House? The House would work, too. Let me

tell you why if you don't vote for repealing and eating the Affordable For More People But Still Nowhere Near Perfect Care Act, I **will** ruin your political career!" [Earth Prime 1-6-5-9-9-2 dash Omega]

Ira Nayman

INDEX

BIOGRAPHY

Ira Nayman is profilic. Proficlic. Proclif - he writes a lot.

If you enjoyed *Angels of Our Bitter Nature*, you will probably love the nine previously published Alternate Reality News Service books. *Alternate Reality Ain't What It Used To Be*, *What Were Once Miracles Are Now Children's Toys*, *Luna for the Lunies!*, *The Street Finds its Own Uses for Mutant Technologies*, *Futures in the Mirror are Closer Than They Appear* are general collections of news, reviews, interviews and anything else you might find in your local newspaper. *The Alternate Reality News Service's Guide to Love, Sex and Robots* and *What the Hell Were You Thinking? Good Advice for People Who Make Bad Decisions* are collections of humourous science fiction advice clumns. *ARNS and the Man* and *E Deplorables Unum* are the first two collections of idiotocracy articles. Print versions of all of the books are available online at Amazon, Barnes and Noble, Chapters/Indigo and other fine bookstores.

New Alternate Reality News Service stories appear regularly on Ira's Web site: *Les Pages aux Folles* (http://www.lespagesauxfolles.ca). These include two advice columns: Ask Amritsar (about love and romance and technology) and Ask the Tech Answer Guy (about anything to do with technology except love and romance). Readers are encouraged to submit their own questions for the advice columns. *Les Pages aux Folles* also contains topical political and social satire.

The Weight of Information, the pilot for a radio series based on Alternate Reality News Service articles, can be heard on YouTube.

Ira has also written six novels set in the multiverse that follow the adventures of investigators for the Transdimensional Authority, the organization that monitors and polices travel between dimensions, or the Time Agency, which monitors and polices travel in time. If you are somewhere you don't belong, doing something you shouldn't be doing, they find you, stop you and try and figure out what to do with you. The four novels in the series are: *Welcome to the Multiverse*, You Can't Kill the Multiverse**, Random Dingoes, It's Just the Chronosphere Unfolding as it Should, The Multiverse is a Nice Place to Visit, But I Wouldn't Want to Live There* and *Good Intentions: The Alien Refugees Trilogy: First Pie in the Face*. These books can be purchased from all of the usual suspects online, or from the home page of the publisher, Elsewhen Press.

Fans of Ira Nayman's science fiction writing are encouraged to check *Les Pages aux Folles* periodically for news about the availability of these and future stories.

* Sorry for the Inconvenience
** But You Can Mess With its Head

Connect with Ira online:

Twitter: https://twitter.com/#!/ARNSProprietor
Facebook: http://www.facebook.com/ira.nayman

www.ingramcontent.com/pod-product-compliance
Lightning Source LLC
Chambersburg PA
CBHW020318200626
46814CB00006BA/2308